THE
WATER
SEEKER

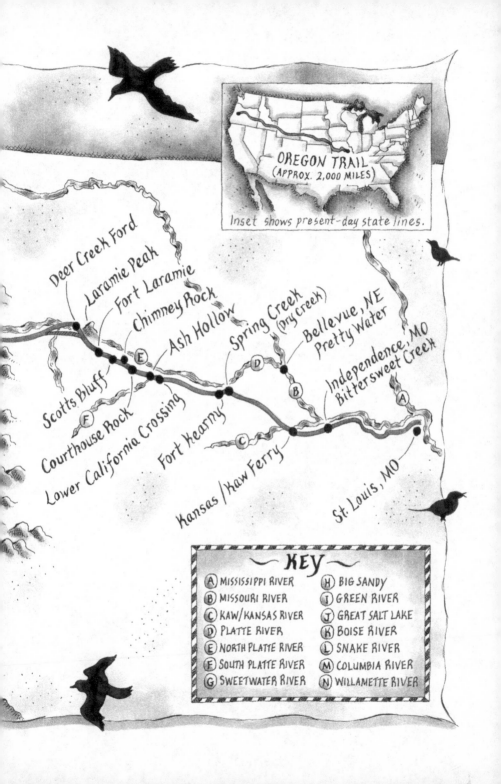

Deer Creek Ford
Laramie Peak
Fort Laramie
Chimney Rock
Ash Hollow
Spring Creek (Dry Creek)
Bellevue, NE
Pretty Water
Independence, MO
Bittersweet Creek
Scotts Bluff
Courthouse Rock
Lower California Crossing
Fort Kearny
Kansas / Kaw Ferry
St. Louis, MO

ⒺⒹⒷⒶⒻⒸ

OREGON TRAIL
(APPROX. 2,000 MILES)

Inset shows present-day state lines.

~ KEY ~

Ⓐ MISSISSIPPI RIVER   Ⓗ BIG SANDY
Ⓑ MISSOURI RIVER   Ⓘ GREEN RIVER
Ⓒ KAW/KANSAS RIVER   Ⓙ GREAT SALT LAKE
Ⓓ PLATTE RIVER   Ⓚ BOISE RIVER
Ⓔ NORTH PLATTE RIVER Ⓛ SNAKE RIVER
Ⓕ SOUTH PLATTE RIVER Ⓜ COLUMBIA RIVER
Ⓖ SWEETWATER RIVER   Ⓝ WILLAMETTE RIVER

KIMBERLY WILLIS HOLT

THE
WATER
SEEKER

SQUARE
FISH

Henry Holt and Company

NEW YORK

SQUARE FISH

An Imprint of Macmillan

Library of Congress Cataloging-in-Publication Data
Holt, Kimberly Willis.
The water seeker / Kimberly Willis Holt.
p.   cm.
"Christy Ottaviano Books."
Summary: Traces the hard life, filled with losses, adversity, and adventure,
of Amos, son of a trapper and dowser, from 1833 when his mother dies giving birth to him
until 1859, when he himself has grown up and has a son of his own.
ISBN 978-1-250-00475-8
[1. Coming of age—Fiction.   2. Fathers and sons—Fiction.   3. Dowsing—Fiction.
4. Overland journeys to the Pacific—Fiction.   5. Frontier and pioneer life—Fiction.
6. West (U.S.)—History—19th century—Fiction.]   I. Title.
PZ7.H74023Wat 2010   [Fic]—dc22   2009024149

Originally published in the United States by
Christy Ottaviano Books/Henry Holt and Company
First Square Fish Edition: June 2012
Square Fish logo designed by Filomena Tuosto
mackids.com

5   7   9   11   13   15   16   14   12   10   8   6

AR: 4.8 / LEXILE: 730L

This story is dedicated in loving memory
to Jack and Pearl Holt, who raised a fine son.

—K. W. H.

When God created water, he made the Kincaids. For water flowed through their veins like blood. So much so, they knew how to draw it deep from the earth. That was their gift. That was their curse. Father to son. Father to son. Father to son.

—SHANNON RENEE HOLT

CHAPTER
1

BITTERSWEET CREEK 1833

JAKE KINCAID WAS KNOWN as the dowser. With a forked branch, he'd made his way from the Arkansas Territory to Missouri, stopping at farms to find water for new wells. His plan was to raise enough money so he could do what he wanted and never pick up the branch again. But the dowsing was a gift. And a gift might be abandoned, but it will always be there, waiting to be claimed.

One farmer didn't have money, so he paid Jake by giving him a parcel of land with a cabin. Since winter was settling in, Jake decided to stay there until spring, when he'd take up trapping. His cabin sat a hundred steps from Bittersweet Creek and about a mile, as the eagle flew, from the Hurd place. When their oldest daughter, Delilah, showed up at his door, begging for a place to stay, he'd not been with a woman in a long time. Without thinking, he said, "Well, I reckon I could marry you."

A few months later, Jake went west to trap. He left each fall and returned in the summer after the trappers' rendezvous. The life suited them. Delilah had a safe haven from her pa's temper, and Jake had someone to come home to. And most satisfying to them both were the months of solitude that they craved.

DELILAH STROLLED through the woods, thinking about how that day felt especially hot. Jake would be making his way from Green Valley, and when he arrived he'd expect a clean house and a hot meal. She hurried home to prepare for him.

Anticipating Jake's arrival always brought on dread and excitement. Every year, Jake traded for supplies with an artist who painted the mountain man's way of life. Delilah looked forward to getting new paints, brushes, and paper. But she also loved her time alone in the woods. And the birds. She loved the birds.

Delilah treasured walking among the pines and cypress trees. She'd grown to appreciate the smell of her own sweat and the way it mixed with the musky smells of the earth. Now she'd have to wash all that away. Jake's return meant she'd have to bathe more often, keep house, and cook meals.

From him, she'd learned how appearances deceived. Her pa, Eb, was a small man who looked as gentle as a cat, while Jake was stocky, barrel-chested, and furry like a bear.

He could talk until the sun fell out of the sky, but Jake didn't have a temper. To Delilah, listening to Jake drone on and on about his trappings was a good trade-off.

A FEW DAYS later, Jake arrived. He grabbed hold of Delilah and pressed his lips against hers. When it seemed he'd never let go, she wiggled free and grabbed his leather satchel in search of the new paints and brushes. She moved so quickly that the bag dropped with a *thump* to the floor, causing a glass to crack. Staring down at it, she could clearly see her own reflection. "What's that there?"

Jake sighed and collapsed upon a chair. "A mirr-o. Was one."

She took off his boots and fed him a bowl of vegetable and bacon soup. Jake gulped down the broth in less time than it took to sneeze. Then he fell asleep.

Delilah carefully set the hand mirror on the table next to her tablet and stared into it. The crack ran the entire length of the mirror, but what she saw fascinated her. She touched her red hair that frizzed like the threads on a ball of wool. When Delilah was a young girl, her ma braided it in a long pigtail and smoothed the wild hairs with lard. Delilah's finger stroked the lines of her nose and her wide chin. She smiled, not just because she was amused, but because she wanted to see what would happen to her face. She had a space next to her black tooth. She'd lost the tooth when Eb punched her for not milking the cow a few years back. Delilah was amazed that a piece of glass could reveal the history of her life. A fire burned inside her, and she began to draw.

IN THE MIDDLE of the night, Delilah heard Jake ease out of bed and pull on his boots. She knew what was next. He did it every summer when he returned. And she knew for sure he thought she didn't know. Last fall, she'd lifted the rock under the oak tree, hunting crickets for fish bait. She discovered the muslin sack buried in the ground under the rock. When she saw the money inside, she fell back on the ground and laughed. Jake didn't know her at all. Money didn't mean a thing in the world to Delilah.

For three months, Delilah cooked and cleaned for Jake, all the while gazing outside the window, praying for cool weather to come. Several weeks before the leaves turned crimson and orange, Jake packed up his mule and headed toward the mountains.

A month later, a sour taste formed in Delilah's mouth and she vomited her breakfast of bread and blackberry jam. Immediately she felt better, but the next morning, the sickness returned. Two months later, her belly began to round out like a melon. She cursed Jake's name to the trees, even threatening to kill him.

Then one November night, as if the heavens had heard her cries, light poured through the cabin window, awakening Delilah from her sleep. She hurried to the porch and discovered streaks of light streaming across the sky. All the stars are falling, thought Delilah. But instead of being afraid, she settled on the top step and watched. There were thousands, too many to count. She just waited and watched. The light was so bright she could clearly see a doe and her young buck in the thick of the woods. The heavens had given her a gift. And hours later, when the shower of light ended, she felt sad.

The next day, Delilah awoke craving bread. Before sunset, she'd baked twelve loaves and eaten three. She tore the other loaves in tiny pieces and scattered them on the porch. In the morning, the birds had discovered her offering. She pushed the table next to the window and began to paint.

By the time winter arrived, Delilah's resentment had disappeared and a softness for the life inside her was growing, though at times she believed they were in conflict with each other. When Delilah curled up in bed to sleep, the baby kicked hard, until she got up and walked the floor. At which time the baby became still. Whenever Delilah settled at the table to draw, the baby caused a burning inside her gut that made her drop the pencil and give up for the day.

She began to dream the same vision each night. In her dreams, she heard a baby cry. Then she saw herself standing by a long winding river. A baby floated by, his little arms stretching toward her. But try as she did, she could not reach him. Downriver, a woman picked up the baby and handed him to another woman. That woman handed him to yet another. And so it went, the baby being passed down through a chain of women along the river. This dream occurred so often, Delilah started to think of it as a premonition. No matter what, she believed her child was destined for trials and tribulations. He would struggle. Delilah was certain of it.

Spring arrived, and Delilah spotted new nests every day. She discovered them in tree branches and corners under the porch cover. She even found one in the hole of the barn wall. The birds crafted their nests from bits of twigs, dead grass, corn husks, and Delilah's hair. She loved seeing her red strands woven in with all the other textures. She always believed she was a part of nature. This was proof of it.

In May, the baby birds began their flight lessons, and a feeling came over Delilah that she, too, was about to spread her wings and take off. She couldn't explain it, but the feeling became stronger each day.

One afternoon, as she walked through the woods, an old blackbird called out to her. *A-mos*, it said. *A-mos, a-mos.* The wind began to howl, but she could still hear the bird's chant. *A-mos, a-mos, a-mos.*

When it was time for her baby, she had no choice but to fetch her ma. She set out for their cabin, walking the mile through the dense woods. Even though it was May, the mornings remained cold. And since there was no worn path, Delilah followed the smell of smoke rising from her parents' chimney. The pain in her womb kept her from noticing the cloud of birds flying above the treetops that towered over her head.

As she'd predicted, her brother Silas was hoeing the garden with Eb.

"I heard you coming the whole way," Eb said. "I could hear those dad-gum birds. They's always following you."

Eb feared birds ever since one swept down and pecked him in the nose. The incident happened three years ago after he'd taken a strike at Delilah. That was the day she took off for Jake's cabin.

A huge flock of crows landed in the garden. Silas removed his hat and waved it overhead as he ran about trying to scare them away. His long, thin limbs caused him to resemble a scarecrow that suddenly came to life. The birds flew away from Silas's reach, circled the garden, then returned.

"Shoo! Shoo!" Silas hollered as he flapped his hat, turning to his right, then his left. He started to spin.

If she'd not been in pain, Delilah would have laughed.

Eb narrowed his eyes at Delilah's stomach. "Looks like you got yourself in a heap of mess, gal."

"I had me a man to help."

Wiping his forehead with his sleeve, he said, "I can see that."

"Jake's my husband."

"I reckon you want your ma. Lolly's in the house." He turned away from her and joined Silas in his crusade, stomping his feet at a group of crows.

Delilah felt the air close up around her. Just returning there had brought back all the bad thoughts. Then Daisy, her seven-year-old sister, ran over and hugged her legs. The girl stared up at Delilah's big stomach and said, "You're as fat as an old grizzly bear."

Delilah stroked her sister's golden red hair. "And you're as tiny as a little squirrel."

Her other siblings acted as if she were a stranger, cowering behind the ladder that led up to the loft. That bothered her most, more than seeing her pa. They've been poisoned against me, she thought. Or maybe they resented her for leaving because Eb had gone to hitting one of them. Her eyes searched each of their faces and arms for bruises, lingering longest on Daisy's. Relieved to discover none, Delilah figured she was probably the lone thorn in her pa's side.

Delilah wanted to return to her cabin for the baby to be born, but Lolly insisted on finishing Eb's dinner first. The sharp pangs came quicker, and Delilah paced on the front porch until Lolly finally joined her. They were making their way through the woods, heading back to the cabin, when Delilah's water broke. Before the sun was down, she was crying out for Jake.

The birds' chatter grew so loud that Lolly hollered, "Them birds are driving me crazy!"

The labor was long and hard, which puzzled Lolly since she'd merely grunted and pushed one time to bring each of her babies into the world. And when Lolly saw more blood coming from Delilah than she'd ever seen with all her own births put together, she suspected the outcome wouldn't be good.

Delilah's screams turned to groans, and her groans became whimpers.

Lolly went outside and found a stick, then gave it to Delilah. "Here, bite down on this."

Delilah yanked the stick from her mouth and flung it across the room. "It tastes like mud."

When the baby finally came, he was red as a ripe raspberry. Wails escaped from his wide mouth as he shook his tiny fists in the air.

Chuckling, Lolly held him up. "This boy is mad." She placed him next to Delilah's breast to suckle. "He's a strong one. What you reckon you'll call him?"

Delilah's lips brushed the light fuzz on his head, and she closed her eyes. Her words came out soft. "Amos is a good name."

"Amos?" Lolly mused. "Where in tarnation did you get that from?"

Delilah didn't answer. She just said, "Tell Jake I done my best. Don't let my baby forget me."

With that, she took her last breath. The cabin and the world outside the window grew silent. And every bird at Bittersweet Creek flew away.

CHAPTER
2

AUGUST 1834

THE RENDEZVOUS had been held at Ham's Fork that year, and Jake tarried a little longer than usual. He'd met up with Isaac Bolton and some of the other free trappers that he'd missed in Green River the year before, when he'd hurried to get home to Delilah. Isaac was a legend in the trapping world, and Jake liked being seen with him. As if by doing so, he'd raised his own worth.

When Jake finally arrived at Bittersweet Creek, he noticed right off that something wasn't right. He couldn't quite put his finger on it, though. Then he found Daisy on the porch.

"Hi, Jake," she said, looking up at him from a squatting position. She was playing with a corncob doll.

"Hi, Daisy." Jake wondered if Daisy had run off from

her ma and pa. The little gal always begged to live with them each time she visited. But Delilah sent her home, knowing Eb would seek revenge.

Inside the cabin, Lolly held an infant. "Reckoned you'd been back before now," she said. "Me and Daisy stayed here waiting for you the last few months. Eb couldn't stand the baby's cries. This baby wails more than any young'un I ever had."

Jake dropped the satchel of paints and pads on the table. "Where's Delilah?"

Lolly pointed to the oak tree behind the cabin, the same oak tree where Jake hid his money. Only now a cross replaced the stone. Jake felt numb.

Lolly stood and walked over to Jake and handed the baby to him. "I'd stay, but I've got my own young'uns to tend to."

Jake stared at her full belly and realized that she'd have another one soon. He peered down at the baby. He wasn't sure what to do with it. A lot had happened while he was away in the mountains.

Daisy ran over to him and touched the baby's toes. "They look like little berries. I want to eat them." She gently nibbled.

"I told you to stop that," Lolly snapped. She held out something to Jake that appeared to be made from some animal's intestine. "Had to butcher your calf to make a bottle."

He didn't bother to ask what had happened to the meat. Last he counted, Delilah had six siblings.

"It's a boy," Lolly said. "Good thing. Girls are so much trouble."

"What's his name?" Jake asked.

"Delilah said she fancied Amos."

From the front window, Jake watched Lolly and Daisy enter the woods heading back to their home. They carried some elk meat that Jake had dried into jerky. He couldn't blame Lolly asking for meat. He'd heard Delilah complain how her pa expected them to live on nothing but the vegetables he grew in his garden. Jake figured if they split Eb open, onions and turnips would tumble out.

As he stared out the window, it came to him what that uneasy feeling had been when he first approached the cabin. The birds. They'd appeared the day Delilah had shown up at his door. Their chirping drove him mad until the sound became a constant hum sinking into his head. Now silence overwhelmed him, and except for a dove resting on the porch rail, not a bird was in sight.

Jake walked to the back of the cabin. Sure enough, the rock was gone. Which, of course, he reasoned, meant the bag was gone, too. *Three hundred dollars.* All the years he'd added money to the bag. Most of the other trappers lived hand to hoof, and those that managed to save extra put their earnings in the bank. Not Jake. He liked knowing where his money was at all times. No doubt Eb and Lolly had it now. If someone had told him the day before he'd been robbed by his in-laws, he'd been ready to clean his shotgun, but today it was all he could do to try and take in what had happened to Delilah.

The baby began to squirm, then started to cry. Jake held tiny Amos close, then scouted around the cabin until he found the bottle. As Amos sucked, Jake tried to focus on his new situation. Soon a warm, wet feeling came from the baby's bottom. He remembered the diaper squares that Lolly showed him. She'd made them from Delilah's old clothes. A lump formed in Jake's throat as he recognized the muslin pieces that had once been Delilah's skirt.

Jake changed the cloth. It wasn't the taking off, but the putting on that was such a challenge. Amos squirmed while Jake clumsily tied the string around the baby's waist to hold the cloth to his body. The dove was still at the window watching him. How could Delilah up and die on him like this? he thought. Then he quickly felt guilty, knowing that in a strange way he was responsible for her death and now for the life of this baby.

He decided to blame Lolly for walking out so quickly. Heck, she and Eb had so many young'uns, what was one more to them? He immediately regretted that thought, too. Delilah would surely come back and haunt him if he left their baby with her folks. And now they had his money, too. Although what was he planning to do with it anyway? Maybe the money would somehow trickle down to Delilah's siblings and that would be a good deed. Something that Delilah would have wanted. Either way, the money was gone. He had other matters to deal with now.

Lolly had made a crib from a wooden box. Jake eased the sleeping infant into it and began to pace. The sight of Delilah's drawings and paintings left a hollow feeling inside him. He ate the bit of stew that Lolly had made while he thought about what was to come.

He could stay put. He could pick up a forked branch and make a fair wage dowsing other men's land. His pa had done it, and it had put meat on their table. He had done it, too. But only when he'd had to. The thought of that life made Jake feel a tightness in his throat, as if someone was choking him. His brother should have been the one with the gift for finding water beneath the ground. Instead, Gil turned to preaching the gospel. The last Jake heard, Gil had started a mission near the trading post at Bellevue. He'd married a pretty gal from Saint Louis. Jake met her five years ago, a month before the wedding.

He hadn't thought of Gil in a year or so, but now his thoughts were fixed on him. Maybe Gil and his woman could take care of Amos while he trapped. The boy would still be his, and he'd visit after each rendezvous, just as he'd returned to Delilah every summer.

The dove pecked at the window, and the baby began to stir on the quilt. Jake made up his mind. He'd leave for Gil's the morning after next.

BEFORE DAWN, Jake was up, gathering supplies he'd need on the journey. His body felt heavy. He'd hardly slept the last two nights, not from fretting of what was to be, but because of Amos wanting the bottle every few hours. Once he'd fallen asleep with Amos in his arms and awakened with a start, thinking how he might have rolled over and smothered the infant.

Gil's mission was at a place called Pretty Water. The way he figured it, that lay two hundred miles away. If he was traveling by himself, the journey would take ten days at most, but the baby needed milk so often the cow had to join them. He'd be lucky to get there in two weeks.

Jake was busy packing the mule when he heard the barn door creak open. Just his sour luck, his shotgun was in the cabin. He squatted, hiding behind the cow. But then he realized Amos was in the box between him and the barn door. He held his breath. Probably that good-for-nothing Eb, trying to see what else he could steal from him.

"Hi, pretty baby," a tiny voice said.

Relieved, Jake stood. "Morning, Daisy. What are you doing up so early?"

"I always get up early."

"Won't your folks be worried?"

"I sneak back before they figure out that I was gone." She knelt by Amos and let him grab her finger. "Where are you going?"

He almost told the girl, but then decided that Daisy

not knowing the complete truth wouldn't hurt. He didn't like the thought of Eb and Lolly knowing his or the baby's whereabouts.

"Gonna see some family." That was not a lie.

"You're going to leave Amos with them?"

The girl might not be able to read or write her own name, but she was smart. "I'll have to see about that." That was the truth, too. Gil may not want the baby.

"I'll miss Amos," she said, "And you. I wish you were my pa."

Jake cleared his throat. He wasn't accustomed to sentimental moments. He felt sorry for her. She was probably destined for the life that Delilah had escaped.

"I'm sure we'll be back this way. It's my land, and it's a perfectly good cabin." Now that was a lie. With Delilah gone, Jake had no plans to return to Bittersweet Creek. His life lay west in the mountains.

Daisy kissed the baby's forehead. "Bye, little Amos." She stood. Then she walked over to Jake, raised on her toes, and kissed his beard. She turned and dashed out of the barn, leaving the door wide open.

For a moment Jake felt stung by what had just happened. He felt a tenderness toward the little gal. What would happen to her? He tried to shake that thought from his head by turning his attention to hitching the cow to the mule. Less than ten minutes later, they set off for Pretty Water.

Amos rode in a papoose that Jake had made from a deer hide framed with sticks. Inside Jake's right pocket was a picture Delilah had drawn of herself. He'd keep the picture to show Amos when he was older, for he remembered what Lolly said were Delilah's last words. He made a promise as he walked away from Bittersweet Creek that Amos would never forget the woman who gave him life.

By noon, Jake noticed a crow resting on the cow's hind quarter, its black eyes staring straight ahead at Jake. "Smart old crow." A blister had formed on Jake's small right toe. He was prone to blisters on his right foot because he favored that leg when he walked. It had been that way ever since his pa had accidentally cut off one of his left toes while they were hoeing in the field.

Two hours later, the crow was still there. The bird's eyes appeared intelligent, at least compared to the cow's and mule's. So Jake began to tell the bird his stories. Before Jake reached the ending of his second tale, the crow flew away. Jake continued to talk, this time to Amos. He told him about two trappers fighting at the rendezvous over an Indian woman, and the autumn night when the sky lit up from all the falling stars. He told him about his meeting up with a bear. "Then I said, 'It's either gonna be me left standing or that bear, and if I have anything to do with it, it sure as heck ain't gonna be that bear.' "

Jake walked until sundown. Then he tied the mule and cow to a tree, leaving enough room for them to graze. He built a fire and laid the blankets nearby. All the while, Amos stayed in the papoose attached to Jake.

"I've turned into a damn squaw," muttered Jake. But at least Amos remained quiet that way. He seemed content watching the world from over Jake's shoulder, crying only when he was hungry. Until then, Jake had never milked a cow more than twice a day. He didn't much care for it, and neither, it seemed, did the cow.

The temperature cooled down at dark, and when the stars filled the sky, Jake was reminded why he loved being out in the wilderness more than anything. He knew in his gut he was doing the right thing for this baby. He heard the soft sound of an owl hooting above his head, and the sound lulled him into a deep slumber.

In the middle of that first night, Amos awoke with such a wail that Jake tried everything. When the bottle didn't satisfy Amos, Jake checked his bottom. But it was dry. He could think of nothing else to do but to sing him a tune.

She was my gal, my gal named Sal
But she had a ma, who was big and tall
She was mean like a snake and couldn't take
The sight or sound or smell of me
And that's why, feller, I'm up here in this tree . . .

Amos quieted, and soon the two of them were asleep.

CHAPTER

3

THE MISSION AT PRETTY WATER
SEPTEMBER 1834

REBECCA STOOD BACK and admired the new schoolhouse. The log frame structure was small, but she doubted many Otoe children would attend in the beginning. She hoped that they would, but she and Gil had started the mission at Pretty Water the year before. They'd confronted challenges breaking through Otoe barriers. Although her husband had tried more than any other man would have. Gil even attended a tribal hunt in order to gain their trust. It didn't help that the post traded whiskey with the Otoe, causing them to get drunk and worked up.

Their life at the mission was not what she'd pictured when Gil had told her of his dream. Her vision had been a romantic one—working side by side, ministering, baptizing, and teaching the Otoe. She was raised in Saint Louis, the daughter of a well-respected minister. When she and Gil took off for Bellevue, she willingly gave up her privileged life, but just once in a while she longed to put on a fine hat and go to a church with a roof and four walls. She felt guilty after such thoughts, because she loved Gil more than anything and wanted to see his dream realized.

Rebecca's only sadness hid buried deep inside her. After losing a baby during childbirth four years ago, she'd been told by the doctor that she'd never conceive again. She had to restrain herself from embracing the Otoe children. Their dark features contrasted against her fair skin and hair, but she'd have chosen any of them and raised them as her own. She kept her feelings at bay, though, concluding that she was put on this earth to do other things instead of motherhood. The schoolhouse was proof of that. Her heart beat fast, thinking of the chairs filled with young people learning to read. And as she walked the few yards home, she had a skip in her step.

GIL KINCAID had one big sin. He loved his wife more than anything or anyone. More than God. His conscience battled with that fact daily, and he knew there would be a price to pay.

He'd learned some Otoe, enough to get by, but not enough to easily translate the Bible as he tried to do each evening. Patience, he reminded himself, but that trait seemed to belong to Rebecca. She could find the joy in such misery.

All he could concentrate on was what hadn't been accomplished and his struggles with the post. If only they'd stop trading whiskey with the Otoe. That's what the Otoe originally wanted in exchange for attending his worship services. Gil refused, and those first Sundays, the Otoe returned to their tribes disgruntled. Gil preached to Rebecca alone, as she sat in the front pew of the open-air church.

Rebecca found a way to fill those pews. She invited the Otoe to eat dinner with them after they attended the worship service. Gil shook his head when he saw thirty Otoe sitting before him. "Dinner for a sermon." He didn't know whether to be amused or disgusted.

"Better than whiskey for a sermon," Rebecca said, smiling. And as always, Gil knew she was right.

The Otoe came the following Sunday, too. They sat, listening to Gil's fervent sermons while thinking of Rebecca's roasted chickens and sweet cakes.

GIL WAS TEN years younger than Jake. The brothers shared a father, but had different mothers, and that had made them different types of men. Gil was like the sprawling branches on an oak tree, reaching, always reaching for more, while Jake was like the sturdy roots planted firmly in the ground, content with his simple life. Jake had never stepped inside a schoolhouse. Despite her husband's objections, Gil's mother had insisted Gil attend school until at least the eighth grade. And when their father died in the middle of Gil's twelfth year, he continued on with his education, eventually studying for the ministry. He and Rebecca read to each other often. That was what they were doing the morning Jake approached their home.

They heard the cow first, causing them to look out the window. A man dressed in fur and leather, pulling a mule, was approaching. A cow followed the man and the mule, its rope attached to the mule's pack.

When Gil noticed the slight left limp in Jake's gait, he headed toward the door. "That's my brother." Five years had passed since they'd seen him. His beard had grown thick, and he'd put on at least thirty pounds.

About that time Amos let out a wail and Rebecca hurried to catch up.

Jake slipped off the papoose and handed the child to her. Fine white hairs stuck straight up on the baby's scalp. "His ma died. Thought you and Gil might lend me a hand."

Rebecca cried and her words came from her heart instead of her head. "Thank you, Jake. I'll be a good mother to him."

Jake cleared his throat. "The boy had a ma, and that ain't you." Then he fixed his gaze on Gil. "And he's got a pa, too. That'd be me."

Rebecca clung to the baby anyway, willing to have any part of him.

MOMENTS AFTER JAKE and Amos arrived, clouds formed in the gray sky, warning of a summer storm. Rebecca caught a glimpse of her reflection in the window. She liked what she saw—a woman like any other mother holding her baby. She studied the image longer than she knew any humble person should have, but the crown of sweet Amos's head pressed against her breast captivated her. When Rebecca's gaze traveled up to her face, she realized the image was not hers at all, but belonged to a woman she'd never seen. A woman with wild red hair. She gasped so loud she was grateful Gil and Jake were in the barn feeding the cow and mule. They would have thought she was insane. Rebecca reasoned that the emotion of the last few moments had caused her to hallucinate because now it was plain that the image in the glass was her own.

The rain began to fall, and four cardinals flew down and landed on the porch. Rebecca laughed and shook her head.

REBECCA STAYED QUIET as she held Amos, doing her best to keep her emotions intact. She didn't want to give Jake any reason to snatch Amos away. He might fear that she would try to become the baby's mother. But it didn't matter what she did, she felt something rising, filling up the empty space inside her.

While Jake ate, he told Gil countless stories of trapping beaver, trading at the annual rendezvous, and a close encounter with a bear. Rebecca was busy in her own thoughts, planning. The thin muslin scraps made terrible diaper cloths. Amos's bottom was covered with the worst rash she'd ever seen. Maybe the Otoe women were smart, placing grass between their babies and the animal skins they used to cover their bottoms. That was in the winter. In the summer their babies went bare-bottomed. It seemed barbaric, but Rebecca had never noticed any rashes on their infants. She decided she'd write her mother as soon as Jake left and ask her to send a bolt of thick cotton from Saint Louis.

And clothes, the baby would need clothing. He was merely wrapped in a soiled blanket. The makeshift bottle was filthy. Had Jake bothered to wash it? If the baby didn't get sick, it would be a miracle. But he *was* a miracle, even if he had arrived in a dirty blanket, delivered by a heathen. Rebecca's thoughts stopped cold from shame. How could she call her husband's brother a heathen? He could have taken this baby to anyone. Surely Amos had a grandmother who would beg to get her hands on her deceased daughter's child. That thought led Rebecca to think of the mother. My goodness, she was going on so with her plans that she hadn't even thought about how Amos had been motherless at birth. In a sudden outburst, she said, "Oh, Jake! I'm sorry about your beloved wife. Did she suffer?"

Jake seemed startled by Rebecca's interruption, and

he paused, staring straight ahead. Then he answered, "I reckon she did. Her ma said she tried real hard to push out the baby. Lolly said she'd never seen so much blood from one person."

With those few words, Rebecca realized how different her husband was from his brother. She was thankful for those differences. Gil would never speak so vulgarly.

Silence filled the cabin. Then Rebecca said, "God bless her."

"I reckon he should have," Jake said, then he turned toward Gil and continued talking about Ham's Fork.

As darkness fell over Pretty Water, Rebecca felt twisted inside. She made a bed for Amos in a chifforobe drawer filled with a folded blanket. She wanted to be near in case the baby needed her, but out of respect and fear, she asked Jake, "Do you want to sleep near the baby? Or if you'd like a good night's sleep after your travels, I'd be happy to attend to him."

Jake nodded. "Much obliged."

Rebecca held back a sigh of relief. She made a pallet on the floor next to the fire for Jake and carried the drawer up to the loft where she and Gil slept.

When Gil slipped into the bed next to her, she grabbed his hand and squeezed.

"Careful, Rebecca," Gil whispered. "He's Jake's child. He could return next summer with a new wife and take him away."

For the first time, Rebecca wanted to slap Gil. Instead

she rolled over and placed her hand on the side of the drawer, ready to assist Amos.

Jake's snores filled the cabin, but Gil's steady breathing made Rebecca finally give in to sleep, only to be awakened by a high-pitched wail from Amos. Rebecca tried the bottle, but he refused. She checked his bottom. It was dry. She felt helpless.

From below the loft, Rebecca heard Jake say, "Oh, hell." Before she knew it, he'd climbed the stairs and was coming at her. She hugged Amos closer.

"Hand him here," he ordered.

Reluctantly, she did, then quickly nudged Gil from his sleep.

"What?" Gil asked, rubbing his eyes.

Before she could answer, Jake had thrown the blanket from Amos's makeshift crib over his shoulder and headed down the stairs. They were out the front door within a few seconds.

Gil fell back asleep, but Rebecca rushed to the window, her head dizzy with thoughts. *He's changed his mind. He thinks I can't take care of a crying baby. They're probably leaving for the grandmother's.*

Watching from the window she realized Jake had not headed toward his mule, but was rocking back and forth on his feet, holding Amos to his chest. Soon she heard him singing something about a gal named Sal.

THE NEXT MORNING Rebecca made coffee, eggs, and biscuits while the brothers talked. She noticed the cardinals she'd seen the day before, but this time a few sparrows and finches were among them. Funny what the rain could drag in. They were the most birds she'd seen in one day since she and Gil had arrived at Pretty Water.

"Jake, do you think I could trouble you to dowse the property up a ways from here?" Gil asked.

"Sure," Jake said. Then he wiped his mouth with the napkin tied at his neck.

"I hope to have a farming family join us soon. I've been corresponding with a couple outside of Saint Louis. They have five sons."

"Good thing for a farmer to have."

Gil nodded. "I'm certain a well would be a welcome sight when they arrive."

"I'll help you dig it, too," said Jake.

"That's fine of you," Gil said.

Rebecca heard the clock ticking on the wall as if it were ticking inside her head. How long would digging a well take? She felt restless with Jake there. As if her new life with Amos couldn't begin until Jake was on his way. A few times, she caught him studying her, not like a man sizing up a woman's looks, but as if he was trying to figure out if she could fit the role of a woman taking care of a baby.

Once she overheard him say to Gil, "I thought you'd have a mess of young'uns by now."

"It wasn't in God's plan," Gil said.

After breakfast Jake and Gil went outside, and from the window, Rebecca watched Jake cut a forked branch from a black willow tree. She'd heard Gil talk about how Jake could find the water flowing beneath the ground like their father had done. Some people called it witching, but Gil believed dowsing was a gift—a gift passed down through the generations. Though he'd been passed by. Gil talked of it as if he were disappointed that the gift had not been his.

"Some people have other gifts," Rebecca said, adding, "Man can't live without God's word."

Gil's eyebrows raised. "Man can't live without water either."

Rebecca watched Jake pace the land that would soon be the mission's future farm. She could make out the forked branch that Jake held, too, but soon she became bored. Besides, it was time to feed Amos.

AFTER DOWSING, Jake stayed the entire week, digging the well with Gil. Each night Rebecca grew weary of his trapping stories. All his adventures started to sound the same to her. On the second night she decided to write her mother about Amos and ask for the supplies she needed. She asked for bottles, but thought of another plan until they arrived by steamboat. She'd noticed an Otoe woman with a newborn at the last couple of worship services. Maybe she would nurse Amos in exchange for some sugar. Looking down at the baby, Rebecca thought she'd even be tempted to trade whiskey if it meant that Amos could be fed the best.

AFTER TWELVE DAYS, Jake packed his mule. Rebecca handed Amos to him before he parted. With the baby in his arms, he stared west as if he were searching for the mountains. He can't wait to leave, thought Rebecca. But when he gave Amos back to her and said, "I'll return come summer with meat. Don't expect you to raise him alone," Rebecca heard the choke in Jake's voice.

CHAPTER

4

THE MISSION 1839

AMOS COULDN'T REMEMBER a day without Sparrow Hawk.
Rebecca explained to him that Sparrow Hawk's mother,
Kanza Mi, had nursed Amos alongside him.

As toddlers, they'd played with the mission's baby
chicks and listened to Rebecca read stories. Now, at five,
they collected garter snakes and escaped to the Platte, where
they skipped stones across the river. Some afternoons they
hid behind a black willow tree and watched Gil rehearse
his sermons in the open-air church. Gil would march back
and forth, his voice rising and falling. At some point, he'd
yell at the empty benches and throw his arms in the air.
Amos wished that Gil would go fishing with him or teach
him to swim like the Block boys. But Gil never had time to
do those things.

Rebecca took Amos to school when he first came to her as a baby. He didn't know much about that time, only that Jake had brought him to her and Gil. And when Jake visited each summer, his stories were about trapping and his years in the mountains. Once Amos asked Rebecca about the time before Pretty Water, but the way she avoided his eyes and talked fast made his stomach spin.

"Your mother died when you were born," she told him.

Amos hated the thought of another woman being his mother, and he never asked her about his time before the mission again.

INSIDE THE SCHOOLHOUSE, Rebecca gave a piece of paper to each child. Amos was happy the steamboat would soon be making its way up the Missouri River with supplies because Rebecca told him they were running low on paper and pencils.

Both Rebecca's parents had died in the last few years, but her father's church continued to support the mission. Paper was hard to come by, but several of the prominent members saw to it that Rebecca's students had enough.

Amos loved to draw. He loved the feel of the pencil between his fingers and the way the lead smelled. Most of all, he loved how if he looked carefully enough at something, he could make the image appear on his page. The other children watched in amazement as Amos drew the words they'd learned to read—horse, flower, tree, bird.

Amos was most fascinated by the birds. There were so many around, but Rebecca said it hadn't always been that way.

One day in class, Sparrow Hawk watched over Amos's shoulder. "Draw a butterfly."

Amos sketched a butterfly that seemed so realistic, the wings looked like they could flutter and fly off the page.

That night, Amos overheard Rebecca talking to Gil about his drawing. "Where does he get that talent from? Was your brother a good artist?"

"Not that I know of," Gil had said.

"Oh." Rebecca had sounded disappointed. Amos wondered why he had to get his drawing talent from anybody. No one had shown him how. He just drew what he saw.

Later, Rebecca settled in a chair next to Amos's bed with a new book a member of the Saint Louis church had sent her. Someone in the congregation had recently emigrated from England and donated the book filled with stories.

Amos leaned against her arm and breathed in her sweet lavender scent. "What's this story called?"

" 'Rumpelstiltskin.' "

Amos liked the part where Rumpelstiltskin turned straw into gold. He wished he could do that.

"How do you spell that word?" Amos asked Rebecca.

"*Rumpelstiltskin*?"

Amos shook his head. "No. *Gold*."

Rebecca pointed to the letters on the page, slowly sounding out each one. Amos let the letters sing in his ears—*G-O-L-D*.

SATURDAY, AMOS CLIMBED the big cedar tree on the side of the barn. The cedar scent grew stronger as his arms and legs rubbed against its branches. He gazed across the field to the mission farm where the Block family lived and worked. John and Henrietta Block had arrived a few years before with their five sons. They appeared as giants to Amos. The brothers had sandy brown hair, except for ten-year-old Samuel, who had hair as red as a robin's breast and freckles covering every inch of his body.

Henrietta was tall and thin, but her head looked like it belonged on a stout woman's body, with its heavy jowls and chin that disappeared into her neck.

That first year, John died from typhoid fever, but Henrietta had stayed on, saying, "There ain't no relatives rich or willing enough to take in a woman with five large sons."

LATER THAT MORNING, Amos pretended to be a pirate with the tree as his ship. Gil called out, "Amos, time to gather the wood."

Amos stayed in the tree, trying to breathe quietly, watching the shadows of the branches wave on the grass. He liked going down to the Platte where they gathered the wood. He didn't even mind the chore. But Gil also used the time to quiz Amos about Bible verses. After Amos had heard the story of Rumpelstiltskin, he wanted to know more about gold. Was it as shiny as the silver serving spoon Rebecca kept polished? Where could he get some? Would he have a lot of gold when he grew up?

The last time Amos had mentioned gold, Gil gave him a Bible verse to learn, James 1:17—*Every good gift and every perfect gift is from above, and cometh down from the Father of lights, with whom is no variableness, neither shadow of turning.*

"Come down from the tree," Gil said.

He had no choice. He stepped to the lowest branch and jumped to the ground.

When they reached the Platte, Gil called out, "James 1:17."

Amos shrugged and continued picking up sticks for kindling.

"James 1, verse 17," Gil repeated. He'd been chopping away at the old tree that had fallen a few weeks before. But when Amos didn't answer, Gil laid down his ax and stared his way.

"I don't know," Amos mumbled.

"Yes, you do."

Something built up inside of Amos when Gil pressured him to recite scripture. The feeling pushed against his gut and made his hands roll into fists.

"You need to be prepared," Gil told him.

"Why?"

"To be a Christian soldier," Gil said. "You never know what great things God has planned for you."

Amos didn't want to be a soldier. He believed there was something wonderful in store for him and it had nothing to do with Bible verses. He wanted to learn to swim and fish. He wanted to learn to spin straw into gold like Rumpelstiltskin. What did Sparrow Hawk do with his father? But Gil wasn't his real father. He forgot that until Jake visited and reminded him. Maybe if Jake didn't keep returning, Gil would teach him the things he really wanted to know.

"James 1:17," Gil repeated.

"I don't know!" Amos yelled, dropping the sticks.

Gil's temple pulsed. "You have a big temper for a little boy."

THE FIRST WARM day of spring fell on a Saturday, so Rebecca suggested a picnic. She filled the basket with smoked chicken, dried apples, and a loaf of bread. Then the three of them rode in the wagon to the Missouri River a few miles away.

Soon after they settled on the quilt, a steamboat made its way up the river, the giant red paddle spinning and spitting water, the horn sounding. What an adventure for Amos! He'd heard about the steamboats that traveled down the river, stopping with supplies, but he'd never seen one.

Maybe he'd be a steamboat captain one day. He didn't need to know Bible verses to do that. But he probably did need to know how to swim.

Some sparrows landed near them and hunted about on the ground. Amos and Rebecca tore the remaining bread and threw the crumbs to them.

SPRING MONTHS FLEW into a scorching summer. July brought more than the heat. Each week fewer children showed up at school. One day Sparrow Hawk didn't come. Later Amos overheard Gil telling Rebecca, "It's the pox."

The year before, a doctor had traveled up and down the Missouri on the *Antelope*, vaccinating as many people as possible with the cowpox vaccine. It had been known to keep the smallpox away or at least keep someone from having a bad case of the disease.

Amos still remembered the sting of his arm being scraped with a knife and the vaccine being rubbed into the wound. He'd had a mild fever a few days later, but that was all. Gil and the Block family had been vaccinated, too, but Rebecca declined, saying she'd been vaccinated as a child in Saint Louis. The doctor recommended that she do it again, explaining that the vaccination might have worn off.

Rebecca had shaken her head.

"You're not doing this because you want to save more for the Indians?" the doctor asked. "That would be foolish because some of them are choosing not to be vaccinated."

Still, Rebecca refused.

Kanza Mi was among the Otoe who declined the vaccine, which meant Sparrow Hawk had gone without it, too. Because of nursing Amos, she'd spent more time at the mission than any other Otoe. The elders of the tribe accused her of losing some of the Otoe ways, so she chose not to be vaccinated, as if by refusing she reaffirmed her place in the Otoe world.

"Why can't I see Sparrow Hawk?" Amos asked Rebecca.

Gil answered before Rebecca had a chance. "The pox is bad, Amos. It's for your own good."

"Is it like the fever?" Amos asked. John Block was the only one he'd known who had died from illness.

"Different," Gil said, "but as bad."

Rebecca stared at Gil.

"You can't shelter him from the truth, Rebecca. He'll find out soon enough."

SOMETIMES REBECCA thought she was going crazy. She never mentioned seeing the woman with the wild hair to Gil. Gil saw things in black and white, and though she struggled with the visions, she knew they couldn't be explained that easily. Because just as soon as Rebecca caught a glimpse of her, the woman disappeared. Lately Rebecca had seen her everywhere—floating in the clouds, emerging from the cornfields, staring up at her from the well water. She fought the urge to scream, "What do you want?" Deep down,

Rebecca knew the answer. But Amos was not someone she was willing to let go of.

In August, summer days became shorter and the corn grew so high it hid the Blocks' cabin from view. Jake would be visiting soon. The day he arrived, Amos was up in his tree. He noticed Jake limping across the grassy knoll toward the cabin, the mule packed down with supplies. Two hogs trotted behind them. He'd never seen a hog before, and when he heard their funny squeals, he was tempted to climb down for a closer look at their snouts. But when Gil and Rebecca came out of the cabin to greet Jake, Amos remained in the tree. Now that he was five, he was afraid Jake would take him away. Away from the mission. Away from Rebecca.

The summer before, Amos had heard Jake tell stories about the trappers and how they met at the rendezvous each year to trade and celebrate the end of trapping season. Most of his stories were exciting, like the year that the rabid wolves attacked some trappers. Jake had leaned over in his chair, his eyes widening as he told the gory tale. "One feller rolled on the ground, foaming from the mouth."

Amos had trouble sleeping that night. He loved listening to the stories, but he also noticed Rebecca acted different around Jake. She didn't laugh as much, and she kept a distance from Amos. Last summer when Jake left, she turned around and embraced Amos so tightly, his breath almost left his body. Then everything had seemed right again.

When Jake disappeared into the house to eat, Amos

climbed down from the tree and went inside the barn where Gil was tending the hogs.

Gil squatted by the trough with a bowl of scraps in his hand. "I'll bet these are the only hogs for a hundred miles around."

"Why does he keep coming back?" Amos asked.

Gil finished scraping out the potato peelings and stood. "He's my brother, Amos." Then he added, "And he's your father. He comes back to see you."

Amos dug his heel into the dirt. "Well, I don't want him to come back."

"You don't know what you're saying."

"Yes, I do," said Amos. Then he turned to leave.

"Wait a minute, young man."

Amos stopped.

"Here." Gil held out a bucket. "Go fetch some water for the hogs."

THAT FIRST DAY of Jake's return they sat on the porch while Rebecca cooked supper. The sun was low and the air had a nip to it. The brothers sat in rockers, their legs stretched before them. Amos settled on the floor close to Gil and noticed how different the men looked from each other— Gil's long lean body and Jake's short stocky frame. Jake reminded Amos of a bear, with his leather clothes, matted hair, and burly beard. Gil had a clean-shaven face and always appeared as if he'd just bathed.

Jake leaned over and held up a trap. "Want to know how to trap a beaver, Amos?"

Amos shrugged, but Jake kept talking. "Let's get out on the grass. We'll say that's a stream."

Jake pulled a thick stick over. "Now, let's say that stick is a fallen log across this stream. That's a prime trapping spot. Them beaver like that."

He showed Amos how to fix the trap carefully so that his hand didn't get caught between its jaws. Amos watched as Jake set the trap and explained how beavers made their lodges from sticks and mud.

"How does the beaver get inside his home?" Amos asked.

"There's two holes in the lodge below the water. When they smell the castoreum on the traps, they think it's left there by another beaver. Castoreum is from a beaver's gland. When they smell that, they'll come out at night, and that's when they meet their maker."

Now Amos was sure Jake planned to take him away. He was getting him ready by teaching him how to trap. Amos returned to Gil's side on the porch and Jake soon followed, settling back into the chair.

Gil leaned forward. "Jake, think you could dowse another well before you leave? You always had the touch, you and Pa."

"Expect I could do that. Your wells ain't run dry already?"

"No, it's the eldest Block boy, Adam. His future bride

will join us soon. She's a distant cousin from Saint Louis. Adam's building a place of his own on the farm."

Jake cleared his throat. "When I stopped at the post on the way home, I heard something you might want to take a heed to."

Gil sighed. "I know I'm not liked there."

Jake stuck his finger in his ear and scratched. "One of the trappers took me aside, knowing you was my brother. Said he heard a man telling the Otoe that sending their children to your school was the cause of them getting sick."

Leaning forward, Gil said, "I'm not going to worry about the foolish talk of one man."

"Just thought you might ought to know. I understand it's the pox. Some of the Indians have been known to kill their own young'uns to put them out of their misery."

Gil shook his head.

Jake reached in his pocket and pulled out a watch attached to a gold chain. "Come here, Amos. Let me show you something."

Amos hurried over to Jake's side because he'd never seen anything made out of real gold. Jake popped the clock's cover open. Inside was a drawing of a woman with frizzy hair. She had one tooth missing and another one was rotten. "Know who that is?"

Amos shook his head.

"That's your ma, Delilah. She died birthing you."

Something clanked inside the cabin. Amos looked in the window and saw Rebecca bend down and pick up the Dutch oven. Then she grabbed a knife and started slicing an onion. Her cheeks looked pinker than usual.

Amos stared back at the picture, then glanced away quickly, wondering if the woman would appear prettier if she had all her teeth. He checked again. No, he didn't think so. Then he squeezed his eyes shut and tried to imagine Rebecca's face in the picture instead. That thought comforted him. But when sleep came to him that night, it was the woman in Jake's picture that he saw in his dreams.

THE NEXT MORNING, Amos watched as Jake cut a forked branch from a black willow tree. His fists gripped the branch palms-up as he kept the stick horizontal in front of his big gut. Amos's eyes traced every step Jake made as he moved slowly across the grass. Soon the branch pointed toward the ground. He marked the spot with a stick, then continued circling.

"Did you find the water?" Amos asked.

"Reckon," Jake muttered, continuing his careful pace.

Amos followed him. "Why are you still looking, then?"

Jake didn't answer, but Gil said, "He's looking for a cross stream. Now come over here and leave him be."

Amos joined Gil, who was leaning against the willow. The wind had picked up, and the way it blew through Jake's hair made him look like a wild man.

The branch pointed toward the ground again. Then Jake peered at Gil and nodded.

"Amazing," Gil muttered.

Jake marked the spot and tossed the branch aside. "I expect about sixty feet down."

To Amos, nothing had happened. The next day the Block boys arrived with shovels to help Gil and Jake dig. Amos hadn't seen Samuel much, not since Henrietta made him quit school because he'd played hooky most days. Now he had to work in the fields with his brothers.

Jameson was Amos's favorite of the Blocks. Sometimes after the Sunday sermon, Jameson gave Amos rides on his horse. He was fourteen, next to the youngest, but also the tallest, with shoulders broad as an ox's and forearms thick like hams. When he spoke, his words came out broken. Rebecca had explained to Amos that Jameson stuttered.

For days, the men and boys dug. Amos grew weary watching. He played on top of the growing hill of dark soil near the hole. Then one afternoon, when the sun hung high in the sky, a small puddle of water emerged at the bottom of the hole.

Gil measured the depth. "Fifty-eight feet!"

That night, Amos couldn't stop studying Jake. His eyes journeyed from Jake's head to his boots, trying to see the magic. Jake reminded him of Rumpelstiltskin.

At dusk the next day, Amos sneaked out of the cabin

and searched until he found the forked branch that Jake had discarded. Amos expected the branch to feel different, but when he picked it up, it felt like any other stick, nothing magical. Then Amos paced back and forth, as he'd witnessed Jake do, holding the stick horizontally in front of him, fists palms up.

He felt like someone was watching him so he peered toward the house. But no one was. He continued tracing Jake's steps. A few crows flew down nearby, but he ignored them and continued pacing. Several feet from the well, his hands felt a strange tingle that traveled from the stick, up his arm and smoothed into a wave. When the stick dipped toward the ground, Amos's breath left his lungs as if someone had snatched it right up. He straightened the branch, but this time it quickly returned, pointing toward the earth at his feet. His hands began to quiver, then his body. Amos dropped the branch and ran until he reached home.

CHAPTER
5

AMOS DIDN'T TELL Rebecca about what had happened when he held the branch. The discovery was exciting and scary, but he had a hunch Rebecca wouldn't like knowing he could dowse. That was Jake's gift. The next morning, though, Amos went back for the forked branch and hid it in the barn.

A week had passed since Jake left Pretty Water. The moment he'd set out with his mule, Amos heard Rebecca say, "I can't believe what that trapper told Jake. The Otoe know we'd never harm their children."

But each day that passed, fewer and fewer children attended, and by the end of the week, Amos and Rebecca sat alone in the schoolhouse. Amos made a game out of the empty desks, trying each one for size. But Rebecca just stared straight ahead toward the door as if she expected to see the children rush inside any second.

Finally she broke the silence. "Amos, take your seat."

"I want to sit here now." It was the desk at the back of the room.

"Very well," she said. Then she told him to write his letters. The morning dragged without Sparrow Hawk and the other children. When recess arrived, Amos was happy that Rebecca let him go outside. But after a few minutes, Amos decided it wasn't much fun to have recess alone. He ran, circling the schoolhouse until Rebecca told him to come in.

"You didn't ring the bell," he said, racing past her.

Smiling, Rebecca picked up the stick and rang the cowbell. Amos stopped running and joined her inside.

On Sunday, Matthew Block was the first to show up for worship, as usual. Amos had heard the other Block boys call him Preacher because he'd started to memorize scripture and many nights he sat with Gil on his porch asking questions about the Bible.

Rebecca and Amos settled on the first row. The only others at the sermon were the Blocks. Gil sounded angry, hitting his fist on the podium and yelling. The heat and flies were bad that day, causing everyone's hands to either fan or swat. When the service ended and they had eaten, no one discussed what had changed until the pies had been cut.

Then Henrietta said, "Gil, you think those injuns are gonna up and attack?" Amos had heard the Block boys use the word *injuns*, but not Henrietta. Just weeks before, Rebecca had told Amos that some people referred to

Indians that way, but she said it wasn't a nice word. "And you're not to use it," she added.

Gil's back straightened at Henrietta's comment. "The Otoe have become our friends. Their children are sick. They don't know what to believe, so they believe the only explanation that's given to them. And no, I don't think they're going to attack."

"Well," said Henrietta, "truth be told, I sure hope we don't regret staying on."

Gil narrowed his eyes. "You're welcome to leave at any time."

Henrietta pressed her lips together, then said, "Come on, boys." Her big sons followed like puppies behind their ma.

Rebecca hurried after them until she caught up to Henrietta's side, with Amos tagging closely behind.

"Henrietta, wait," Rebecca said. "He doesn't mean to speak harshly. We need you and the boys. Gil is distraught because of all the work he's done. The situation will straighten out. God's will be done."

Henrietta's eyes hardened. "If you believe that, Rebecca Kincaid, you're the biggest fool on God's green earth."

At supper, Gil said, "Except for Matthew, I'm not sure there's a good Christian among them."

Rebecca shook her head. "Oh, Gil."

"That woman is rough," Gil said.

"Only a little around the edges. My goodness, think of what she's been through."

"You're too kind," Gil told her. "I suspect they joined this mission for the money, not for doing the Lord's work."

Rebecca chuckled. "Oh, yes, there's so much money in doing the Lord's work, especially farming."

Then they both laughed.

Amos was confused. He didn't know someone could get rich farming.

The next day, Gil decided to travel to Kansas to seek out and convince a doctor to return with him. "If only every Otoe had gotten vaccinated, all of this would be unnecessary."

After Gil packed his horse, he embraced Rebecca.

"Please be careful," she said. "Do you think the doctor will return with you?"

Gil tightened the strap around the horse's gut. "I don't know. But something has to change. We didn't come this far to have to turn back."

He pulled Amos to him and rested his hands on his shoulders. "Take care of your—take care of Rebecca. You're the man of the house now." With that said, he mounted his horse, tipped his hat to them, and rode away.

Amos looked up at Rebecca. Her eyes were wet. "Are you sad?" he asked her.

"When you're older, you'll understand what it is to love someone so deeply that you feel a part of yourself missing when they are away. One day you will have a fine wife and you will know."

"Will she be pretty?"

Rebecca smiled. "Yes, I believe she will be beautiful all the way to her soul."

She wiped her eyes with her apron and went inside to start the day's tasks.

THAT MORNING at the schoolhouse, Amos felt restless, twiddling his fingers while Rebecca wrote on the board. "Do I have to be the only one at school again?"

Rebecca gave him a weak smile. "Let's take a day off."

As they walked back to the cabin, Amos asked, "Why did Gil leave?"

"He wants to win back the Otoes' trust, and that's exactly what I plan to do."

When Amos and Rebecca reached the cabin, she placed a clean cloth over the spice cake she'd made the night before. Amos had helped her beat the eggs and stir the ground cinnamon into the mixture. He had to be very careful not to spill the spice because there was only a small jar and Rebecca said she didn't know when they'd get more.

Rebecca picked up the cake and told Amos, "Come along. You can stay at the Blocks' for a while."

"But I want to go with you. I want to see Sparrow Hawk."

"Another time."

Amos walked with Rebecca as far as the mission farm. The Block brothers were cutting the last crop of summer corn. Henrietta gave Samuel a break from the fields and ordered him to watch Amos.

"I'll be back before dark," Rebecca told him before they parted.

Then Amos watched her until she entered the line of trees that formed a barrier across the knoll.

An hour before sundown, she returned. When asked if she'd seen Sparrow Hawk, she answered yes. But that was all she said.

OVER THE NEXT few days, Amos and Rebecca didn't go to the schoolhouse. Each morning she dropped Amos off at the Block farm and headed to the Otoe camp. Each night though she seemed more tired than the night before.

On Saturday she didn't return to the Otoe camp. Instead Rebecca pulled down a box of baby clothes and began cutting them into squares. Most of the outfits had been sent by Rebecca's mother through the years when she was alive. They'd also included gifts from members of her father's church. Rebecca had kept the letters that accompanied each piece of clothing in an envelope—*Many blessings for your new little one. Congratulations on the new baby.* She read them all to Amos.

Rebecca set a few outfits aside for Adam Block's future child. The rest she cut into little squares. When the pile amounted to a tidy sum of white, blue, and brown, Amos asked, "Are you going to give Adam's baby the quilt?"

"No, Adam hasn't married yet. It will be a while before he has a baby. This quilt is for someone special."

"Who?"

Rebecca glanced up at Amos and smiled.

Amos watched her pin the squares together, but he grew bored when she threaded the needle and made tiny stitches. He went back to his tablet and drew.

That night, Rebecca sewed until darkness filled the cabin and the only light came from the sliver of moon. On the fifth evening, when she'd gotten halfway through the quilt top, she tucked Amos in.

"Can I sleep with my quilt?" Amos asked.

"It's not finished."

"That's all right."

Rebecca fixed the quilt top over him.

Amos felt warm and happy. Maybe Jake would let him live at Pretty Water forever. And then Gil would forget that Jake was his father and teach him to swim and fish and love him as much as Rebecca did.

By the middle of the next week, they started watching out for Gil, but he didn't return. That morning they heard Henrietta on the porch. She held a basket of freshly-picked corn. Her sleeves were rolled above her crusty elbows and Amos noticed a brown mole on her forearm in the shape of a pickle.

Rebecca selected an ear of corn and peeled back the green husks. "What pretty corn."

"I've been canning this morning," Henrietta said. "You reckon Gil will be able to fetch that doctor?"

"God willing," Rebecca said.

"Humph." Henrietta stared at the growing quilt on Rebecca's lap. The right corner of her mouth curled up. "I recognize all those clothes."

Rebecca started toward the stack of clothes she'd set aside in the corner. "That reminds me, Henrietta. Please take these clothes for Adam's first child. With him getting married next year, he may need them soon."

Henrietta took the clothes from Rebecca and turned to leave. "It sure is quiet out here. Kind of eerie, if you ask me." She shuddered, then out the door she went.

Amos wondered if she meant the Otoe might attack. Later he watched the horizon from his tree, trying to be the man of the house like Gil had told him to be. But everything was quiet, except for the occasional sounds of laughter coming from the Block boys working in the fields.

Rebecca fed Amos the beans and bread she'd made the day before. Then she told him, "I'm going to lie down for a while."

A few hours later, when the sun set low in the sky, Rebecca was still asleep. And when there was nothing but darkness, Amos dressed into his night clothes and put himself to bed.

The next day, Amos awoke on his own and was surprised to find Rebecca still in bed. He decided to do his chores, but when he finished, she had not come down from the loft. He climbed the stairs and noticed her face was white as the linen sheet on her bed.

"Rebecca?" he whispered. When she didn't answer, he touched her forehead. It was hot. She smelled odd, too, like milk that had gone bad.

Amos tried again. "Rebecca?"

Rebecca raised her eyelids half-mast. "Get Henrietta."

Amos rushed down the stairs and out of the cabin. He passed the cedar tree where a group of crows called out to him. He raced across the grass and tore through the cornfields. By the time he'd reached the Blocks' cabin, he was panting like a dog. Jameson met him at the door. "W-Whoa, young f-feller. What's your h-hurry?"

"It's Rebecca. I think she's sick. She told me to fetch your ma."

Jameson swung around and went for his mother.

When Henrietta appeared at the door, she said, "You better wait here with the boys."

Amos told her, "I'm going back home."

"Suit yourself," Henrietta said, marching on ahead of him.

"It's g-g-gonna be all right," Jameson called out to him.

Amos hung back a bit and watched Henrietta's scuffed boots smash the patches of clover as she walked to his home.

Back at the cabin, Henrietta ordered Amos around. "Fetch me a bucket of water. Get me a clean rag. And I mean a clean one, mind you."

Amos did as she said. He could barely carry the bucket of water up the stairs, having to stop at each step to rest before easing it to the other. Water sloshed over the rim. By the time he reached the loft, Henrietta looked annoyed. Her hands flew to her hips. "Well, it's about time."

She started to lift Rebecca's nightgown over her head, then paused and turned toward Amos. "You run along now."

Rebecca looked his way. Dark circles had formed half-moons under her eyes. "I'll be fine, Amos."

Amos left the loft, slowly going down each step. He picked up his tablet, then quickly dropped it. He didn't feel like drawing. He went out to the tree and climbed to the top branch, searching for a sign of Gil. What if some Indians had killed him? Amos had heard stories from the Block brothers about Indians killing white men, but those stories never seemed real to him. The Otoe had been his friends. He missed Sparrow Hawk. He knew Kanza Mi and Sparrow Hawk would never hurt them. A bluebird landed on a nearby branch and began to sing. Amos watched and listened until the bird flew off.

When the sun was straight up in the sky, Amos grew hungry. He suddenly realized he hadn't eaten all day. He slipped back in the cabin and heard Rebecca heaving.

Henrietta held Rebecca's shoulders. She swung around when she saw Amos easing up the stairs. "Fetch your night clothes and get on to my house. You'll be staying there tonight."

"Why? What's wrong with Rebecca?"

Henrietta scowled. "Never you mind. Just do as I say."

Amos gathered his nightshirt and tablet. He started toward the door, then turned back and grabbed the quilt top.

THE BLOCK BOYS took turns leaving the fields to occupy Amos. Jameson showed him how to juggle three small red potatoes. Samuel stood on his hands and walked across the front of the house. Caleb and Matthew arm wrestled each other. But Amos didn't feel like being entertained.

When Jameson noticed Amos drawing in the tablet, he asked to see it. "S-Snakes alive, Amos. Your p-pictures are like looking at a s-storybook."

Then all the boys passed the tablet around, flipping through the pages. Samuel held the pictures up close to his face. "I can see the tiny feathers on that bird's wings. How'd you do that?"

"You just have to look," Amos said like it was nothing. Still, their compliments lifted his spirits.

Henrietta returned right before sundown. Her bun was lopsided atop her head, and her dress was soiled and smelled like sour milk.

"You boys are going to have to fend for yourselves at dinner. There's a pot of beans left from yesterday. I just came back to change." Henrietta unlaced her boots, pulled them off, and rubbed each foot.

Samuel walked over to her. "What's wrong with her, Ma?"

"If I didn't know better, I'd swear she had the pox."

From the chair across the room, Matthew said, "But we got vaccinated years ago."

Henrietta's left eyebrow shot up. "Most of us did, but she claimed she'd already been vaccinated when she was a little girl. The doctor told her it might not hurt for her to be vaccinated again, but she wouldn't hear of it. 'I wouldn't want to waste what could go to one of the Otoe,' she'd said. Now look at how thankful they are."

Jameson peered sideways at Amos. "I'll bet it ain't the p-pox. I'll bet it's s-something else that she's going to get over with p-pretty quick."

"Humph." Henrietta walked past the table where Amos had put the tablet and the quilt top. She stopped and swung around. "Why'd you bring this into the house?"

"It's mine. Rebecca made it for me."

"She's been touching that all week. We can't stand to take a chance." She grabbed the quilt top and threw it into the fire.

Amos felt a fire of his own flicker inside him. He stood and shoved Henrietta, who lost her footing and fell to the floor.

Matthew helped her up while Caleb grabbed Amos's wrists.

Henrietta brushed the loose hair from her face and

said, "I'll forgive you for that, considering the circumstances. But you better never try anything like that again."

None of the boys said a word as Amos watched the flames spread over the quilt top and burn until there was nothing left.

THE NEXT FEW days, the boys lived on fried eggs, leftover beans, and stale bread while Henrietta trotted back and forth between the two cabins. In the mornings they grabbed a piece of bread before heading out the door. They ate lunch on the outskirts of the fields and took their dinner on the porch in the evenings.

The fourth day that Amos had been at the Blocks', he was sitting on the porch with Samuel when he saw Henrietta heading their way, swinging a dead chicken by its neck.

She handed Samuel the chicken. "Here, pluck this clean for me."

Samuel's shoulders slumped as he took the chicken from her. He plopped on the porch steps and started yanking the feathers off.

Henrietta shook her head. "Laziest boy I ever did see." She turned toward Amos. "Rebecca's fever broke."

Amos jumped to his feet and gazed toward home.

"You can stay put," Henrietta said. "She needs to be well a few days before you start getting underfoot."

Amos's hands curled into fists. He wouldn't get in

Rebecca's way. He'd help her. After all, Gil said he was the man of the house.

Henrietta spent the rest of the day in the kitchen, humming as she worked. It seemed funny to Amos that she frowned while she hummed a tune. Cooking seemed to make her happy. And when the house filled with the aroma of biscuits baking and chicken stewing, Amos's mouth began to water.

That night the dinner table was covered with thick slices of smoked venison, biscuits, gravy, green beans, corn, stewed chicken, and a huge shoofly pie. Amos didn't know how they'd possibly eat it all.

The boys sat at the long table, and Amos settled between Jameson and Samuel. They bowed their heads, and Henrietta said a quick blessing. As soon as *amen* slipped out of her mouth, the boys lifted the bowls and scooped some of the contents onto their plates. Then Samuel grabbed the bowl and repeated the process. Amos held his hands up, but the boys were so tall and focused on the next dish, they didn't seem to notice him. Everything happened quickly. Amos's head began to swirl. Almost all the bowls had passed him by before he figured out the procedure. No one spoke. The only sounds were forks and spoons scraping against the plates.

When the bowls completed their journey around the table, Amos thought he finally had his chance, but they were empty except for the one with a lone biscuit. He grabbed the biscuit and gobbled it down. Even Henrietta didn't seem to notice Amos's slight dinner. She was too busy licking the prongs of her fork.

After dinner Henrietta left with some chicken broth and a biscuit that she'd put aside for Rebecca. Amos figured she'd stay the night with Rebecca, but twenty minutes later she was back with an announcement. "The reverend has returned."

Amos stood as if to leave.

"Sit down," she said. "He told me he'd come fetch you later."

But Gil didn't return that night. Amos knew he didn't because even after he was sent to bed with Samuel, he stayed awake. Once, he dozed off, but he awoke when he heard a coyote howling somewhere in the distance. Finally when early light began to squeeze through the crack in the curtains, Amos heard Gil's voice on the porch. He started to bounce out of bed, but something in the hushed tones stopped him. Instead, he pressed his ear against the curtained window and tried to hear the words.

"She seemed better yesterday," Henrietta was saying.

"The eye of the storm," Gil said. "It's the pox all right. I saw enough of it in Kansas. That's why the doctor couldn't come back with me. He was heading southwest after that. Said it was worse than ever down there."

"Apparently it can wear off after so many years. If only we'd known."

"Mm-hm." Henrietta rocked back and forth in her

chair. "Being around those children gave it to her. You can't trust an injun."

"She wouldn't have had it any other way."

Amos could make out their forms through the thin weave in the curtain. Gil stood. Amos held his breath, waiting to hear Gil mention his name. Then he heard him say, "Do you mind keeping Amos for a while longer?"

"He's no trouble as long as he keeps that temper tamed."

Gil made his way down the steps and Amos slid back in bed, pulling the covers up to his chin. Amos wished he'd recited all those Bible verses Gil had wanted him to learn. He knew most of them. Maybe if he'd shown Gil how he'd memorized them, Gil would think of Amos as his son and take him home.

Stale bread and scrambled eggs for breakfast. Beans for lunch. The bland meals would have stuck to his ribs, but Amos didn't feel much like eating all day because of what he'd heard that morning. He kept waiting for Henrietta to tell him something, but she never did. She just kept busy doing the laundry and preparing dinner. By five o'clock the scents of her hard work at the stove had entranced him, and this time he had a plan.

At dinner when Henrietta said "amen," Amos immediately stood. That way he'd be on the same level as the seated Block boys. This time, when a bowl came his way he grabbed it. He quickly scooped a helping out onto his plate and let Samuel to his right take hold of the bowl. Then he caught the bowl to his left from Jameson. He ate and ate, but instead of feeling satisfied, Amos had a deep hunger, thinking of the slower-paced dinners he'd shared with Rebecca and Gil.

The next afternoon, Henrietta pointed Samuel toward the fields. "Your holiday is over." Then she turned toward Amos. "And if you can't busy yourself, you're welcome to join him."

Amos took out his drawing pad and drew. But as soon as he heard Henrietta humming, he took off for home. When he started, he walked backwards, watching out for her and the Block brothers. But Henrietta stayed inside the house and the boys were too busy clearing the dried corn husks from the fields to notice he was missing.

The wind blew hard that day. Several times Amos stopped to rub the dust from his eyes. As he reached the cabin, he slowed his pace because he heard whimpers and moans. He stared inside the window. Gil would not expect him, and as much as Amos wanted to see Rebecca, he didn't want to startle her. Rebecca was no longer in the loft, but resting upon Amos's bed on the first floor. Gil faced her, blocking Amos's view, but he could see some of her golden hair sprawled on the pillow. He listened as Rebecca spoke.

Her voice sounded tired. "Do you see her?"

"Who?" Gil asked.

"The woman. She's always following me."

"Henrietta?"

"No." She moaned.

Gil wet a rag in a bowl of water and wiped her neck.

"Please, Gil. I can't take it anymore."

"Not that again."

Amos wondered if they were still talking about the woman that Rebecca saw. It didn't sound like it.

"You must," Rebecca cried.

Gil shook his head. "Rebecca, I can't. I won't." He walked to the table and set the bowl down.

When he moved, Amos saw Rebecca. Her face, neck, and arms were covered with blisters filled with pus. If it weren't for her hair and eyes, Amos wouldn't have recognized her.

His stomach churned as he raced toward the farm. A few yards from the fields he collapsed on the ground and vomited. Then he rolled over and buried his head in the tall grass. The sun beat down on his back while the wind swept the blades, singing out a song to him. He wished the song would lift him up and carry him back to the day when Rebecca was well and beautiful, telling him what a very good boy he was.

AMOS AWOKE. Someone was gently shaking his shoulder. He opened his eyes, but the sun was so bright he could only see the large shadow of a man above him.

"You sure f-found a f-funny place to take a n-nap, Amos." Jameson scooped him up and carried him to the Blocks' cabin.

"Draw some water from the well," Henrietta told Jameson as she pulled the soiled clothes off Amos. When the barrel of water was filled, Amos stood on a chair and stepped into the water.

The whole while, Amos didn't say a word. He just let Henrietta bathe and dress him. The year before, he'd started bathing himself, but that day Henrietta could have told him to climb on top of the barn and jump and he would have.

THE NEXT MORNING, Amos awoke to a gunshot. Samuel sprang from bed first. He opened the door to flee, but Henrietta broke his stride. She yanked the collar of his nightshirt and took him back in to where Amos was pulling on his shoes. "You boys stay here. The older boys will tend to it."

Samuel stomped his feet. "Aw, Ma. I always have to miss everything."

As soon as she shut the door behind them, Amos and Samuel parted the curtains and watched as the four older Block boys took off across the field. Amos's heart pounded so hard he heard it beating in his ears. Maybe Gil shot a rabbit.

Soon, Jameson had returned. "It's b-bad, Ma. She's dead. Shot s-straight through the head. Gil won't come. Won't let go of her. He's in there, s-sitting on the floor, r-rocking her."

Henrietta shook her head and flopped into a rocker. "Leave him be for now."

Amos tore out the door, and this time Henrietta didn't

try to stop him. But Jameson did. He swooped him up, and when Amos kicked him in the ribs, Jameson didn't flinch. Amos sobbed and beat his fists into Jameson's chest.

"It'll b-be all right," Jameson whispered, carrying him back into the cabin.

"Who killed her?" Amos yelled.

No one said anything for a long moment. The only sound was the wind moaning against the cabin walls.

Then Henrietta stood and shook her finger at him. "I'll tell you who killed her. Those injuns killed her. That's who."

Amos looked up into Jameson's eyes. "They did?"

Jameson blinked, then softly said, "Yeah. That's who k-killed her all right."

A COUPLE OF HOURS later, Henrietta told her sons, "Go fetch him."

The four older boys went, and when they returned with Gil, Amos was waiting in the doorway. But Gil didn't seem to notice him as Adam guided him through the house and to the back room where Adam and Caleb slept.

After Adam and Gil disappeared into the room, Henrietta told Amos, "He just needs to be alone awhile." The words came out softer than Henrietta's usual harsh tone. Then she twisted around and grabbed her broom. Amos listened to the *swish-swish* sound, wishing he could scream. Instead he escaped into Samuel's room and fell back on the bed.

At dusk, the older Block boys buried Rebecca's body a few yards from Amos's cedar tree. "We'll have a funeral when Gil's good and ready," she told Matthew, who insisted on reciting a few words of scripture. Matthew flipped open the Bible; Henrietta shook her head and walked toward the house.

Later when Amos went to bed, he smelled smoke. He looked out the window, and saw flames blazing from his home and the schoolhouse across the fields. Samuel led Amos away from the window and pulled the curtains together. "Ma said they had to do it, on account of the pox."

That evening, Amos didn't say his prayers. Instead he closed his eyes and whispered, "I hate injuns."

CHAPTER
6

THE DAY AFTER Rebecca died, Henrietta prepared a pot of chicken and corn soup. She added a handful of chopped carrots and was about to put it over the fire, but thought she'd give the soup a good stir first. When she dipped the spoon into the stock, she glanced down only to discover a woman with wild hair staring up. The image startled her, but Henrietta was a no-nonsense person. She frowned and began to stir faster, trying to make the vision disappear. She stirred and stirred, but even the vicious mixing didn't cause the woman to leave. Henrietta hung the pot over the fire and threw on another log. She rubbed her hands together and said, "There. That ought to do you." Then she vowed to quit stealing that nightly swig from her late husband's whiskey bottle, which she kept hidden under her pillow.

LIFE AT THE Blocks' came with a price—chores. But the routine offered Amos some comfort. Helping the boys in the fields at least kept him away from Gil, who did nothing but sit in a chair by the fire and stare at the flames. Gil never spoke, and his hair now had two gray streaks that had appeared the day after Rebecca died.

When Amos tired of his chores, there were no trees on the farm to escape to. Henrietta did not like trees. She wanted to see clear to the horizon. "We'll have a good head start if those savages cause a ruckus," she said to Gil as if he were listening.

Even though Gil didn't respond, she continued. "I'm not like Rebecca. Letting that Otoe woman come inside the cabin and sit at her table. I'd never have an injun step inside this house."

THE BLOCK BROTHERS hardly got through the day before one of them jumped the other and wrestled. The first time Amos witnessed the rumble, he thought they were sore at each other. Arms and legs flew through the air. Bodies rolled. But they finished with smiles and deep belly laughs.

"There they go again," Samuel said. Then he grabbed hold of Caleb by the leg who was busy pinning Jameson to the ground.

Amos stepped back to a safe distance and sat down to enjoy the rest of the fight. When the boys finished, they rolled over flat on their backs, panting like dogs.

"Don't you get hurt?" Amos asked.

"Nah," said Samuel. "Only a few bruises. Unless you count that time Jameson broke his arm or the time Adam broke his nose. That's all." That explained Jameson's oddly placed elbow and Adam's crooked nose.

Amos gave up trying to talk to Gil. He'd become a stranger, spending his days peeling potatoes, washing jars, or doing any other small tasks Henrietta gave him. Otherwise, Gil sat in the rocker and sharpened pencils all day. The pencils started out full size, but by the time he was finished, he would have whittled them down to a nub. The shavings dusted the floor around his chair like fallen flower petals scattered on the ground. Mostly, Gil sat in the rocker and stared at the fire.

Weeks passed and Amos began to see his chores as a way to escape his thoughts about what used to be. He liked the brothers, and soon he joined their wrestling. He had a hunch the boys were gentler with him, but it felt good to be a part of something, even if it meant getting jabbed in the ribs once in a while. During one playful brawl, Matthew's hand dangled inches from Amos's mouth. Amos chomped down hard.

Matthew pulled away, rubbing his palm. "No biting!"

Amos's face burned. He scooted back from the boys and stared down at the grass.

"I don't know about that," Adam said. "He's the runt. And the runt should have some advantages."

"Yeah," said Samuel, raising his head high. "He's the smallest here."

"S-Sounds f-fair to me," said Jameson. So it was decided right there in the edge of the fields that no one except Amos would have the privilege of biting. After that discussion, though, Amos noticed the boys kept him at arm's length, rolling away from him whenever he showed his teeth.

BY EARLY OCTOBER the crops of pumpkins and winter squash were ready to harvest. Henrietta filled the jars with pickled squash and stewed pumpkin pulp. One day when they'd cleared the last pumpkins from the field, Jameson took Amos aside and said, "You w-wanna see a g-giant?"

Amos nodded. Rebecca had told him stories about giants that were so tall their heads were above the clouds.

Jameson dug in his coat pocket and pulled out a small wood carving of a man about three inches long. Amos was disappointed.

"That's not a giant," Amos said.

"You sure a-about that?" Jameson's hand returned to his pocket. Then he opened his fist, revealing a half dozen tiny wooden people no bigger than thimbles. "N-Now it is."

He let Amos play with the carvings whenever he wanted. Amos made a village for them from hollow pumpkins and crookneck squashes. The giant knew how to spin straw into gold. Some days Amos pretended the tiny people were

Otoe. When they weren't looking, the giant stomped on them.

THE WORK SLOWED in the winter, and Amos stayed busy drawing in his pads and playing with the village he'd created. He tried not to think of Gil, until one day he did not think about him at all. But with Rebecca, it was different. Every day he thought of her. He thought of her in the morning when he smelled eggs frying. He thought of her at night when he went to bed without a story. He tried to remember all she had told him—the fairy tales, how one day he would marry someone beautiful all the way to her soul, how he should look for the goodness in everyone. Yet he could not shake his hate for the Otoe.

All the months that had passed, they never saw another one. Caleb said he heard that they'd up and moved closer to the trading post.

Henrietta smirked. "Humph. Closer to the whiskey, no doubt."

But Matthew said he'd heard that they'd lost so many from the pox that they were joining up with another tribe. "The Omaha, I believe. They're all related along the river anyway."

WHEN THE DAYS began to warm into spring, the Blocks became busy with the crops and with the upcoming arrival of Adam's bride to be, Esther. Adam spent the late afternoons and early evenings on their future cabin. And sometimes when Henrietta shamed them, the other boys reluctantly joined him. But usually they left the work to Adam.

"She ain't my bride," Samuel said.

"She ain't mine either," Caleb repeated. Soon the boys sang the same song, even Amos. But Adam continued to build the home, no matter if they helped or not. The cabin wasn't finished in mid-April when Adam drove the wagon over to the dock near Bellevue where Esther and her mother would arrive by steamboat.

Adam had not seen Esther since he was six years old and she was four. Now he was twenty and she was eighteen. On her mother's suggestion, they'd started writing letters to each other after John Block's death. At first the letters were spare and formal. But the last two years, their correspondence became so personal, causing Adam to hide the letters from his brothers. Each Friday, Adam would meet the steamboat to retrieve word from her. "He took after his father, always the romantic type," Henrietta had said, like Adam had been afflicted with some terrible disease. "No telling what he wrote in those letters."

The boys had teased Adam that morning about the trouble he'd encounter at the dock.

"I'll bet she has a hook nose," Samuel said.

"Yeah," Caleb said. "What kind of gal is so desperate she has to come all the way to Indian territory to get hitched?"

But when Adam returned to the cabin, the boys cocked

their heads for a good look. Esther's hair was black as an Otoe's, but she had creamy skin and eyes bright as blue-bells. One look at her, and Amos decided right off he didn't like her. Her beauty made him uncomfortable. When she was introduced to him, he walked away to the other side of the porch.

"Look at him, getting shy," Henrietta said. Then she told the older woman, "Melba, come on in and take your bonnet off."

Amos had learned that Esther's mother, Melba, was Henrietta's second cousin. The women couldn't have been more different. Henrietta's bun always slid to the right side of her head, and her dress was wrinkled and faded. Melba's white hair formed a perfect sausage roll at the nape of her neck, and fine ruffles layered her skirt.

Amos didn't like the way the boys acted strange around Esther. As soon as Adam lifted her out of the wagon, the brothers stumbled over each other to greet her. And by the end of her second week there, Adam and Esther's cabin was miraculously finished.

The wedding would be held three weeks later on May 26. When Amos heard Melba announce the date, he asked her, "What's today?"

"May fifth," she said. Then with a broom in her hand, she went to meet Esther.

Henrietta swallowed the last of her coffee. "Well, what are you standing around for?"

"It's my birthday," Amos said. "I'm six years old."

"In this house we add on a chore for every birthday." Henrietta wiped the cup with her apron before returning it to the cabinet.

Amos didn't bother to ask about a birthday cake. Eight months had passed since Rebecca had died. For a month he'd wept into his pillow before falling asleep each night. Whenever Henrietta spoke harshly to him, for a split second, he'd forget what happened to Rebecca and start to head home. Then when he saw the empty space where the cabin and schoolhouse had stood, he was reminded of it all.

Although the tree and barn still remained, Amos had been afraid to return to them. But it was his birthday. Being six years old should mean he was braver and stronger. He wanted to get the dowsing branch. A few minutes later, he crossed the field and faced the barn door. The cow, hogs, and chickens had been moved to the farm before the Block boys had set fire to the house. Then why was his hand frozen on the barn latch? He held his breath and slowly began to open the door. When he heard the noise, he stopped.

Coo-coo. He knew that sound. The doves. He'd heard them each morning at home. Relieved, he sighed and swung the door wide. A wave of doves took flight above his head, their wings flapping madly as they escaped the barn. At first they startled him but then he felt strangely comforted by the sight of the birds flying toward the clouds. The doves must have slipped in through the holes in the barn walls. When he could no longer see them, he searched for the dowsing rod. He found it in the corner where he'd buried it. Then with the branch in his hand, he headed back to the Blocks', leaving the barn door open in hopes that the doves would return.

Henrietta and Melba decided that dusk was the perfect time for the wedding. "The day will have cooled off by then," Henrietta reasoned. They moved the long table outside and lined lanterns along the porch so when the sun set, there would be enough light to eat by.

To Amos's surprise, Gil performed the ceremony. Except for the white streaks in his hair, Gil seemed like his old self that day, delivering his sermon. After the ceremony Amos felt a bit of hope. Although he didn't know what he was going to say or do, he moved slowly toward Gil. But as Amos came near, Gil walked toward the cabin and never came back for the rest of the celebration.

When the sun set, they feasted on roasted chicken, corn, peas, and squash. Melba added two jars of honey to the meal. She'd carried them all the way from Saint Louis. By then, Amos had long since mastered the circling of bowls from Block to Block. However, Melba's eyes blinked and her mouth flew open at the quick pace that the bowls passed her by.

Esther paid no attention. She was too busy gazing into Adam's eyes. After they'd finished the cake, Adam lifted his bride and carried her across the grass and inside their home.

"Glad she ain't my bride," said Amos. Melba and Henrietta laughed, but none of the Block brothers said anything. They were watching the couple until their cabin door shut behind them.

Melba left for Saint Louis the next day, and the short time they'd had to celebrate ended. Winter was over and it was time to plant. Amos dreaded the end of the carefree days he'd had to draw and play. When he reached the fields that first morning with the brothers, someone was already there, slicing the dark soil with a hoe. It was Gil.

CHAPTER

7

IN EARLY AUGUST Samuel and Amos noticed an old man on a mule approaching the cabin. He wore a raccoon hat over his long silver hair, and a patch covered his right eye.

"Afternoon, young fellers," he said, dismounting the mule.

"Are you a pirate?" Amos asked him.

The man laughed. "Just call me Pirate Paul." He winked with his good eye.

Henrietta and Esther stepped outside with a bushel of peas and a bowl. Even with her hair wrapped in a tight bun, Esther was beautiful.

"If you're looking for the post," Henrietta said, "you're a few miles off." She settled in a chair next to Esther and started to shell the peas.

Pirate Paul pulled off his hat and dug out a letter from his pouch. "No, ma'am. I'm here to deliver a message from Jake Kincaid to his brother, Gil. Does he live nearby?"

Henrietta ran her thumbnail down the spine of a pea pod. "You found him."

"You ain't his wife, are you?" Pirate Paul asked, giving Henrietta a good looking over from head to toe.

"She's dead. But Gil lives here now. He's working in the fields."

He handed the letter to Henrietta, who passed it to Esther. "Read this. I broke my glasses years ago and haven't been able to read a word since."

Amos wondered if Henrietta could read. They didn't have any books in the cabin except for Matthew's Bible.

Esther's cheeks turned scarlet. "But it's Gil's letter."

Henrietta smirked. "And when do you think he'll get around to reading it?"

Esther looked to Pirate Paul, who took off his hat and wiped his forehead.

"I'm sure it will be fine, ma'am."

As Esther carefully opened the envelope, Pirate Paul turned to Amos. "You must be Jake's boy."

Amos didn't say anything, but Henrietta said, "That's right. He was raised here at the mission."

Pirate Paul ignored her. "He talks about you all the time. Of course he talks all the time, but I reckon you know that."

Esther read Jake's letter. "Dear Gil, I'm not going to be

coming your way this summer. I need to get a jump on the trapping and sir—" Esther paused. "I think he meant *circumstances*." She continued to read, "and circumstances have arisen. Here's some money to help with Amos. Tell my boy he can expect to see me next summer. Your brother, Jake."

Pirate Paul shook his head. "Everyone else figures that was the last rendezvous. But not Jake. The trapping life is over, but Jake just won't give it up. Well, maybe it ain't over for him. He could always sniff out them beaver better than anyone I know. I swear he's part beaver."

Henrietta grabbed the envelope and peered into it. "Where's the money?"

Pirate Paul tapped his leather pouch. "I've been instructed to give it to Gil personally."

"Samuel," Henrietta said, "go fetch Gil."

Samuel took off toward the fields.

Henrietta stared down at Pirate Paul. "What's Jake mean by 'circumstances'?"

A slow grin spread across Pirate Paul's face. "Oh, when was the last time you seen ole Jake?"

"A year ago. He dowsed a place for that new well." Henrietta pointed to the well in front of Adam and Esther's cabin.

"I reckon he had nothing but his mule with him?"

"And two hogs that he gave Gil."

"Well, let's just say Jake ain't traveling so light anymore." He fixed his hat on his head. "I guess I'll make my way to the post, seeing as you ain't offering me anything to eat."

"All you had to do was ask," Henrietta said. "You can wash up at the well."

Gil reached the house just as Pirate Paul finished splashing water on his face.

Amos didn't care what the circumstances were. He was happy he would be with the Blocks for at least another year.

The week after Pirate Paul delivered the message from Jake, Esther asked Amos, "How would you like me to teach you to read?"

He'd done his best to avoid her since she'd been at the farm, but she'd caught him alone on the porch, playing with Jameson's wood-carved giant and people.

"I know how to read," Amos told her.

She handed him a book. It looked just like the book that Rebecca had read stories from. The book that he thought had burned with the house. "Can you read this?"

"Where did you get that book?" Amos asked her.

"My aunt sent it to me from England. They're German stories."

He was right. The book had burned. Rebecca hadn't finished reading the stories, and he'd wanted to know all of them. "Can I learn to read *that* book?"

Esther smiled. "Of course. I'll need to speak to Henrietta about you getting out of some of your chores before we begin."

Later when Esther asked Henrietta, Samuel overheard. "Can I go too, Ma?"

"Amos can," Henrietta said, "but you ain't. You already proved schooling ain't your calling."

"Well, chores ain't my calling either." Samuel stomped out of the house, slamming the door behind him.

EACH MORNING after breakfast, Amos headed to Adam and Esther's cabin. They read from the book, but she sneaked in arithmetic and spelling, too. She owned a map of the world and made him point out places he'd read about in the book. He began to awake with anticipation, but when Esther touched his arm in a way that reminded him of Rebecca, he shrugged from her reach. After that, they settled into their roles of teacher and student, nothing more.

The first time Amos came for his lessons, Esther thought she felt the presence of another person. She never saw the person, but she assumed it was Rebecca. There were some things about herself that Esther had not told Adam. And one of those things was that she believed in angels. She always had. When she was a small child, her grandmother had visited her moments after dying. Even her mother did not learn of the death until months later when word traveled by ship from Italy. Esther believed loved ones who passed on watched over those left behind. It made perfect sense to her that Rebecca would be looking after Amos.

ONE AUTUMN AFTERNOON when they were harvesting pumpkins and squash, Samuel motioned for Amos to follow him
away from the field. The older boys were so focused on the
task, they didn't notice Samuel and Amos slip away.

Soon they reached the woods that bordered the farm
and the Platte. Amos asked, "Where are we going?"

"You ever seen a steamboat on the wide Missouri?"

"Yes," Amos answered, remembering the day of the picnic. A sadness started to fill him, but then Samuel grabbed
his hand.

"We better hurry."

Samuel and Amos raced through the woods, dodging the
trees, stopping only when they needed to rest. Then they
were running again. They arrived at the river in time to see a
steamboat making its way down to the trading post.

"I'm gonna ride a steamboat one day," Samuel said.

"Can I go, too?" Amos asked.

"Yep, if you want to get rich." Samuel leaned back, resting on his elbows. "I'm gonna find a lot of gold and marry
me a pretty woman."

"I'm going to marry a pretty woman one day." Rebecca
had told him he would. "And I'm gonna be rich, too," he
added.

After the steamboat disappeared from their sight, Amos
asked, "Can you teach me to swim?"

Samuel hopped to his feet, "Nothing to it. Follow me."

Amos stayed right behind Samuel as he raced into

the water. For as long as he could remember, he'd wanted to learn to swim. Samuel made it look easy, and Amos believed it was until he took a step that caused the water to cover his head. He tried to jump, but his toes couldn't reach the river bottom. He opened his eyes, but all he saw was darkness. The river was taking him to the world below. Finally his body floated up and his head bobbed above the surface.

"Help," he cried before sinking again. Amos flapped his arms and kicked his feet. Somehow he managed to reach above again. He looked into the sun. Black dots circled in the sky. Just as he realized the dots were crows, he sank again. His heart pounded against his chest. A second later, he felt a yank and a force thrusting him out of the water. Someone was holding him up. Was it Samuel? But when his vision cleared, he saw Samuel on the riverbank watching him.

"Hold on, little mister!" the voice said as he carried Amos through the water. The voice was thick and unfamiliar. When they reached the bank, Amos was placed next to Samuel.

Amos looked up. A dark man, darker than the Otoe, bent over, his hands resting on his knees as he tried to catch his breath. Water glistened on his tight curls. A few seconds later, he stood and grabbed a cloth sack from the ground. Two apples and a fiddle fell out.

Samuel snatched the fiddle just as the man's hand reached toward it. "You a runaway slave, ain't you?"

River water dripped down the man's face. "No, sir."

"Yes, you are," Samuel said. "You're one of them Missouri slaves."

Amos had first heard about slaves in the Bible from Rebecca. And Esther told him that some men owned slaves today. She'd shown him where they came from on the map—a place called Africa.

The man didn't say anything. He just stared at the fiddle, then looked toward the line of trees skirting along the river.

"Where are you heading?" Samuel asked.

"Are you going back to Africa?" Amos asked, wanting to prove to Samuel he knew some things, too.

"No, sir. I's going west."

Amos looked down at the man's bare feet. If he meant the West, where Jake went, that was a long way. How would he walk that far with no shoes?

Samuel dangled the fiddle by its neck. "Is this here your fiddle?"

"Yes, sir." The man looked toward the trees.

"Tell you what," Samuel said. "You give me this fiddle. I won't say I seen you."

The man's eyes met Amos's.

"I won't tell, either," Amos said. He suddenly felt chilled and wrapped his arms around his body.

"My pappy made me that fiddle," the man said.

Samuel plucked one of the strings. "I hear there's big rewards for information about runaway slaves."

The man swallowed and picked up his sack. He dug inside until he pulled out the fiddle's bow. "You need this if you's gonna play. If you's works at it some, da fiddle will sing."

"Hope you make it west," Samuel said, taking the bow from him.

The man took off walking fast, his pace soon turning into a run. Amos watched the pale bottoms of his feet until he disappeared into the woods.

As Amos and Samuel headed their own way, Samuel rubbed the bow against the neck of the fiddle. Then he stopped. "You know we can't tell about this, Amos."

"I'm not going to tell," Amos said.

"Never." Samuel narrowed his eyes.

"Never," Amos repeated. If it weren't for the man, he'd still be in the dark world underneath the Missouri. He'd never tell as long as he lived.

"I tried to save you," Samuel said.

Amos was not so sure about that.

As they walked back to the mission, Samuel rubbed the bow across the fiddle. It made an awful screech. "Maybe I'll get rich playing this fiddle. Or maybe it will help get me a pretty girl."

Amos walked beside him thinking that Samuel would need to practice a lot before either of those two things happened.

Henrietta met them at the edge of the fields. The other

Block boys stopped their work and watched as she grabbed hold of Samuel's ear and pulled him toward the cabin.

"Ow! Ow, ow!" Samuel hollered.

Amos followed at a slow pace.

Henrietta glared at Amos from over her shoulder. "If you ever sneak off swimming with this sorry fellow again, you'll be traveling back to the cabin the same way."

Amos's ears burned.

At the cabin, Henrietta quizzed Samuel and Amos about the fiddle.

"Found it in the woods," Samuel said, the whites of his eyes growing wider. "Someone must have dropped it."

She let him keep it, but she separated Samuel and Amos when they worked in the fields. Samuel had to stay near Caleb, and Amos was assigned to Jameson. That suited Amos just fine.

A week later, two men on horseback rode up to the farm. Amos had just come from his morning lesson with Esther. The men wanted to know if they'd seen a runaway slave traveling through the area.

"Jeremiah's a dark one," one of the men said. "And he had a fiddle with him. He'd never part with that."

Henrietta stared at the man. "Nope, can't say I seen him." She turned and headed into the house.

Amos was surprised when Henrietta didn't mention the fiddle. Later Caleb asked, "Who were those men, Ma?"

"Two men looking for a runaway." She picked up a sock and began to darn. "Never met a slave owner I cared to know."

NOT A DAY had passed by since Rebecca's death that Henrietta had not seen the woman with wild red hair. When cutting out her evening swig of whiskey did not keep her away, Henrietta decided to double the dose. She slept sounder than ever each night, but still the vision would appear the next day. Henrietta began to accept the woman's presence and thought, as long as she was there, she might as well talk to her. Rebecca had never been the type she could burden, and Esther seemed to be cut from the same cloth. Henrietta became so comfortable with their one-sided chats that she'd forget to make certain they were alone.

The boys and Esther caught her mumbling to herself often, and they started to wonder if Henrietta was losing her wits. But when she noticed them staring at her, Henrietta would snap, "Don't you have something better to do than watch an old woman talk to herself?" Her remark assured them that she had not crossed entirely to the other side, and they left her and went about their business.

BY WINTER every hair on Gil's head had turned white. He spoke more, but only when someone asked him something. When spring arrived, Gil sometimes talked about the crops like he used to recite scripture, repeating the remarks over and over again. "A good rain would do well for the corn," or "No time to toil. The fields must be hoed." Amos had long since quit trying to communicate with him.

One night after dinner, Esther excused herself early from the table. She went to her cabin, then returned with a pound cake and something wrapped in fabric. "Happy birthday, Amos."

Amos had forgotten. He'd turned seven years old that day.

A hearty round of birthday wishes came from each Block brother. Even Henrietta wished him well, and Gil smiled his way. Samuel attempted a tune on the fiddle. He practiced every evening until Henrietta snapped, "Enough of that!" But that night she listened to him as he stood in the middle of the room and slid the bow across the strings. Whenever he hit a wrong note, which was often, Amos noticed her wince.

When Adam began to dance with Esther, Caleb tied on Henrietta's apron and danced with Jameson. Henrietta shook her head. "Well, if this ain't the most ridiculous bunch I've birthed into this world."

Later Esther handed him the wrapped gift, which turned out to be *German Popular Stories*, the book with "Rumpelstiltskin" and other stories he now loved.

JUNE BROUGHT a lot of rain, which kept the boys out of the fields and under Henrietta's feet. The morning the sky cleared away, Henrietta went from bed to bed and yanked the sheets off them. "Rise and shine. Time to work." It was the best mood she'd been in since the rains.

They worked a long day, tromping through the mud. Even Amos had to skip his lessons and help out. During dinner he fought to stay awake, his head bobbing, until he finally slumped over, his face landing in the mashed potatoes.

Everyone laughed except for Gil, who'd retreated early to his chair. After dinner, Adam and Esther returned to their cabin. While Henrietta washed dishes, the others sat on the floor listening to Samuel try to play his fiddle. A few minutes later, the dogs went to barking.

Henrietta dropped a spoon. Caleb grabbed the gun. Samuel lowered his bow. All eyes focused on the door. A hush fell inside the cabin except for the sound of Gil's rocker knocking against the floor.

"Hello there," a deep voice bellowed from the other side of the door. "Anyone home?"

Amos recognized Jake's voice right off. His heart pounded.

"It's Jake Kincaid. I'm looking for my brother, Gil."

Caleb put the gun down. Henrietta walked to the door and swung it open.

There stood Jake, and next to him was an Indian woman. He scanned the room over Henrietta's shoulder. "I'm here to get my boy."

The Indian woman dressed fancier than any Otoe Amos had seen—moccasin boots with beaded trim, stone necklaces, gold bangle bracelets, duck feathers tied to her hair. The woman's eyes sat wide apart on her round face.

Henrietta froze in the doorway. She had not asked them in yet.

Finally, Jake said, "I'd planned to stop at Gil's. Saw the house had burned down and noticed Rebecca's grave."

"It was the pox," Henrietta said.

Jake looked past her, his eyes searching until they found Amos. "That's a damn shame. Rebecca was a good woman."

Amos wondered why Henrietta didn't tell Jake the Otoe had killed her. Why had she lied?

"Gil got the money I sent by Paul, didn't he?"

From across the room, Samuel hollered, "Pirate Paul?"

Jake snorted. "Old Man Ferguson? He ain't no pirate. Just an old trapper with one good eyeball."

Henrietta opened the door wide and stepped back, leaving room for them to come inside. She studied the Indian, her gaze traveling up and down the woman's body.

Jake seemed to take notice. "Pardon me, ma'am. This here's my wife, Blue Owl."

"Your wife?" Henrietta's face screwed up, working on Jake's words. She glanced at Amos, then told Jake, "Well, pull up a chair."

Caleb offered his chair, and Jake dragged it across the floor until he reached Gil's side. Amos and the Block boys stayed silent, staring at Blue Owl.

"The pox." Jake shook his head. "I think the Indians have it pegged right. They call it 'rotting face.'" He took off his fox hat, revealing matted hair.

"I expect you're hungry." Henrietta headed toward the fire. "We already ate. I'll have to warm up some food."

Blue Owl stood between Henrietta and where Jake sat as if she wasn't sure where to go.

"Blue Owl will be glad to help you," Jake said.

"I'll be fine," Henrietta said. "Never cottoned to another woman in my kitchen."

"No, 'spect not," Jake said.

Blue Owl's bangles jingled as she moved across the floor and settled at Jake's feet.

Jake leaned forward, stopping when his face was a few inches from Gil's. "It's me, little brother. Jake."

Gil's eyes were empty, but he nodded.

"You been through a time, ain't you?" When Gil didn't answer, Jake turned his attention toward Amos. "You done growed."

"I'm not as tall as Samuel yet," Amos said.

"Which one of you is Samuel?" asked Jake.

Samuel stood with his fiddle tucked under his arm, his back erect, and his chin raised.

Jake gave him a good look-over. "Nope, not yet."

Then Samuel quickly asked, "Sir, how'd you get that Indian wife?"

Jake leaned over the way he always did when he was about to tell a long story. "I knew her pa. Met him a few years back at the rendezvous. A lot of Shoshone show up there each year. After Delilah died, he said I could have any of his daughters whenever I wanted. For a good long time, I didn't want no wife. Who needs the trouble? Until last summer when I sized up all three daughters. All of them was purty 'cept this one. But I picked her because I watched her work. And she can work. Purty fades. You should have seen her sisters' faces when I chose Blue Owl. They looked like they'd been slapped good."

Everyone in the room twisted their heads toward Blue Owl. If she understood what Jake was saying, she didn't seem upset.

Henrietta placed a plate with a chunk of ham on the table. She told Blue Owl, "If you have a notion to, you can cut the ham." She spoke loud, as if Blue Owl was hard of hearing.

Blue Owl stood and walked over to Henrietta who held out a butcher knife to her.

Amos wondered how Henrietta went from never having an Indian in her house to handing a knife to one.

"Ain't you gonna talk to me, brother?" Jake said to Gil. Then he turned his head toward Henrietta. "He ain't worth much now, is he?"

Henrietta ignored him and placed the plates on the table with a loud thump. Amos wondered if she didn't like Jake, but then again, he couldn't tell if Henrietta cared much for anyone.

Suddenly Gil asked, "How was trapping?"

"Well, trapping was not so good," Jake said. "And trading was even worse. Sorriest year I've ever had. Last year at the rendezvous, there was a lot of talk about how people back East were getting tired of beaver. That it's going out of fashion in Europe. Others said the creeks were trapped out. That's why I didn't come last summer. I aimed to prove them wrong, and I wanted to get an early start. I swear their sour talk ruined it. You should have seen—"

"Food's on the table," Henrietta snapped.

Amos figured Henrietta had saved them from hearing one of Jake's long stories that would surely lead to another tale.

The boys didn't say a word. They just watched the two visitors eat. Blue Owl ate with her fingers. Jake started to, but then he noticed the fork and knife. He sighed, lifted the utensils, and put them to use. He finished by sopping up the last of the gravy with his bread. Then he gulped down a mug of water and wiped his mouth with his sleeve.

"What happened to Gil's cabin?" Jake asked.

Henrietta's eyebrows raised. "Burned it down after the burial. On account of the pox."

"Care if we bed down outside your home?" Jake said. "We'll move on tomorrow with my boy."

Amos felt sick in the pit of his stomach.

"Where are you going to take him?" Henrietta asked.

"Back to Bittersweet Creek. I'm gonna have to dowse for a while. Lots of people moving into the Missouri Territory. They'll be needing wells. And with Rebecca dead and all . . ." He glanced over at Gil. "Well, you see how it's gotta be."

Henrietta settled into her chair next to Gil. "One more mouth to feed ain't no trouble. You can leave Amos here with us."

"I can't."

"Why not? I just said you could."

Jake sucked his teeth. "You ain't kin."

Blue Owl began to gather the dishes.

"Just leave those," Henrietta snapped.

Blue Owl returned the plates to the table. Then she walked outside the cabin.

Amos's heart pounded in his ears. He hoped Henrietta would say something else about him staying, but she pulled a shirt from her mending basket and started to sew.

Before stepping outside, Jake paused and stared at the floor. "I can't take Gil, though."

Henrietta pulled her needle through the fabric, not bothering to look up. "He ain't a problem. Besides, he's getting better."

Amos wondered why Henrietta would lie for Gil but

wouldn't help him. All night Amos stayed awake, staring at the moon and listening to Samuel's slow breaths. He thought of running away, but where would he go? He wondered if the runaway slave made it west with his bare feet and two apples.

The next morning, Amos rose early and went into Gil's room. He tapped him on the shoulder.

Gil opened his eyes.

"Don't let them take me, Gil," Amos begged. "Please. I want to stay here." He didn't add "with you" because it would have been a lie. Gil was not the same person he remembered. He meant here with the Block boys. They'd become like brothers to him.

Gil stared at him with empty eyes.

A lump gathered in Amos's throat. "Gil, please. I promise I'll be a Christian soldier." Between swallowing sobs, Amos recited, "James 1:17—Every good gift . . . and . . . every perfect gift . . . is from above, and cometh down from the—"

"Go with your father," Gil said. Then he rolled over and Amos stood alone.

THE BLOCK BOYS lined up like pickets in a fence. Adam was first. He held out his hand, and Amos shook it firmly like he'd been taught by Gil. Matthew and Caleb followed.

Jameson tousled Amos's hair. "Got s-something f-for ya."

He dug in his pocket and pulled out the carved giant. "He'll p-protect you f-from anything. K-Kind of like a good l-luck charm."

Amos took the giant from him and slipped it into his pocket. An aching filled him when he thought he'd never see Jameson and Samuel again. He'd miss them the most.

And as if Jameson read Amos's thoughts, he added, "Watch for me. You never know when I m-might c-catch up with ya."

For a moment, Amos felt hopeful. Samuel stepped forward and instead of a handshake, he punched Amos in the shoulder. His shoulder stung, but it kept his mind off his gut.

Esther came from the cabin with Henrietta. She went over to Amos, bent down, and kissed his cheek. Amos longed to reach his hand toward her arm, but resisted. He didn't need anyone now.

Henrietta gave a muslin sack with Amos's clothes to Jake. Jake looked in the sack and pulled out Amos's gray wool pants and white shirt. Rebecca had starched them each Saturday for the Sunday worship services. Amos hated those clothes. They made his entire body itch. But when Jake said, "Won't be needing these," and handed them back to Henrietta, Amos suddenly wanted them more than anything.

Hugging the sack, Henrietta looked down at Amos. "I'll put the clothes away for Adam's first son. Don't forget to clean behind those ears." Her lips twitched a bit and she quickly turned around to leave.

Amos didn't bother to say good-bye to Gil, who was inside the house, probably staring at a wall. He didn't care if he ever saw him again. Gil had rejected him, and Amos would never forgive him.

Jake finished packing the mule with jars of pumpkin and squash Henrietta gave them. They were about to leave when Samuel said, "Wait!"

He raced back into the cabin and returned with the fiddle. "I'll send you off with a song." Positioning his chin on the fiddle, he placed his bow on the strings and screeched out something that sounded like "The Campbells Are Coming." Then with the river serving as their guide, they set off by foot, the three of them—a water seeker, his Shoshone wife, and a boy with a giant in his pocket.

CHAPTER
8

JUNE 1841

THE BOY'S FEET hurt, Blue Owl was certain. Halfway through the first day of the journey to Bittersweet Creek, she noticed Amos walking on the balls of his feet. Probably blisters, she reasoned. The shoes were a poor choice for a long walk. She would make moccasins for him that night. Her head was busy with thoughts as Jake rattled on.

"Trapping gave me a good life," he told Amos. "But this last year, them mountains turned into a scorned woman. Where I used to trap five beaver, I'd get only two. Yes, sir, God was laughing at me."

The sun danced on the river. A pyramid of geese flew overhead, honking. Jake stopped talking and quickly went for his shotgun in the mule pack. He aimed at the geese, then hesitated, returning the gun.

"Why didn't you shoot?" Amos asked, even though he was relieved Jake hadn't.

"Ah!" he grunted. "We got plenty of food. Did you know that geese mate for life?"

Amos shook his head.

"Once when I was a boy, a flock of geese flew over our farm. I figured they were heading south. My pa shot one. If he aimed at something, he shot it. It was Christmas Eve, and we thought a blessing had fallen out of the sky. A Christmas goose! The next morning, while I tended to the animals, I saw one old goose waddling around like he was lost. Gil's ma told me, 'That's because your father shot his spouse.' Never could quite enjoy the taste of goose after I learned that."

"What happened to him?" Amos asked.

"I had me a pet goose for a while. Called him Widower. Then one night a coyote got him."

He should have shot the goose, Blue Owl thought. Her father could kill a goose in mid-flight with a single arrow. Blue Owl cared about a lot of things in this world, but a goose was not one of them. Birds were to be eaten. At the last rendezvous, she'd tasted her first apple pie. The sweet fruit oozed from the flaky pastry, but that night she dreamed of a pie filled with sparrows and wild onions. She awoke, her mouth salivating. Now sparrows seemed to sense her desire, fleeing from her sight when she looked their way.

THEY MADE CAMP at twilight. Amos removed his shoes in haste. Blood spotted his socks where the blisters had broken. Jake didn't notice. He was too busy gathering wood for a fire. But Blue Owl stared at his feet. Amos tucked them under his legs and frowned.

Amos watched Blue Owl pull a pan from the pack and mix cornmeal with water. She formed flat cakes that she cooked in a skillet over the fire. She served the corn cakes with smoked elk, and though Amos was hungry, he didn't want to eat anything that Blue Owl had made. He turned away from his plate.

"Eat!" Blue Owl said.

Amos gasped, taking in so much air that he started coughing. Finally he caught his breath. "You can talk?"

Jake chuckled. "Sure she talks."

"But she hadn't talked," Amos said.

Blue Owl glanced toward Jake. He filled all the quiet, always had.

"She don't much care to talk," Jake said.

AFTER THEY'D EATEN, Blue Owl walked over to Amos and gently held his foot. Amos frowned and wiggled it free from her grasp.

She sighed, then grabbed his shoe and went back to her place across the fire. With a porcupine needle, she began to sew small pieces of deerskin together.

"You want to know how she got her name?" Jake asked.

Amos shrugged.

"She was born with her ma's cord around her neck. Face was as blue as a jaybird. That's what they say. They thought she was dead, but then she went to breathing. The *Owl* part is on account of her round face and how her eyes are kinda wide apart."

Amos stared in the opposite direction, but Blue Owl caught him peeking at her a moment later. Jake thought he knew everything about her, but he didn't. She had dreams he'd never know, and one of them was about to come true. She'd traveled with Jake the last two years while he trapped. She'd wintered at Powder Creek with the other trappers, cooking for strangers. The other women were Indian, too, but not Shoshone. They might as well have been white. Most of all, she'd disliked the rendezvous, where the men drank too much and fought over Indian women.

Jake thought he'd chosen Blue Owl, but she had prayed to the Great Spirit that he would choose her instead of one of her beautiful sisters. This man of stories had intrigued her. And she'd seen him find water with the branch. This was a man with gifts. That was before she grew tired of his stories and discovered he despised dowsing. Now she suspected he'd performed the act to impress her father.

But soon she would have a cabin. No longer would her feet have to move west through mountains and snow.

Blue Owl continued sewing after the sun set. Jake slept, but Amos fought it, stealing glances at her through half-closed eyelids. She felt him watching her as she sat in the orange glow of the fire, pulling the needle through the deerskin. Long after he fell asleep, she finished and laid the pair of moccasins at his feet. She felt someone else watching, too. She'd felt it ever since they'd left Pretty Water with Amos. The wind picked up and stirred the fire. The face of a woman appeared in the flames. The discovery did not cause her fear. She believed spirits walked with the living. And without ever having seen her, Blue Owl knew this spirit was the boy's mother.

In the morning she waited with anticipation as Amos discovered the moccasins. When he did, he quickly turned his head, studying Jake from head to toe. Jake wore a hat made from a fox, a buckskin shirt with fringe and beading, and moccasins. Blue Owl had stitched every piece.

Jake mentioned the moccasins. "Better put them on. You'll never want to wear those silly buckled shoes again."

Amos didn't move. Blue Owl waited, too, sitting with a stiff posture. A moment later she went to the fire and placed the coffeepot over the low flames.

Jake stared down at Amos's feet, then said, "We'll be moving out shortly. We have about nine days of walking ahead of us before we reach Bittersweet Creek."

They ate leftover corn cakes and loaded the mule with the supplies. By the time they finished, the moccasins were on Amos's feet.

THE CLOSER they came to Bittersweet Creek, the quieter Jake grew. Instead Blue Owl filled the silence with questions about Jake's cabin.

"How many windows?" she asked.

"Two," Jake said.

She pondered on that. Then a few miles later she asked, "Dirt floor?"

"Yep," Jake answered.

This disappointed her. She'd wanted a wood floor like Henrietta's.

"It was good enough for Delilah," Jake said.

Blue Owl had not heard Delilah's name since before she became his wife. She didn't say another word until the next day, when she asked, "Water?"

Jake sighed. "The well is about twenty steps from the front door."

"How much longer?" Amos finally asked.

"Soon," Jake snapped. Then he softly added, "Tomorrow."

CHAPTER
9

BITTERSWEET CREEK

AS THEY APPROACHED Bittersweet Creek, the smell of chimney smoke filled the air, and before long a cabin came into view. Jake slowed his pace.

On the porch stood a young man, who held a rifle aimed at them. He cocked the trigger. "Just hold it right there, mister."

They did as they were ordered.

"That's my porch you're perched on," Jake called out to him. His voice was calm and tired.

"Says who?"

"Jake Kincaid. That'd be me."

The young man was almost as thin as the rifle he held. He kept the barrel aimed toward the trio and hollered, "Daisy! Get out here!"

A moment later, a pretty girl with golden red hair came onto the porch. She was small except for her round belly that reminded Amos of the Otoe women right before they had babies.

"He said his name is Jake Kincaid," the young man told her.

Daisy smiled and waved at them. "Hi, Jake!"

"Well?" asked the man. "Is he?"

"I said hi to him, didn't I? Come on in, Jake."

The gun was still aimed at them.

Amos stepped forward, but Jake caught him by the collar.

Daisy snapped her tongue and released a loud sigh. "Put the gun down, Homer."

Homer relaxed his arm but forgot to ease the trigger back and the rifle went off, making a hole through the porch floor.

Amos jumped.

"You just put a hole in my porch, boy," Jake said.

"Sorry." Homer's face turned scarlet.

"This here is Homer," Daisy said. "My husband."

Homer offered his hand. He had tiny eyes and a possumlike grin. "Pleased to meet you."

Jake shook Homer's hand. "Sure you know how to use that thing?"

"Oh, yes, sir. I know how to use it just fine. I shot a couple of squirrels this morning."

"He was aiming at a deer," said Daisy.

"Shoot dang. Was not." Homer yanked at his pants' waistband.

Daisy ignored him. "He can't see too good." She studied Amos. "You're Amos, ain't you?"

Amos nodded. How did this girl know him?

"I'm your aunt Daisy. You can call me Daisy, though. I don't feel old enough to be an aunt."

Jake rubbed his beard. "You were just a little thing when I saw you last."

Daisy straightened her back, causing her belly to stick out more. "I'm fourteen years old."

Jake chuckled. "That ain't old."

Daisy stared at Blue Owl. "I ain't never seen an injun before."

Blue Owl frowned.

"Blue Owl's my wife."

Daisy's mouth dropped open, but nothing came out.

"You live here now?" Jake asked.

She stopped staring at Blue Owl and said, "No one was living here, and we figured there'd be no harm. Reckon you'll be wanting us to move on."

Jake settled in the chair at the table. "I didn't say that."

Amos noticed how Blue Owl narrowed her eyes at the back of Jake's head.

"Your folks still live around here?" Jake asked Daisy.

"Ma and Pa do, but they're both meaner than snakes.

Ma had a baby that was born dead. My brothers and sisters have scattered like a stirred anthill. Silas was the only one who stayed on, but he died last winter. He got the fever."

Jake stirred in his seat. "Sorry to hear that."

"I made some stew," Daisy said, "And thanks to Homer, it's got squirrel."

"Two of them," Homer reminded her.

Amos scoped out the cabin, but nothing seemed familiar. Drawings covered most of the walls. Right off, he recognized one of Jake. Amos couldn't get over how much the drawing looked exactly like Jake—the wild hair, the untidy beard, the broad chest.

"Your momma did those," Daisy told him. "There's a pile over there. I saved them from Homer. He was using the pictures as kindling." She shook her head. "You want to see?"

Amos nodded. He sat down at the table and studied every drawing—mostly they were of birds, but also squirrels, a creek, a thinner Jake, a thicker Jake, several of Delilah with a growing stomach, and a picture of a little girl that resembled Daisy. When Amos put the pictures in a certain order they told a story.

"I saved the empty tablets, too," Daisy said. "You can have them."

That night Daisy and Homer slept in the bed that had been Jake and Delilah's. Daisy offered it to Blue Owl and Jake, but Jake told them no, thanks, they would sleep on the floor.

Amos placed his blanket a few feet away from Blue Owl and Jake, just as he had on the journey. The fire was dying down, but Amos watched the two forms nearby. When the house became quiet except for the crackling fire and Jake's snoring, he saw Blue Owl shove Jake's arm.

Jake stirred. "What?"

Blue Owl whispered, but Amos heard her sharp tone. "You tell them go."

"I ain't a-gonna do it," said Jake. Then he rolled on his side and quickly fell back to sleep.

CHAPTER
10

THE NEXT DAY Amos explored Bittersweet Creek. He walked across the log that formed a bridge over the water, then settled on the middle of it and watched two squirrels chase each other around a sycamore. He listened to them chatter as a cold wind blew and shook the bare trees.

Later Amos strolled around the back of the cabin and discovered a cross under an oak tree. He knelt next to it. Someone had scratched *Delilah Kincaid* on the cross. A couple of doves flew down and pecked at the earth covering the grave. Amos watched them for a while, then he noticed a piece of cloth sticking through the ground. He gave it a yank, wondering if the cloth could be Delilah's dress. His heart pounded. When he felt some weight, he wondered if it could be her bones. He stopped. Then he gently pulled until he uncovered a sack. And after he saw what was inside, he dug in the ground and buried it again.

"I'm rich," Amos whispered to the doves. Not with gold, like he'd always dreamed about, but paper money—three hundred dollars. He wished Samuel was around so he could show him the buried treasure. He'd made his fortune, and he was only seven years old.

AUTUMN ARRIVED LATE to Bittersweet Creek. The men built a back room onto the cabin so that Jake and Blue Owl would have a place to sleep. As the season shook the leaves from the oaks and the days became shorter, the five settled into a familiar routine. Jake and Homer spent their days hunting; the women cooked and canned together. Daisy taught Amos to fish.

Together they sat, barefooted on the cross log, holding sticks with crickets tied to the end of their strings.

"Your momma taught me to fish," Daisy said. "She could sit for hours with a stick in her hand."

"What was she like?" Amos surprised himself by asking the question. But now he wanted to know.

Daisy pressed her lips together and looked up at the sky. "Well, I was just a girl when she died, but I'll tell you what I remember. She had a fiery temper if she was pushed too hard. She and Pa were like two starved dogs fighting over a bone."

"She must have liked birds," Amos said.

"I don't know if she liked birds, but they sure enough liked her. They were always around her. I guess she fed them or something. After she died, we hardly saw a bird around this place. They've been coming back lately, though. I'm glad. I kind of like hearing the birds sing in the morning."

Amos couldn't imagine what it would be like to not have birds. He couldn't think of a day they hadn't been in his life.

ONE COLD NOVEMBER night, the wind blew hard against the cabin walls, causing the glass in the windows to shake. Amos played marbles while Blue Owl and Daisy prepared venison stew and cornbread. Like most evenings, Homer sat near the fire across from Jake, listening to his stories as if Jake was offering him fresh biscuits from a Dutch oven.

Jake turned to the incident when he shot the bear. Homer had heard the story at least four times. They all had. But Homer leaned forward with his hands on his knees as if it were his first.

Tilting back in the rocker, Jake held his head high. "Then that old bear reared up on his hind legs. You ever see a bear stand tall?"

Homer shook his head. "No, sir."

"Well," said Jake, "I hope you never do. 'Cause you've never seen such a sight as a bear looking down on you."

"Shoot dang," Homer said, "I expect there ain't nothing like it."

Jake's eyebrows shot up and his lips twitched. This was his favorite part. "I told Isaac, 'Either that bear or me is going to have to die, and—' "

"It sure as heck ain't gonna be me," Daisy hollered, then she burst into a string of giggles.

Jake lost his balance and rocked forward. "Did Blue Owl tell you about the bear?"

She shook her head and managed to say, "No, Jake. You did."

Amos wanted to laugh, but he shot a marble across the room instead. It rolled toward the table where Blue Owl was setting down the plates. She stopped the marble with the toe of her moccasin, and Amos crawled over and grabbed it.

Daisy pulled out a jar of honey. "Homer got it in Independence last summer. Some old couple raises honeybees nearby. Have you ever had honey?" she asked Blue Owl.

Blue Owl shook her head.

Daisy lifted the cornbread out of the pan. Everyone gathered around the table and spooned the golden syrup over thick slices. Amos hadn't eaten honey since Adam's wedding. The sweet taste brought him back to that evening and a lonesomeness filled him up inside. He liked Daisy and Homer and living at Bittersweet Creek, but if he'd learned anything, it was he couldn't allow himself to feel settled anywhere. Because whenever he did, it was taken away.

That night when the household was asleep, Amos awoke to a *tink*, *tink* coming from the other side of the room. The moon cast a dim light through the window and he could make out the shadow of someone sitting at the table. It was Blue Owl scraping a spoon inside the honey jar.

BEFORE WINTER ARRIVED, Daisy went into labor. She didn't have Homer send for her ma. Instead Blue Owl helped bring the baby into the world. She shoved Homer, Jake, and Amos outside and closed the door.

Jake began to tell a story about an Indian woman who gave birth at a rendezvous. "She birthed her baby after breakfast that morning, then cooked a supper of buffalo steaks that night. It was the finest—"

Daisy began to scream and Homer covered his ears with his hands and began to pace. When she screamed again, Amos took off.

He hadn't meant to go far, and before he realized, he'd wandered over to the Hurd house. On the side of the cabin was a garden covered with hay and a huge tree loaded with pecans. Some nuts were scattered on the ground. Amos thought about gathering them. Then he discovered an old man and woman on the porch. The woman's long silver hair hung to her waist, and she seemed to be staring at nothing in particular. She reminded Amos of Gil sitting in the rocker. The old man stepped off the porch. His cloud of white hair stuck straight out above his ears, and he walked with his legs wide apart. With each step he took, onions and turnips rolled out from under the hem of his pants.

Amos started to turn back toward the cabin when the man hollered.

"Come here, boy!"

Amos thought of running, but the force of the man's voice drew him closer.

"I said come here!" The man flicked his wrist. "Come here so I can get a good look at you."

Amos turned to face the man that he now realized was Eb Hurd, his grandfather.

Eb moved toward Amos, shaking his finger in his face. "Are you the little thief that's been stealing my pecans?"

"No, sir." Amos noticed the trail of vegetables behind Eb, leading to the porch.

Eb pulled back his fist. Amos dropped to the ground and crawled through the man's legs. Then he took off running, his heart pounding so hard he thought it might flee from his chest. He glanced over his shoulder and what he saw made him stop, turn, and stare. A group of humming-birds swirled like a giant spinning top in front of the old man. Eb swung at them, but he lost his footing. He flapped his arms. His hair stuck out on end, causing him to resemble an old bird trying to take flight. A few seconds later he fell.

Amos didn't wait to see if Eb could get up. He headed for the woods. Now he understood why Delilah and Daisy had run away from his grandfather. He thought about the veg-etables dropping from Eb and the hummingbirds coming to his defense. It was not yet spring, and he'd never seen hum-mingbirds except for in the summer. A shiver ran down his spine. He decided Bittersweet Creek was like the places in the book Esther gave him. It had buried treasure, an old man made of turnips and onions, and hummingbirds in the winter.

When he returned, Daisy had stopped screaming and everyone had gathered around her bed.

"Come meet your cousin." Homer's face was lit up like a moonbeam. "Amos Kincaid, this here is Finnegan Johnson. But I reckon we'll call him Finn."

Amos inched toward Daisy and the infant. The baby was so tiny he could fit in Jake's wide palm. He glanced at Blue Owl, who was doing something that Amos had never seen her do. She was smiling. Jake, too, seemed to be under the spell of Finn. He wondered what was so special about a baby.

Daisy pulled the blanket from Finn's face so that Amos could see. "He's going to look up to you, Amos. You'll be like a brother to him."

Then Homer dug his hand inside his bulging pockets. "Almost forgot, Daisy. Look what I fetched you." He pulled his hand from the pocket and opened his palm, revealing a dozen cracked pecans.

CHAPTER
11

SPRING 1842

AFTER THE LAST snow melted, Amos left Bittersweet Creek
with Jake and Blue Owl for Independence. Two days later,
they arrived at the town. There they saw a lot of folks
starting their journey west and others buying supplies
for their Missouri farms. It was the latter group Jake
wanted to meet up with.

"This is the best place to find a dowsing job," Jake
explained to Amos. At the general store, they found a family that planned to farm nearby. The Bighams weren't much
older than Daisy and Homer and already had two children.
Karl Bigham became Jake's first client. He didn't have
much money to spare, but Jake told him that he'd dowse a
place for a well free of charge.

"If you're satisfied, tell other folks," Jake told him.
"That'll be payment enough."

Blue Owl set up their tent on the farm near the river's bend while Amos followed Jake to the dowsing. Amos wondered if Henrietta had found the branch he hid under Samuel's bed. He thought of telling Jake that he could dowse, too, but Jake seemed bitter about the gift. Amos decided to keep what happened at the mission a few years before a secret. But at night, he dreamed about dowsing, and when he awoke, his hands tingled like the time he'd tried dowsing with Jake's branch at the mission.

The dowsing at the Bighams' did not go quickly. A couple of hours into Jake's pacing, the farmer's wife moved in closer and watched Jake like a hawk sizing up a mouse. Jake took until noon to discover the best place for a well. After he staked the spot, the farmer's wife pointed to a place thirty yards away and told her husband, "Then I want the cabin right there."

Karl nodded. "I suppose that'd be as good as any."

His wife frowned. "What do you mean that would be as good as any? *That* is the best place for our cabin. It will be close to the well."

Karl's face flushed and he stole a glimpse at the ground.

"I expect you'll need help building a well," Jake said to Karl. Then he turned to Mrs. Bigham. "Or do you plan to help him?"

"Me? I can't build a well. I've my babies to tend."

Jake ignored her. "I'll be happy to help you," he told Karl.

"I couldn't pay you worth your time."

"It costs the same as the dowsing."

He tipped his hat. "Mr. Kincaid, I'm much obliged."

"Just call me Jake."

Later that night, Jake said, "She's a bossy little gal. Karl said she got educated out East. An education like that won't do you any good on a farm."

The next morning, Amos joined Jake again, this time to work. While the men dug, he carried buckets of dirt to a pile away from the well, excited that Jake had given him a chore, but by the end of day, his arms and back hurt. His thoughts turned to the bag of money buried beneath the tree.

After dinner that night, he asked Jake, "How much money do you need to be rich?"

Jake was in a drowsy state. "Oh, I figure enough that a man can live out his days as he sees fit."

"Is three hundred dollars rich?" Amos asked.

Jake was wide awake now. "What made you pick that amount?"

Amos shrugged. "I don't know. Sounds like a lot of money to me."

"Well, it's a lot of money to lose, but it ain't enough to be rich." Jake closed his eyes and soon fell asleep.

Amos looked at Blue Owl, who was spreading the blankets for his bed. He didn't care what Jake said. Three hundred dollars was going to make him a rich man one day. He knew it.

Though it was spring, the day was hot as summer and their shirts clung to them like a second skin. By mid-afternoon the next day, Karl's wife walked out with a child on each hip. "You sure there's water down there?"

Jake narrowed his eyes at her.

"Nora, the man is a dowser," Karl snapped. "I figure he knows how to find water."

With his sleeve, Jake wiped the sweat from his brow. "Ma'am, I ain't no miracle worker. It takes time to get to the water."

"It just seems like you'd have some sign," Mrs. Bigham's voice quivered, and she softly added, "by now."

"I can stop this minute and leave," Jake said, standing and holding the shovel as if he could drop it.

Mrs. Bigham blushed. "I was just asking." She turned and walked away.

The young man stayed quiet until she was a safe distance away. "Women."

Jake laughed.

By the end of the week, the men hit water.

Mrs. Bigham smiled weakly and handed a sack of dried beans to Jake. "Thank you, Mr. Kincaid."

Jake accepted the gift, but Amos noticed that he didn't tell Mrs. Bigham to just call him Jake.

THE NEXT MORNING they packed up the tent and went west until they reached another farm. The owner told Jake of a nearby family that had just settled there. They traveled three miles until they reached the split mulberry tree the man had mentioned as a landmark. The tree had been struck by lightning. Half of the tree was dead, all bare branches, while the other half thrived, covered with leaves and berries. Amos tried to memorize it. He had brought a satchel of paper and pencils. He planned to draw it when he had a chance.

They found the man with his family sitting around a campfire, near their covered wagon. The family stared at them and two of the little ones hid behind the woman's skirt. An uneasy feeling filled Amos's gut.

"You looking for someone?" the man called out.

Jake stopped walking. Amos and Blue Owl followed his lead. "Your name be Joseph Woods?"

"What business is that of yours?"

"My name is Jake Kincaid. Your neighbor told me you might be looking for a dowser?" Jake stepped forward, offering his hand.

The man ignored it and asked, "You can witch a well?"

Jake's arm returned to his side. "Yes, sir."

"I'm Joseph Woods. I got a need for a water witch, but we don't have a need for her." Woods glared at Blue Owl. Then he turned his head and spat on the ground.

Blue Owl looked straight at the man.

"Mister, she's my wife," Jake said.

"That's your worry. You and the boy are welcome, but the injun will have to stay out of sight."

"Now, look here," Jake said, stepping forward.

Blue Owl touched Jake's arm. And though she touched him lightly, it stopped him from going further.

"There's a creek about a mile away," Woods said. "She can wait there. To get there she needs to go back to the split tree and head south."

Amos watched Blue Owl turn and leave. He felt twisted inside. Ever since Rebecca's murder, he didn't care for Indians. He guessed that included Blue Owl, but he didn't like Joseph Woods either.

Jake placed his hand on Amos's shoulder. "Come on, boy." Then he said to Woods, "I'll be back at sunrise."

"You ain't aiming to start today?"

"No, sir, I'm not," said Jake.

Then Jake and Amos walked away and caught up with Blue Owl.

The three made their way to the creek, Jake cursing Joseph Woods under his breath the entire way. When they reached the split tree, Amos decided he didn't much feel like drawing it after all.

WHILE AMOS HELPED Jake put up the tent, Blue Owl waded into the creek with a thick branch about a foot and a half long. She stood calf-deep in the water, and the branch held high above her head. A second later, she brought the branch down in a swift smooth stroke. Then she dipped her hand beneath the water and pulled up a fish.

Amos couldn't keep his eyes off Blue Owl. She fascinated him.

Jake seemed to take notice. "She's been doing that since she was younger than you."

Blue Owl pointed the club toward the sky, again. She made two more hits and got two more fish. Jake helped her split the fish open and they scraped away the insides. "I'll bet you know folks that eat that, don't you? Diggers will eat anything."

He winked at Blue Owl, then he turned toward Amos. "You know what diggers are?" As usual, Jake didn't wait for an answer. "Some folks say they're lowlife Indians because they'll eat things from the ground—grasses, seeds, insects. I watched a Shoshone boy wait a whole hour until he could hook a lizard. Yeah, some folks call that a lowlife way of living, but I think it's smart. Hell, I can remember a time or two that I was near starved and would have killed for a grasshopper."

Jake built the fire while Blue Owl ground up corn until it turned into a mush. Then she cooked the fish and the mush over the fire. Amos was hungry. He sure wished he could have a biscuit.

When Blue Owl flipped the fish over, Jake said, "That's done enough for me. Don't want it dried out like jerky." Blue Owl placed a fish on a tin plate and served

Jake first. Then she dished up some for Amos, leaving the smallest fish for herself. After the first bite, Amos decided this was the best meal he'd eaten since they left Bittersweet Creek. And he bet it tasted better than any grasshopper or lizard.

CHAPTER

12

THE SECOND EVENING at the creek, they were eating another dinner of fish and corn cakes when they heard bushes rustle. Amos froze and watched Jake grab his shotgun. Before he could aim it a voice hollered, "Don't shoot, Jake. It's me, Paul Ferguson."

Jake set down his shotgun and the man parted the bushes and moved closer to the campfire. Right off, Amos recognized the man with an eye patch. He was Pirate Paul, the man who'd stopped by at the Block farm with the message from Jake a couple of years ago. Amos was excited.

"Ferguson," Jake said, shaking his head, "you ought know better than to slip up on a man that way. I almost killed you."

Pirate Paul took off his hat. "Well, if it ain't Amos Kincaid. How's ole Jake treating you?"

"Good," Amos said.

Blue Owl placed a fish and a corn cake on her tin plate and gave it to Pirate Paul.

Ferguson nodded toward her and said, "Ma'am."

"What brings you out this way?" Jake asked Pirate Paul.

"I'm on my way to Independence. Gonna scout for Isaac's wagon train." Pirate Paul picked a fish bone from his mouth. "You ever thought about it?"

"Ain't that many going out West, are there?" Jake asked.

"More and more each day. I plan to stay once I reach Oregon City. Maybe open a business. Sure you won't come along? I'm sure Isaac could use another scout. He'd probably be excited to get the great Kincaid."

"Never gave scouting much thought. Most folks ain't cut out for traveling West. Don't know if I could herd a group of tenderfoots."

Pirate Paul chuckled. "Well, I reckon I'll find out soon enough. I heard Bernard has started buffalo hunting."

"I'm too old for that," Jake said.

"Yep," Pirate Paul said, "he's young and foolish. Should suit him well."

Amos thought buffalo hunting sounded exciting. He'd never seen a buffalo. "What does a buffalo look like?"

"Like a furry ole bull," Jake said. "And when they stampede, move out of their way. I've known a few men got trampled to death from a buffalo stampede."

Jake began to tell some of his stories. Amos had heard them all by now, but Pirate Paul had stories, also. He offered Jake a swig of whiskey, but Jake shook his head. Amos listened as Pirate Paul talked about happening upon a thousand mountain sheep high in the Rockies.

"I heard a shot, and I'll be dern if a sheep didn't fall from the cliff and land at my feet. I thought about taking it for my own use, especially when the feller who shot it didn't show up after twenty minutes. But then I got curious how far away that feller was when he shot that sheep. Forty minutes later, I heard him a-whistling. He told me he walked three miles." Pirate Paul slapped his knee and leaned toward Amos. "Imagine that, three miles?"

Jake spat on the ground. "That ain't nothing. I seen a man shoot a grizzly off a cliff four miles away."

Amos hung on every word, but Blue Owl got up and walked along the bank of the creek. He wished Pirate Paul would tell a story about what it was like at sea with other pirates. Finally he asked him, "Did you find a lot of treasure on your ship when you were out at sea?"

Jake raised an eyebrow as Pirate Paul rubbed the silver whiskers on his chin.

"Oh, I'm a land pirate."

Amos didn't understand. "But where did you find your treasure?"

Pirate Paul leaned over until he was inches from Amos's face. "I found mine in the creeks."

"The creeks?"

"Yes, sir. Why do you think me and Jake trapped for so long? Have you ever seen a beaver?"

Amos shook his head. "No, sir."

Pirate Paul's one eye squinted. "Well, those beavers' teeth are made from gold and silver."

Jake laughed.

Amos's face felt warm. He knew when he'd been had.

Pirate Paul's voice grew soft. "But my treasure-finding days are over."

"Ain't that the God's truth," said Jake. Then both men were quiet.

The next morning Pirate Paul accompanied Jake to the Woods farm. Jake had offered him some pay if he'd help dig the well. Amos wanted to go, too, but Jake told him he needed to stay at the camp. He thought Jake was treating him like a little boy until Jake said, "You need to protect Blue Owl."

His remark made Amos think of the time Gil went for a doctor and told him that he was the man of the house. That was shortly before Rebecca became sick. Maybe he just wasn't good at protecting people. Amos took out his drawing pad and concentrated on the one thing he knew he could do.

THE MEN FINISHED digging the well after four days, and Pirate Paul headed toward Independence. Amos expected that they'd be moving on, too. Instead Jake leaned toward Amos and took a long whiff. "Boy, you and me are stinking like wet dogs. Let's go bathe before Blue Owl takes off without us."

Amos couldn't remember the last time he'd bathed. Even then he had stayed on the banks and splashed the water onto his body. Blue Owl went inside the tent, and Amos followed Jake to the creek, where they shed their clothes. Jake eased into the icy cold water. "Snakes alive!"

It took Amos a few minutes to adjust to the temperature. He squatted in the shallow end near the bank. Jake swam underneath the surface, and when he emerged, his hair was slicked back from his face, revealing his long forehead. It reminded Amos of Gil's.

A second later, Jake hollered for Amos to join him in the deep end.

"No, sir."

"Can't you swim?"

Amos stayed silent. After almost drowning in the Missouri, Amos was afraid of the water.

"Well," said Jake, "I guess you ain't had a chance to swim much." He swam back to Amos and took hold of his wrists. "Best you learn now."

He let Jake pull him out to the deep water. His heart pounded as he listened and tried to follow Jake's instructions. First, Jake taught him to float on his back. "That's it," he said when Amos got the knack of it.

Amos liked floating, but when Jake flipped him over, he panicked and kicked his legs. Jake let go of his hands and Amos sank beneath the surface. He closed his eyes and the world became dark and hollow. He opened his mouth to scream and the water filled his insides. Amos was certain he was going to die. Then he felt Jake's hands around his waist. When Jake lifted him, Amos began to cough up the water.

"Now you done been baptized," Jake said.

While Amos tried to recover and catch his breath, Jake continued. "You can't let the water know you're a-feared of it. If you do, it will get the best of you, for sure."

Amos grew tired and hungry. He was relieved when Jake said, "Let's go back to camp. We'll try again tomorrow."

After his second near-drowning episode, Amos wasn't looking forward to another attempt. But the next day, Jake's calm instructions and his frequently stating, "You're doing fine," caused Amos to relax. He was able to move his arms and legs in a way that kept him at the surface, although his strokes were not the same as Jake had taught him.

"I'll be. You swim like a frog, boy. But if that's what's natural for you, I ain't got no complaints. You never know when swimming might come in handy."

The weather was growing colder, and the second night, Blue Owl frowned at Jake when he told Amos it was time to swim. "Amos will get sick."

"He ain't gonna get sick. A boy learning to swim is natural."

They stayed camped at the spot near the creek for an entire week, and each day they spent more time in the water than they had the day before. By dusk Amos was exhausted, but the practice had turned him into a better swimmer. Though even as he improved, he still couldn't quite shake the belief that the water could swallow him whole.

AMOS'S LIFE took on a predictable rhythm. Jake dowsed and built wells while Amos moved dirt. They covered miles and miles. As time progressed, he thought about Rebecca and Gil less and less during the day, but when the moon shone high in the sky, he longed for the storybooks Rebecca read to him, and more than that, he longed for her embrace. Now he listened to Jake's stories while Blue Owl's hands stayed busy cooking, sewing beads on leather, making moccasins to replace the ones they'd worn out. Amos wondered if she listened to Jake's stories, too. He figured she knew them all by heart.

One evening Jake and Amos lay flat on their backs gazing up at the stars. Most nights they did that while Jake talked about everything except the stars. But that night he said, "I remember the year before you were born. It was back in November of thirty-three. The whole dang sky lit up. And I'm not talking lightning. The stars, they were a-falling. Millions. The sky was so bright I could see the freckles on the other feller's face. We had another trapper with us that was a part-time preacher. He went to saying the Lord's

Prayer. He figured the world was ending and he better get right with his maker. Well, you never heard such confessions coming out of his mouth. It got to where the sky wasn't nearly as entertaining."

"Why did that happen?" Amos wanted to know.

"Heck if I know. It never did happen again. Oh, I seen a star or two fall in my lifetime, but ain't nothing ever compared to that."

Jake yawned and stretched his arms toward the sky, then cracked his knuckles. "I feel like that branch is a noose around my neck. Dowsing is choking the life out of me."

"Why don't you quit?" Amos asked. The solution seemed simple to him.

"A man's gotta do something. I reckon this is it. When I was a boy, my pa dowsed to earn extra money when we had a lean year. And when he put the branch in my hands for the first time, I felt a burning inside me because I had the gift, too. If only I'd known back then that Pa might as well have cursed me to hell. I miss trapping. Every day held something new. Just be thankful I didn't hand that gift down to you."

Amos figured it was probably best not to tell Jake that it was too late.

Heavy rains arrived in November. The third day Jake decided he and Amos should go to the Millers' farm anyway. The last dry day, he'd dowsed it, but they still needed to dig the well. Mr. Miller looked at Jake like he lacked any wits when he showed up in the middle of the downpour, but he put on his hat and left his family behind in their tent to join Jake at the site.

Amos trod through the mud, carrying buckets of more mud away from the spot of the future well. The buckets of mud were heavier than buckets of dry dirt. His arms felt like they'd been stretched to twice their length. His shoulders and back pounded in pain. By noon, he began to sneeze.

An hour later, Mr. Miller threw down his shovel. "This is ridiculous, Kincaid. I'm calling it a day. Don't come back until the rain stops."

Jake and Amos walked away, the rain pounding down on them so hard they could barely see their way back to the campsite. When they reached their tent, Blue Owl was waiting inside. Amos's head felt fuzzy and his throat hurt when he swallowed.

Blue Owl pulled off his soaked clothes and wrapped him in a blanket. She'd built a small fire in the center of the tent, but Amos felt cold. He curled into a ball and shivered. She touched his cheek. Her fingers felt cool against his skin. She mumbled something to Jake and he left the tent, then returned a few moments later.

Amos fell into a deep slumber, until Blue Owl awoke him. After raising him to a sitting position, she held the cup to his mouth. "Drink."

He obeyed, sipping the nasty liquid that tasted like dirt. And when he shook, Blue Owl covered him with all the blankets they owned. She lay beside him and held him close until he stopped shaking.

As much as he didn't want her touching him, Amos was too tired to resist. He closed his eyes and thought of Rebecca.

The rain stopped the next morning, but Jake left for the Millers' without Amos. Blue Owl gave him more tea and soup made from fish and corn. He dozed on and off until Jake returned. By the time Jake started snoring that night, Amos was wide awake. Between the flickers of the orange flame, he saw Blue Owl open her eyes and meet his gaze. He glanced away, but quickly looked again.

Blue Owl slid her hand out from under the blanket and pointed to the ceiling. Amos gazed up and noticed a rabbit hopping above him. When he looked closer, he realized Blue Owl had created the animal with her fists and fingers. He watched as the rabbit hopped about, then disappeared. A second later, a bird took its place. Blue Owl's hands moved gracefully—*fingers touching, fingers apart*. The bird flew around and around the ceiling, until eventually sleep found Amos.

CHAPTER
13

FIVE YEARS LATER 1847

THEY USUALLY RETURNED to the cabin every November, but by the end of September, in the sixth year of dowsing, the last robin had flown south and the oaks had dropped their leaves. Winter was setting in early. In October they loaded up the mule, and instead of heading to the next farm, they set out for Bittersweet Creek. Amos was relieved. He was tired of being cold. It didn't matter how many buffalo skins Blue Owl piled on him at night, the damp chill sunk into his bones, making warmth impossible.

When they approached the cabin, Finn flew out the door, heading toward Amos's outstretched arms. Amos liked knowing Finn adored him. Each year that passed, he anticipated more eagerly the season they spent at Bittersweet Creek. Daisy had once said, "Finn thinks Amos strung up the stars and let them loose in the sky."

The six-year-old boy had not grown much since they left last spring. His pants, held up by suspenders, dragged the ground at the hem. Amos lifted him so that Finn's legs straddled his waist.

Homer came out to the porch. "Well, it's about time. Thought you were gonna freeze to death before I saw you."

The smell of venison stew drifted from the cabin, and when they crossed the threshold, Daisy moved away from the fire and gave them each a hug. Amos noticed that, unlike past reunions, Blue Owl didn't pull away.

Even though she'd turned twenty that year, Daisy still looked like a half-grown girl, with her narrow shoulders and hips. "I've been so lonesome for all of you," she said, giving Amos an extra squeeze. "I fell asleep each night thinking of all the things I needed to do before you returned."

Finn hugged Amos again. "Can I see the giant?"

Amos pulled the giant from his pocket. He'd considered giving it to Finn, but always changed his mind. He knew it was childish, but he believed Jameson when he'd said the giant would protect him.

Daisy patted Jake's belly. "Blue Owl's been feeding you good." Daisy had such an ease with Jake, it was as if he was her pa and not Amos's. But then Amos thought on it some and realized Daisy was that way with everyone.

When they entered the back room, they saw the bed.

Daisy grinned and told Jake, "Now you and Blue Owl can stop sleeping on the floor. I've been collecting chicken feathers for the last four years. And Homer bought the muslin and wool in Independence. I'm afraid I had to stuff more grass and wool in it than feathers."

Amos had spent more than half of his almost-fourteen years sleeping on the ground, but he'd never forgotten the comfort of a featherbed. The bed wasn't for him, but a warmth filled him anyway.

"I built the bed frame from pine," Homer said, grinning. The bed took up most of the room.

Jake cleared his throat. "This is mighty fine of you."

That night, Amos made a pallet in front of the fire. Barely an hour had passed when a tap on his shoulder awakened him.

The room was dark, but he could make out Blue Owl's frame, standing before him.

"Go to bed," she told him firmly.

It took Amos a moment until he realized she wanted to exchange places. He went to the back room and climbed in, on the other side of Jake, while Blue Owl took his spot on the floor. Amos fell to sleep quickly, thankful Blue Owl couldn't shake some of her Indian ways.

THE NEXT MORNING, Amos slept late. After waking, he stayed in bed listening to the sounds of the cabin—Finn's feet pattering across the floor, Jake on the porch, yawning like a rousing bear, Daisy speaking in a low voice to Blue Owl. He stretched his neck toward the door, trying to hear their conversation. Blue Owl spoke so seldom that he found himself hungry for her words.

"Don't you like a feathered bed?" Daisy asked her. She sounded a bit hurt, probably because of the trouble she and Homer had gone through.

"Yes."

"Then why don't you sleep in it?"

"All my life, I sleep on ground. Not the boy."

CHAPTER
14

BLUE OWL RAN the cake of soap down her arm and through her hair. Twice a week she bathed in the creek at dusk. It didn't matter that it was winter. Even as a child, her body could adjust to extreme temperatures. She swam under the water and rinsed the lather from her hair. When she emerged, she floated on her back and studied the treetops pointing toward the sky.

She loved everything about Bittersweet Creek. Although Jake had not taken back the cabin from Homer and Daisy, she felt a part of it. It was hard not to like the woman-child who had tried to please her so much. Blue Owl might not sleep in the bed, but Daisy and Homer had made it for her and Jake. That was what mattered. The jars of honey that Daisy secretly put away for Blue Owl amused her. She felt a heavy guilt because she had more affection for Daisy than for her own blood sisters.

She wished Jake would stop dowsing and settle at the creek. They could farm. Homer and Daisy raised vegetables in a garden, but with them joining in, they could grow large crops. Amos could help, too. He was almost fourteen. There were not many moons left before he'd be a man. Although how long a boy walked this earth had nothing to do with it. Choices made a boy into a man.

Sunlight was fading. Blue Owl emerged from the water, retrieved her clothes, and dressed. On her return to the cabin, she heard the bluejays calling out their *jay-jay* sounds. The noise grew louder, and she knew they were close. She looked up and discovered them circling above. A second later, she felt a drop on her shoulder. She wiped the spot and examined it. Just as she suspected—*bird crap*, as Jake called it. Then more drops sprinkled on top of her head like rain. She ran back to the creek and washed her hair again.

While she twisted her locks, squeezing out the moisture, she changed her mind about Bittersweet Creek. She loved everything about the place except for the birds. Ever since Amos had joined them, there had been lots of birds. Birds and the woman spirit. Her instincts warned her that she should think of it as a sign of something bad with the boy. But when Blue Owl thought of Amos, she could see only good.

WHEN THEY GATHERED around the table for dinner that night, Jake suddenly announced, "I can't stand another day dowsing. Isaac said he could use another scout going West and I aim to tell him I'm willing."

Blue Owl felt like a rock had hit the bottom of her stomach.

Before the meal ended, Homer and Daisy decided they'd go, too. The talk turned toward the journey ahead. Everyone had questions except Blue Owl. She didn't understand Jake's yearning to go West. She didn't trust Isaac. She'd met him at the last trappers' rendezvous. He reminded her of a coyote, tricky and vain. Why couldn't Jake be happy with his gift? Her people held great respect for someone who found water where no one else could.

After dinner, Blue Owl washed the bowls and spoons, then handed them to Daisy, who hummed as she dried each item. Foolish girl, she thought.

She couldn't restrain herself from asking, "Why you want to move West?"

Daisy shrugged. "It will be something different."

"You will see the same moon," Blue Owl said.

"Homer wants to go." She began to hum again.

Blue Owl stayed quiet after that. She was tired of moving. She yearned for a home of her own.

AMOS WAS READY to go West. He wanted a new adventure. They decided to leave in early March. The morning of the departure, Amos slipped out of bed before dark and dug up the money from under the tree. Before walking away, he studied the cross above Delilah's grave. Then he opened the trunk inside their room and found Delilah's sketches and paintings. After folding the pictures around the money, he tucked them in the satchel where he kept his drawing pads and pencils.

When they closed the door for the last time, everyone looked forward except Blue Owl who stared back at the cabin with, what seemed to Amos, a longing in her eyes.

CHAPTER
15

INDEPENDENCE
SPRING 1848

THERE WAS SOMETHING powerful about a place where dreamers gathered. So much yearning in one place could create a
strength, mighty enough to carve out a trail through prairie,
rock, and water, and lead the dreamers to their destination.
Independence was one such place. A jumping-off to the big
dream—a new life in the West.

Amos soon learned the dreams were as varied as the
dreamers themselves—free land, an escape from diseases
in the East, a mission to save souls. One man told Amos he
merely wanted to catch the big fish.

Amos, too, believed something big was going to happen
out West. In a couple of months, he'd turn fourteen. He
didn't feel like a man, but he didn't feel like a boy either.
But being a man must mean more than reaching a certain

age. Surely something important had to happen first. Maybe that would occur on the trail. Amos could hardly wait.

They set up camp half a mile outside of town next to a spring where tree limbs covered with birds bent above their heads. Each week more emigrants came and more tents went up until they formed their own city. Among them was a half-breed named Thomas, whom Isaac hired as his second scout.

"Are all these people going to Oregon?" Amos asked Jake.

"Most of them, but a few fools think California is the land of milk and honey."

"Why shouldn't they go to California?" Amos asked.

"It ain't safe yet. What with the Mexican war just ending." Jake spat on the ground, his way of saying it was the God's truth.

Even with all the people coming to Independence, Isaac said, "It's not as much as last year. Seems Saint Joseph and Westport are becoming more popular. Me, I'll go with what I know best."

Five years before, Isaac had traded his fox hat for a black felt one. Before fixing it on his head each morning, he combed every white hair into place. It seemed to Amos that as much as Jake had trouble shedding the trapping life, Isaac had embraced his new role as a trail captain.

A couple of days after they arrived, Jake gave Homer seventy dollars to buy a wagon that was about ten feet long and not quite four feet across. A good many years had

passed since Jake had bought a wagon. He'd underesti-
mated the cost. The next day he sent Homer back with more
money for a cover. On the trail, Homer would guide the
oxen team by walking on their left side. He planned to build
a small seat, barely enough room for tiny Daisy or Finn to
rest when they weren't walking. Blue Owl and Amos would
need to walk the entire way. Amos was no stranger to walking, but this would be his longest trip ever—two thousand
miles.

At first Jake thought he'd wait on purchasing the oxen.
"No reason to trouble with livestock this far out. We won't
be leaving for at least another month."

But when he learned the best oxen were sold first, he
changed his mind. That would also give them time to be
broken in.

They'd have to wait for the ground to dry from the spring
rains and for the grass to grow enough to feed the livestock.
"Hopefully," Isaac told them, "we'll be leaving Independence by May. We want to reach the Willamette Valley
before the hard winter sets in."

Part of Jake's job was to recruit families for their wagon
train. After Amos and Homer accompanied Jake for a couple of days, Jake sent them out to do the same. Like Jake,
they were to tell the potential emigrants about Isaac and his
strengths as the trail captain. Amos had his own way of
talking to folks, and he soon proved better than Jake. When
Jake found a prospect, he got caught up in an old trapping
tale and people begged off. Homer tried to imitate Jake, but

he muddled his words and always ended up saying, "Shoot dang!" so much in a cloud of nervousness, folks hurried away.

Amos would simply start out asking, "Have you heard of the famous trapper Isaac Bolton?" Even if they hadn't, most people wouldn't admit it, and before long Amos had recruited another family.

THEIR SECOND WEEK in Independence, Amos and Finn arrived in front of a mercantile store. A tall woman and her shorter, stout husband exited the store. They were well-dressed, finer than any of the other emigrants he'd seen so far. Amos had started to approach them when the woman turned and called out, "Come along, Gwendolyn." At first, the woman's accent sounded odd to Amos, until he realized it was British. Jake had dowsed for a family that had come to Missouri from England.

A girl wearing a straw hat on her orange hair appeared in the store's doorway. She towered above the couple, even though she hunched her shoulders as if to seem smaller. The shadow of her hat's brim kept him from getting a close look, but when she stepped into the sunshine, Amos saw. Pink scars covered the girl's left cheek, and her eye on that side was noticeably larger than the one on the right.

She pointed to a line of pigeons resting on the store's rail. "Look, Mother, there they are again, the birds."

"Seems we can't escape them," her mother said with a hint of disgust.

Amos was about to step forward to begin his pitch when he caught Finn staring at the girl with his mouth open.

The girl noticed and stuck out her tongue at Finn. Amos felt paralyzed, and the family walked past him before he had a chance to speak.

"Did you see that ugly girl?" Finn asked. "She stuck out her tongue at me."

"You were staring at her, Finn. It's not nice to stare." But the sight of her had shocked Amos, too. The girl seemed about his age. He wondered if she was born that way. In his entire life, he'd never seen anyone so horrifying. He watched as the family made their way down the road. Every passerby gawked as they caught a glimpse of her.

"Why does she look like that, Amos?" Finn asked.

"Hush, Finn." Amos turned his head and tried to forget what he'd seen.

Next door, a flaxen-haired girl gazed in the milliner's shop window, her eyes fixed on the fancy hats on display. Nearby a boy, who appeared to be close to Amos's age, tossed two small balls high in the air. He did a fine job catching them, but then he missed and one ball rolled into the road. The boy raced after it, unaware that a wagon was rushing in his direction. The driver had a panicked look as he tried to stop the wagon without success. Amos expected the boy to return to the girl's side, but the boy seemed focused on the ball. Even the sound of the horse's hooves didn't make him flinch.

The girl's scream shook Amos from his daze, and he

dashed out into the road. He yanked the boy by his collar, pulling him to safety. The wagon missed them by a few inches, so close that Amos's breath left his body. He snapped, "Couldn't you hear that wagon?"

The boy, who didn't as much as glance in his direction, rushed back out into the road and retrieved the ball.

"No," the girl said to Amos, "he couldn't." Then she took the boy by the shoulders, turning him toward her, and pointed toward Amos. Her fingers formed exaggerated signals. "This young man saved you, Elijah."

Elijah turned toward Amos and grinned, offering his hand.

Amos shook Elijah's hand.

"Can't he talk?" Finn asked.

"No," the girl said, "and he can't hear either. My brother had the fever when he was a baby. God spared his life, but he can't hear." She inhaled a big breath, as if to calm herself, then she turned toward Amos. "Thank you. My name is Jubilee McBride. This is my brother, Elijah."

Amos nodded, his face heating up. He couldn't help noticing Jubilee's violet eyes and dark pink lips.

"I'm Finn," said the tiny boy.

"Hello, Finn." Jubilee gazed at Amos, waiting, but Amos felt speechless with this pretty girl being nice to him.

Finn sighed. "This here is Amos Kincaid. He's my cousin."

Jubilee smiled. "Nice to meet you, Amos. I'm most grateful to you for saving my brother."

Amos's lips parted, but the words lodged in his throat. Jubilee was beautiful.

Elijah cupped his hands over his ears, then pointed toward Amos.

"No," Jubilee said, shaking her head. "He's not deaf."

"Nope," Finn said. "He can hear, all right."

Amos had still not managed to say anything when a man and a woman walked out of the store and approached them. The man's wide-brim hat shaded his eyes, and he wore his spectacles low on his nose. He knew they must be Jubilee's and Elijah's parents because the woman resembled Jubilee. Her forehead was deeply lined like someone who'd worried a lot, but the eyes were the same violet as her daughter's.

Jubilee stepped toward the couple. "This is Amos Kincaid and his young cousin, Finn. Amos saved Elijah's life when he chased the ball into the road again."

The man offered his hand to Amos. "Thank you, young man." His voice was gentle. Then he turned toward Elijah, his palm up.

Elijah didn't hesitate. He gave a ball to his father.

The man waited, his hand out until Elijah gave up the other one. Then Elijah locked his hands behind his back.

Jubilee's father tucked the balls into his pocket. "I'm Gideon McBride. This is my wife, Mrs. McBride."

"Father is going to start a church in the West," Jubilee said.

Finally Amos found his tongue. He focused on Reverend McBride. "Have you heard of Isaac Bolton? The famous trapper?"

And for the first time, Amos heard someone say, "No, Amos. I can't say that I have."

That caught Amos by surprise, but he quickly recovered. "Well, he's been to the Oregon Country many times. He knows the best route. He'll get you there quick before the snow melts."

"I'm not looking for speed, Amos. I want the safest route for my family."

"Then Isaac is your man," Amos said, surprised to hear such conviction in his own voice.

Finn tucked his thumbs under his suspenders and rocked on his toes. "Yes, sir, Isaac is your man."

Amos wanted to trip Finn. He caused Amos to sound silly instead of smart like he'd wanted to seem to Jubilee's father. Amos frowned at his cousin and continued. "Isaac holds a meeting inside Dimmet's Mercantile at sundown every night. He can answer any questions you might have."

Reverend McBride nodded. "Well, then, Amos Kincaid, perhaps we'll see you at sundown. First I have to see about our belongings and find out where to purchase our wagon and mules." He tipped his hat to Amos. "Thank you again for looking out for my son."

"Good day, Amos," Mrs. McBride said. "We're so grateful."

"Good day," Amos said.

"Good day!" hollered Finn.

Amos watched in the direction Gideon McBride and his family headed. Numerous boxes, three large trunks, and a piano were stacked in the alley between the store and the milliner's. Amos wondered what Jake and Isaac would say when they discovered all the McBrides' possessions. And he'd heard mules weren't the best choice for pulling wagons. They'd wear out faster. The oxen might be slower, but they were strong and gentle, a better choice on a long journey.

AMOS AND FINN started back toward camp. The wind swept down and a cloud of dust arose from the street and blocked their vision. They covered their eyes, and when they opened them, a man on a horse galloped up and stopped at their feet.

"Pardon, y-young fellas."

Amos stopped walking. "Sir?"

The man on the horse pushed his hat back, and Amos could tell he was not so old, even though he had a full beard. Something about the man seemed familiar.

The man got off his horse. "I'm l-looking for a g-group to g-go out West with. Heard of any?"

Now Amos was certain he knew the man. He couldn't believe it, but it was him. "Jameson?"

"D-Do I know you?" Jameson asked.

"I'm Amos."

"G-Good g-god, Amos. You've g-grown."

"He's thirteen," said Finn.

"I'm almost fourteen," Amos said, frowning.

Finn stood on his toes. "I'm Finn, and I'm six."

"Amos, is it really you?"

Amos dug in his pocket and pulled out the wooden giant.

"I'll be d-dang, boy. You still have that?"

Amos didn't know if Jameson meant the giant was a toy he should have put away years ago or if he was amazed that Amos could have kept track of something that long.

"He always has it with him," said Finn. "It gives him good luck."

Amos thought he really needed to figure a way to get rid of Finn. He was as annoying as a sticker burr under a saddle.

Jameson gently punched Amos's shoulder. "Is your pa still trapping?"

"No, but he's going West." Then remembering his pitch, Amos added, "Have you heard of the great trapper Isaac Bolton?"

"Heck, yeah. I even saw him once at the f-fort."

"Jake's scouting for him. We're leaving around April or May, as soon as the grass dries. He's back at the camp, if you want to follow me."

AT THE CAMP, they found Jake straddling a barrel, playing poker with Homer and Thomas. Jake frowned, his eyebrows lowered, as he studied the cards. That meant he held a bad hand. Amos learned a long time ago that Jake didn't have a poker face. He didn't gamble much, probably because he lost most games.

"Remember Jameson?" Amos asked him. "He wants to go West."

Jake stared up from his cards. "One of the Block boys, eh?"

"Yes, sir," Jameson said.

"Grew into quite a good-size man. You as strong as you look?"

Jameson's shoulders were broad enough to hold buckets, and his neck was short, but thick. "Yes, sir," he told Jake. "I'm p-pretty strong. Not afraid of hard w-work neither."

Jake sighed at his cards, folded, and crossed his arms in front of his chest. "I'll talk to Isaac. I think he's looking for another cowman to keep an eye on the livestock."

"I could d-do that."

After Jake folded his cards, he stood and faced Jameson. "How's my brother?"

"F-Fine."

Jake's left eyebrow shot up. "What's that mean?"

"He's f-farming and . . ." Jameson swallowed so hard Amos swore he saw a wad of spit travel down his throat.

"And?" Jake was leaning toward him.

"He m-married M-Ma." Those three words seemed to exhaust Jameson. He removed his hat and wiped the sweat off his forehead.

"Was that his idea or your ma's?" Jake asked.

Jameson shrugged.

Amos felt dizzy from the news. Gil and Henrietta Block? Whenever he'd allowed himself to think of Pretty Water, he'd assumed everything was the same as when he left. Now he knew life had gone on there without him.

"How's Samuel?" Amos asked, trying to move away from the subject of Gil.

"He ain't changed. Still d-dodging work, talking about heading West. Every time he goes to leave, he claims his side is aching something awful. Ma says that's because he don't really want to go. All my other b-brothers married and started f-farms around M-Ma. Except for M-Matthew. He went out East to p-preach."

ALL THE TENTS along the spring sat close together except for one, which left enough room for at least twenty tents. Amos was trying to figure out who was in the lone tent when he noticed the scarred girl he'd seen earlier emerge from it.

"I just learned about those fancy folks," Jake said.

"Why do they camp so far from us?" Amos asked.

"Thinks he's too good." Jake added a pinch to his tone and said, "They're from London."

Amos couldn't imagine such a journey.

"Yes, sir," Jake continued. "They came over on a ship. Then they traveled from the East to Saint Louis before getting on a steamboat. Seems Mr. Hale Winthrop was somebody important over yonder in England. He had a store back there. Now he plans to have 'the finest mercantile store in the Oregon Country,' as he puts it. When he reached for a box, I caught a glimpse of that money belt he wears tied around his belly. I wouldn't be surprised if that man's entire savings is rubbing his navel."

Amos wondered what Jake would think about him if he knew about the money hidden in his art satchel. "Are they coming with us?"

Jake shrugged. "Oh, when I mentioned about Isaac's fine reputation, Winthrop wrinkled his nose and said, 'I'll be the judge of that.'"

"Have you seen their daughter?" Amos asked.

"Hard to figure that homely thing could be birthed from such a good-looking woman. Don't matter how purty you dress her up, there ain't no denying her looks. That gal's teeth hang out like a jackrabbit's. She's badly burned, too. Anyhow, if Winthrop thinks his tent is gonna be all by its lonesome, I can't wait to see his eyeballs bulge when tents start to set up near him the next few days. Folks are beginning to pour into this town like a heavy rain filling a barrel."

CHAPTER
16

GWENDOLYN WINTHROP looked toward the other tents. She noticed the boy who'd stood outside the mercantile store that morning with the rude little brat. He had stared, too, but unlike the younger boy, he turned away. She didn't know what bothered her most, the gawking or the shunning. She should be accustomed to both by now. In London the reactions subsided after the customers encountered her a few times. Still, when people spoke to her there, it was as if they didn't know where to focus. They stared over her shoulder, searching for her mother to rescue them from the awkward situation. Now in this new country, she would have to start over again.

If they only knew she could tell so much about them by just a quick sniff. In London, she'd known Agatha Peabody pined for their delivery man because of the lilac perfume she wore exclusively on Thursdays when he made deliveries. And when Mr. Boden complained about someone breaking into his home and stealing his tobacco and best pipe, she knew the thief was his young son, Charles. She knew about affairs of the heart, gluttons who ate bread pudding for breakfast, and her own father's penchant for rum. She was the keeper of secrets and the credit belonged to her nose.

Gwendolyn watched the older boy sitting next to a burly man dressed in leather and fur. If that was his father, he looked nothing like him. The boy's hair appeared as if it had been bathed in sunlight, and unlike the man, he was tall and lean. Thank goodness for the safe distance between them. He couldn't see her gaze tracing every inch of his body. She began at his head and worked her way down his neck, over to his shoulders, then his arms. Even from where Gwendolyn stood, she noticed his long fingers. She wondered if he was a musician or a poet.

Gwendolyn scanned her way down Amos's legs, and when she reached his moccasins, she allowed her eyes to travel all the way up his body again. She wondered what he smelled like. Inside the tent, her father grumbled to her mother. Gwendolyn detested him. He was the reason she'd never have the life she dreamed of—a simple life—an adoring husband and children. At least she had books. A heavy sadness overcame her as she glanced back at the boy.

While she admired the boy, she caught a glimpse of the familiar woman dashing behind his tent. The woman always appeared in moments of sadness and pain. The first time she showed up was in London at the home over their store. Gwendolyn was eight years old and had just endured the first of her father's many beatings. That one merely split her bottom lip and bruised her left cheekbone. Gwendolyn couldn't remember what she'd said, but her remark had been defiant enough to set off Hale's quick temper.

After the blow to her face, she escaped to her bedroom and threw herself on the bed, crying into her pillow. When she found the courage to check in the mirror, she noticed a woman with scarlet hair standing behind her. She turned to face the woman, but she had disappeared. She should have been frightened, but she wasn't. The woman smelled of pine and earth, and somehow Gwendolyn sensed goodness in those things.

Try as she did, Gwendolyn could not tame her tongue enough to suit her father. More beatings followed. The results were an eyeball that appeared larger than the other and the scarred right side of her face. The burn happened the day her father had finished off a bottle of rum. Before she could reach her room, he threw a lit candle her way. The flame and hot wax met Gwendolyn's right cheek. The woman was there then, too. Over the years, no words were uttered between the two, but Gwendolyn found comfort in her presence. She waited for another sign of her, but as usual the woman appeared briefly and then she was gone.

THAT WINTHROP GIRL was staring at him. Even with the distance between their tents, Amos could see her. She made his skin crawl. He was thankful when Blue Owl told him to find wood for the fire.

When the sun started setting, Isaac walked toward Jake and Amos. Except for his neatly trimmed mustache, his face was clean shaven and he wore a fresh shirt.

"Aw, you got all purty," Jake said to him.

"I might be an old trapper, but I don't have to look like one all the time." Isaac winked.

Jake didn't seem to mind looking like an old trapper. He introduced Jameson to Isaac. "I think you might have your cowman."

With a single glimpse at Jameson, Isaac agreed, and just as easy as that, Jameson became a part of the Isaac Bolton team.

Amos wished he could do something important for the wagon train. His days would probably consist of keeping an eye on Finn.

"How did my best salesman do today?" Isaac asked Amos.

"Good," Amos said, his spirits already lifted from Isaac's remark. "Can I tag along to the meeting tonight?"

"Yep," said Finn. "Amos wants to see that pretty girl again."

Amos shoved Finn so hard that the small boy stumbled to the ground.

"Watch yourself," Jake ordered.

Amos's ears burned. Finn was right. He was hoping to catch another glimpse of Jubilee. This time he'd say something intelligent, though he hadn't quite figured out what.

"Come on along, Amos," Isaac said. Then he and Jake started toward the store. "You might want to come too, Jameson. See what you're in for."

A few yards away from camp, Isaac said, "Amos, your ears are as red as a saloon gal's petticoat."

All the men fixed their eyes on his ears, and Amos felt like they'd been set on fire again.

Jubilee was not at the gathering, but when Amos noticed Elijah and Reverend McBride, he was relieved. That meant there was a chance the McBrides would join their train. By sundown, a small crowd had formed, and Amos recognized a lot of the people because he'd spoken to them earlier that day. Pride swelled inside him, and he told Isaac, "There are the McBrides. He's a preacher. That's Mr. Elroy. He has a bunch of daughters." Then Amos pointed to a man standing next to a gawky, skinny younger fellow. "And next to the counter are Mr. Sanford and his son, Ker."

"Good job, Amos," Isaac said as he surveyed the group.

"Takes after his pa," said Jake.

Elijah leaned against a pole next to the reverend, but when he saw Amos he smiled and waved at him. Amos waved back.

Isaac went to the front of the crowd. "Gentlemen, if I could have your attention please. I'm Isaac Bolton, captain of the Bolton wagon train. My plan is to get you and your families safely to the Oregon Country. I've made the trip many times, and I know the safest way. I hope you'll consider joining up with our party."

A man in a tall beaver hat interrupted. "I heard there is a cutoff that would let us avoid taking on the Columbia. Are you planning to use it?"

"No, sir, I'm not. You're referring to the Barlow Road. That's only a couple years old, and I don't yet trust it. Besides it costs five dollars a wagon."

Then Mr. Sanford spoke. "Five dollars seems like a small price to save your hide. I've heard of men being sucked under that river."

Isaac paused briefly, then said, "You'll have to decide for yourself. All I can say is that I've traveled that river many a time. It can be treacherous, but I've never witnessed a man go under."

A few men shook their heads and mumbled to one another. Amos had heard the question before at another meeting, though. They'd lost some joiners because of it, but Isaac later had said, "I'd rather lose foolish men now than have to deal with them on the trail. There can only be one leader."

That night Isaac continued as if the question hadn't been asked. "I plan to head our party out of Independence as soon as the grass and the dirt dries. If we're lucky, that will be in a couple of weeks. Worst case, we're probably looking at a month. Some of you might have your sights on California, but I won't take any part-wayers. I aim to end with the folks I start with. And that's to the Willamette Valley. I'll need you to add your name to this paper if you want to join our party. Any questions?"

Questions flew from the men's mouths. Hale Winthrop raised on his toes and peered over a taller man's shoulders. "How many times exactly have you made the journey?"

"Five as trail captain," Isaac answered. "And more times than I can remember as a trapper."

"How many Indian attacks?" Hale asked.

"None." Isaac turned his head, searching for another question.

Hale wasn't finished. "What is the greatest danger traveling on the trail?"

"Carelessness."

Amos watched the reverend closely. He couldn't tell if he would sign on, but after Isaac answered every question, Reverend McBride got in line to add his name to the list. Amos thought of Jubilee and her pretty yellow hair. He wished she'd been there that night. She was older than him, at least fifteen or sixteen. But that wouldn't matter, he reasoned, since he was more mature than most boys his age.

The Winthrop girl stood next to her father. When she looked in Amos's direction and smiled, Amos quickly glanced away. Jake was right. Her teeth were long. He felt guilty, but it was hard to look at her. Besides, the way Hale Winthrop had frowned during the entire meeting and then asked so many questions, Amos doubted that they'd be joining them.

A moment later, Elijah and Reverend McBride made their way over to Jake and Amos.

"Evening, Amos," the reverend said.

"Evening, Reverend McBride."

"Is this your father?"

"Yes, sir."

Jake offered his hand. "Jake Kincaid, first scout for the Bolton party."

"Glad to meet you. I'm Gideon McBride. I plan to start a church in Oregon."

"A man of the cloth, huh?" Jake nodded and eyed him suspiciously.

"This is my son, Elijah."

Smiling, Elijah held out his hand.

Jake took hold of it and shook.

"I'm buying our wagon tomorrow," the reverend said. "I'd planned on buying mules, but I keep hearing different opinions about that."

"No, sir," Jake said, "you don't want to do that. They may be faster than oxen, but they wear out faster, too."

Reverend McBride rubbed his chin. "I see."

"Yep," Jake said, "ain't you heard that saying 'stubborn as a Missouri mule'?"

"I appreciate the advice," said Reverend McBride.

"Amos, looks like your family has helped our family twice in one day. We owe you."

"Ain't no debt owed here," Jake said.

On the way back to the camp, he asked Amos, "That boy can't talk, can he?"

"No, sir," Amos said. "He can't hear either."

"That's a damn shame."

Amos believed not being able to talk would probably just about kill Jake.

MANY OF the emigrants had lived in cities. Blue Owl could tell she was one of the first Indians they'd seen up close. Young children hid behind their mothers' skirts when she walked by, and the women watched her with suspicion. She was used to white people's attitudes toward her, but Daisy seemed unnerved by it. When the women greeted Daisy, inviting her to join their sewing circles but not extending an invitation to Blue Owl, Daisy smiled sweetly, and answered, "Oh, me and Blue Owl have to get the washing done," or "Me and Blue Owl got more to do than we can shake a stick at."

Mrs. McBride didn't join the sewing circles, or *clucking circles*, as Jake called them. She and Jubilee stayed busy at their tent, washing clothes, cooking, or dusting their piano. When Mrs. McBride spoke to Blue Owl, she didn't act afraid or superior. Her words bounced from her mouth like laughter. A happy woman, thought Blue Owl.

The other women chattered like magpies in their circles. The longer their session, the louder they became. Blue Owl overheard Mrs. Elroy talking to some women outside a nearby tent. She was sewing blankets together, leaving an opening at the top, large enough to slip in a body.

"A coffin of cloth," she explained. "In case the worst happens. I've heard about the animals and Indians digging up the deceased. Why, my cousin said she saw a man's arm along the trail. God willing, we won't need these things, but if it is so, I won't have any of my loved ones go through that."

Expressions of horror covered the other women's faces, but Mrs. Elroy kept on telling the women all the things her cousin had warned of in a letter about the trail. Blue Owl wondered why Mrs. Elroy had bothered to join on. She couldn't blame the animals for hunting a meal. And if white people wouldn't bury their dead with their boots and shoes, Indians wouldn't bother digging up the bodies.

The Elroys' tent was set up next to theirs. They had four golden-haired daughters who constantly giggled and a black cat that called out to the moon until daybreak. One night they awoke Jake, causing him to growl, "Those darn Elroy girls make my head feel like it's gonna bust open from all their carrying on. And I wish like hell a coyote would eat that cat."

The next to the youngest, five-year-old Eliza, had a round face and wispy hair that stuck out from under her bonnet. When Finn noticed her, he was smitten. After that first encounter, he inched his way closer and closer to the Elroy tent each day until he and Eliza became pals. They played endless games of tag and hide-and-seek around the campsite.

One morning he tossed a small rock at the Elroy tent. The pebble slid down the tent, hardly making a sound. Finn then threw a larger stone. The thump awoke the entire family and caused the Elroy baby to wail.

Mr. Elroy poked his head through the tent and snapped, "Finnegan Johnson, Eliza will not be playing with you today. Perhaps tomorrow you will study on it some before you decide to throw a rock at our tent."

A moment later, Mr. Elroy changed his mind. Blue Owl was amused that a tiny girl was responsible for Amos's freedom from his tag-along. While she scrambled a skillet filled with eggs, Blue Owl noticed a mockingbird staring down at her. Daisy had bought the eggs the day before at the mercantile store. But the way the bird glared with her black-beaded eyes, it was as if she thought Blue Owl had stolen them from her nest. Not a bad idea. Blue Owl began to salivate as she stirred, thinking of mockingbird eggs fried in butter and served with bread and honey.

AMOS WENT to town with a belly filled with scrambled eggs and biscuits. He was thankful for Eliza Elroy. She'd made it easier for him to escape Finn.

The first man that he approached about joining the Bolton wagon train interrupted Amos's pitch. "Son, you can stop right there. I'm not going to Oregon. I'm heading toward California. Yes, sir. I want to get to the West alive."

Before lunch, Amos heard about a man who'd arrived in Independence that very day to warn people about the dangers of the journey to the Oregon Country. That same man, he learned, was taking a party to California.

Amos also ran into a couple of people who had put their names on Isaac's list the night before. Now they were going to California. He decided he should warn Isaac or they might not have anyone left in their party.

When he reached the outskirts of camp, he was met by Finn. He made giant circles with his arm. "You gotta see this, Amos."

"Not now, Finn. I have to find Isaac."

Finn jumped in place. "But—"

"Oh, all right. But this better be good."

Amos followed Finn to the top of a knoll. They hid in a patch of trees and watched Hale Winthrop struggle to drive the mules. Panic covered his face as he pulled the reins to the right and the left. He yanked the reins toward his chest. The mules ran one way, then the next. There seemed to be confusion on both Hale's and the mules' parts.

"He's gonna get killed," Amos muttered.

Hale kept calling out, "Whoa, whoa!" Each time his plea grew louder.

"I don't think he knows how to drive," Finn said.

Amos put his right foot forward like someone about to race off. He tried to decide if he should help or not. Hale Winthrop thought he knew everything. Let him figure it out. Finally Mr. Winthrop managed to stop the mules. He hopped off the wagon and rested against it, glancing around as if to see if anyone had noticed his poor attempt. He took out a handkerchief and wiped his red puffy jowls.

Finn started to holler, "Hey, Mis—" but Amos covered Finn's mouth with his hand. Then he grabbed hold of Finn's suspenders and pulled him in the direction of the camp.

Amos found Isaac polishing his boots. He told Isaac about the California man, his words rushing from his mouth so fast he had to gasp for air between sentences. "He's telling them they'll be lucky to make it to Oregon alive."

To Amos's surprise, Isaac didn't get upset. He pulled on his boots and gave them a last look-over. "There's nothing we can do about greed."

But that night when Isaac spoke with more potential joiners, he peppered his talk with the dangers of wagons that turned toward California. "The Sierra Nevada can be treacherous and, of course, the Mexican War hasn't been over with that long. Not everyone honors a treaty."

Amos wanted to ask Isaac what made him change his mind, but when the meeting ended and they headed back to camp, Isaac plucked the question right out of his head. "Nothing wrong with a little warning or two."

HALE WINTHROP wasn't the only man having trouble learning to drive a wagon. A lot of farmers were heading West, but the Bolton party had their fair share of people coming from Saint Louis and New York City. Amos and Finn passed the time watching the city slickers fumble through the process.

Reverend McBride's wagon was larger than any of the other emigrants'. Most people knew that their loads needed to be as light as possible to endure the trip, and Amos wondered why no one had warned the reverend about the dangers of too much weight. Jubilee said he needed a wagon large enough for their piano. The reverend believed it would be a big draw when he started his congregation in the Oregon Country.

EVEN HOMER had to practice driving the oxen, but after a dozen *shoot dangs*, he caught on. By early April, Homer was teaching Amos. He wondered how many moccasins he'd wear out before reaching Oregon.

The next day they bought the provisions for the trip. They purchased flour, sugar, coffee, bacon, dried beans, and pickles. They also bought soda to bake with and salt to season their food. Amos had never seen so much food in his life.

One evening Jake told Isaac, "Some of these folks packed their entire cabins in those wagons. It's gonna slow us down. Ain't you gonna tell 'em they need to get rid of some of those belongings?"

Isaac shook his head. "I've already warned them. But so many of them don't want to throw out their great-aunt Sadie's chair. They'll figure it out on their own."

At night Amos walked the camp where hundreds of wagons parked from various parties that planned to leave in the next two weeks. Forty wagons had joined the Bolton party. To his surprise, the Winthrop wagon was one of them.

Amos heard the music before he discovered Jubilee playing the piano. He knew the song. Rebecca had taught it to him. "Stand Up and Bless the Lord."

This was one night he didn't mind that Finn tagged along. Somehow Finn's presence gave him an excuse to approach Jubilee.

Elijah stood by the piano, and when he noticed them, he smiled and waved.

Jubilee greeted them, her fingers still hitting the keys. "Hello, Amos. Hello, Finn."

"That sure is pretty music," Finn said, rushing up to the piano.

Jubilee smiled. "Thank you."

"Have you played for long?" Amos asked as he joined Finn's side.

"I've been playing since I could sit on the bench. By the time I was your age, Finn, I was playing for the church."

Elijah swayed to the rhythm, and Amos noticed he had his palms spread flat atop the piano.

"I thought he couldn't hear," said Finn.

"He can't," said Jubilee. "He's listening with his hands."

"Huh?" Finn scratched his head.

"Put your hands on top of the piano near Elijah's." As Jubilee instructed them, her fingers never left the keys.

Finn's fingers barely reached the top of the piano, but he stretched, standing on his tiptoes until he fit fingertips to knuckles over the surface.

Finn moved his fingers from the piano as if he'd touched fire. "I can hear like Elijah!" he hollered. "I can hear with my fingers, too. You try, Amos."

Jubilee glanced up at Amos with a small smile, and something tugged his heart. His feelings were jumbled inside. He liked when Jubilee smiled at him, but he'd never felt so on guard before, as if he stood inches from a cliff, ready to teeter over into danger. Although when he studied Jubilee, there was nothing dangerous about her.

Amos slid his palms between Finn's and Elijah's. When the vibration of the music bounced against his hands, Amos understood how Elijah kept rhythm.

Out of nowhere, Finn asked Jubilee, "How old are you?"

"Sixteen," Jubilee said.

"I'd marry you," Finn said, "but you're too old for me. Anyway I'm gonna marry Eliza."

Jubilee laughed. "That doesn't seem like a bad alternative."

Amos saw the Winthrop girl strolling by. Jubilee noticed too, because she stood and called out to her. "Hello, there."

The girl glanced over as if she wasn't sure the greeting was meant for her.

"Would you like to join us?" Jubilee asked.

"No, thank you," the girl said in her British accent. "I need to return to our tent. My parents will be worried."

Amos was relieved, mainly because he didn't know how to keep Finn from staring.

"Will you be traveling with the Bolton party?" Jubilee asked, her neck stretching in the girl's direction.

"Yes."

"We'll be seeing you, then. My name is Jubilee McBride, and this is Amos Kincaid."

"Hello," Amos said softly.

The girl nodded, but she was not smiling.

Jubilee touched Elijah's shoulder. "This is my brother, Elijah, and Amos's cousin, Finn."

Nodding again, the girl walked quickly away.

"And your name?" Jubilee asked to her back.

The girl stopped, but didn't turn around. "Gwendolyn." Then she dashed off.

Amos decided that Gwendolyn was as unfriendly as her father. He shook her from his thoughts as he watched Jubilee's fingers return to the piano keys.

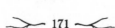

GWENDOLYN REGRETTED her reply. All the way to her tent, she muttered the words she wished she'd said, "Yes, thank you. I'd love to join you." She repeated the words over and over. But she had said "no" because accepting would have meant magnifying Jubilee's beauty even more to Amos.

Safely inside the tent, she slipped into her nightgown and went to sleep, thinking of Amos Kincaid's voice. Hello, he'd said to her. *Hello, hello.*

CHAPTER
18

APRIL 1848

BY THE END of April, the ground had dried and the grass was green enough to keep the animals fed along the trail. Isaac announced they would leave the next morning.

At daybreak, the wagons met at Independence Square. More than half of the wagons were pulled by oxen, but some of the emigrants had chosen mules or horses. The first wagon belonged to the Winthrops. Hale had parked there hours before most of the others. Amos had learned from Jake that the first wagon spot was the best because the wagons kicked up a lot of dust.

"You can tell he's a merchant." Jake said in a way that made a merchant sound like the lowest profession on earth. The McBrides volunteered to go last, which caused Jake to say, "I ain't one for churchgoing myself, but McBride seems like a genuine man of the cloth."

Amos wondered what Jake thought about Gil.

"Well, Winthrop may be first today, but the last wagon goes to the front tomorrow." With that said, Jake mounted Smokey and joined Thomas. They'd get a forty-minute start before the wagons. Staying a couple of miles ahead of the party, they'd watch for danger, but also scout for a place to stop at noon and to camp each night.

While Jake and Thomas made a head start on horses, Jameson would wait with Syd, the other cowman, for the wagons to get out of sight before they followed. That way they could gather any animals that might have wandered off the trail. Amos wished he could ride up front with Jake or behind with Jameson. At least then he could ride a horse. Anything but walking alongside the wagon. Still, an excitement stirred inside him. After this journey, Jake planned to return to Independence and scout for Isaac on future trips. The way folks were heading West, he could be scouting for years. Maybe if Amos proved himself on this journey, Isaac would let him scout or be a cowman on the next.

Isaac gave the signal and it was time to go. A few of the emigrants had painted *Oregon or Bust!* across the back of their wagons. The wagons did not leave in the perfect straight line Amos had imagined. Some of the emigrants had yet to master steering the oxen. Amos couldn't help but think it could be *Bust* before they made it out of Independence. A few miles from town, the oxen seemed to give in to their destiny and the drivers' faces and shoulders eased.

THE SUN BEAMED down, and for a while, Amos amused himself watching his giant shadow moving along the grass. Blue Owl followed him most of that first day, while Daisy rode up front in the wagon. Finn started off walking with Amos, but when his steps slowed, Amos lifted him and handed him to Daisy. He soon fell asleep on her lap. Thirty minutes later, he was walking with Amos again.

Amos's legs ached. He'd never walked so much in one day. Even when they'd headed back to Bittersweet Creek, they weren't on a tight schedule. Jake had taken the journey slow, his pace mirroring his reluctance of leaving the trapping life behind. Isaac planned to cover fifteen to eighteen miles a day. "Of course," he'd said, "that won't always be possible, but it's a reasonable goal."

Homer's wagon tracked along in third place after the Elroys'. When Eliza awoke from her nap, Mr. Elroy set her down, out of the wagon.

"Can I take Penelope with me?" Eliza asked.

Mrs. Elroy handed her the cat, and she raced to Finn until they were walking side by side. Penelope jumped from her arms but tagged closely behind.

"Do you know 'Buy a Broom'?" Eliza asked.

"No," Finn said.

She opened her mouth, beginning softly. Each line of the song came out louder than the previous. By the time she reached the ending she was belting, "Buy a broom, buy a broom," so loudly that three wagons in front and behind them heard the girl's high-pitched voice.

Next she sang "Old Dan Tucker" followed by "Yankee Doodle." By the end of the day, Finn had learned every song in Eliza's head.

The following morning, Amos showed Finn how to jump off the wagon without Homer having to stop. Careful, Finn would stand on the seat and jump into Amos's arms. By the middle of the afternoon, Finn had jumped off the wagon four times. He and Eliza played tag and when they discovered a meadow of wildflowers, they joined Mrs. Elroy and Eliza's sisters to pick bouquets.

The Elroy girls' hair glistened like wheat in the sunlight as they bent down to snap the flowers at the stems. The baby, Lou Ann, picked the petals off the flowers, leaving the stems naked. Amos thought the Elroy girls were beautiful and he stopped on the side of the trail to draw them. Too bad the sisters can't stay that way, he thought—gentle and dreamlike, instead of erupting into giggling spurts.

That evening, the party quit before sundown, and the wagons circled to form a corral for the oxen, mules, and horses. The cows grazed on the grass outside the corral.

The only wagon that didn't become a part of the circle was the Winthrops'. Hale Winthrop parked his wagon about a hundred yards away from the others.

"Humph!" Jake snorted when he noticed the lone wagon.

"He told Isaac that night could be a dangerous time among strangers. I reckon he uses that money belt for a pillow."

Amos gazed around at the wagons. Laughter and voices scattered about. He wondered what Jubilee was doing at that very moment.

The day had been long, but after everyone was fed, the color returned to folks' faces. An old bearded fellow blew into a harmonica while Jubilee played the piano. The music filled the night air and people began to dance. Amos watched Daisy and Homer twirl around the circle until Daisy spun away from Homer and pulled Amos to his feet.

"About time you learned to dance, Amos Kincaid," she said.

He felt awkward and self-conscious. He knew his ears were red without anyone telling him. But he followed Daisy's lead, and soon he was moving around the circle. The fine hairs around her face clung to her damp forehead.

From the piano, Jubilee smiled up at him. Reverend McBride took her place. She wiped her hands on her skirt and watched the dancers. When Daisy and Amos made their way to where Jubilee stood, Daisy pushed Amos in her direction. "Take this boy for a spin and let me have some rest."

Jubilee laughed. "Should we dance, Amos?"

"Sure," Amos said.

They stood there a long moment, Jubilee reaching toward Amos, Amos staring into her violet eyes. "Well, I guess we could join in now."

Amos nodded.

Jubilee waited, her arms still stretched toward him. "You might want to take my hands, Amos."

"Oh, of course." His ears burned. He took hold of her hands and they joined the circle.

Amos's heart danced—the music playing, the campfire's orange glow, Jubilee's soft hands.

GWENDOLYN TAPPED her feet to the music. The tunes were new to her, nothing like the symphony concerts her parents took her to in London. These were songs of cheer and hope. Her parents retired early to the tent, but she remained outside, listening to the music and watching the dancers. She wished her father had not chosen to make camp so far away from the corral. That way she could get a closer view.

She closed her eyes for a moment and imagined dancing with Amos. He was smiling as he held her hands and guided her around the circle. And when she opened her eyes, she was surprised to see her dream come alive. For there was Amos dancing, moving to the music with such glee. Then she looked closer and noticed his dancing partner. Gwendolyn's face stung. She slipped into the tent, promising herself that she would not waste any more time with such foolishness.

WHEN THE SONG stopped, Jubilee followed Amos over to his campsite. "I want to tell your family good night."

Amos had never heard anyone refer to them as his family. It sounded odd, but he realized she was right, partially anyway. He wasn't related to any Indian. Blue Owl just happened to be married to Jake.

When they reached the spot, he noticed Jameson sitting by the fire eating a plate of beans. He felt glad that Jameson would see him with Jubilee. Maybe he'd think she was his girl.

Jubilee smiled at them all. "Isn't the journey exciting?"

"It's only the first day," Jake said, winking at her. "Might see how you feel in a week or two."

The plate of beans fell off Jameson's lap as he stood and removed his hat, staring at Jubilee.

Daisy held in a giggle as she bent over and picked up Jameson's plate.

"S-Sorry," Jameson blurted out.

Amos swallowed and told Jubilee, "This is Jameson."

"P-Pleased to meet you, ma'am."

"Nice to meet you, too." Jubilee studied the grass at her feet, appearing shy for the first time since Amos had met her.

"You sure can p-play that p-piano," Jameson said.

Amos was relieved Jameson was too old for Jubilee. He must have been at least twenty. And he was glad he stuttered. He felt guilty and cruel thinking that, until Jubilee glanced up and stared into Jameson's eyes. Amos quickly did the arithmetic in his head and came up with twenty-three.

Jameson had to be twenty-three. He had nothing to worry about. But he sure wished they'd stop staring at each other.

Suddenly a cowbell rang, followed by Isaac's voice. "Folks, we're off on a great journey. I'm thankful for this smooth start, but we've got to make better time than we did today. We only made eight miles, and on a day like this we should have covered twice that."

The thought of covering more miles made Amos's legs ache, but when he stretched out on the pallet under the wagon next to Finn, his mind stayed busy with the evening's events. He concentrated on the dancing, trying to forget about Jameson meeting Jubilee.

THE NEXT MORNING, Amos awoke to Daisy's singing out, "Rise and shine."

The sky was dark and moonlit, but Amos had to yoke the oxen before breakfast. Though they were gentle, they shook their heads, protesting Amos's attempt to position the wood frame. He dreaded this part. He was not much for sweet talk, but that's what Jake had done the day before to calm them. Calling each by name, he whispered encouragements. "Good day, Samson, pretty boy. It's going to be a fine day on the trail."

When that failed, he kept the same soothing tone and said, "Hello, Samson. You'd make a mighty fine stack of steaks, boy. Roasted over the fire, then served on a plate.

So what's it going to be? Are you going to let me yoke you? Or will I have to choke you?"

Samson finally stilled, his enormous eyes showing his trust in Amos. By the time he finished yoking the oxen, light had begun to crawl up the horizon, a blue bleeding into gray. Amos allowed himself a single moment to appreciate the view. If only he could capture the early light and shadows with paint. If only he had time. Most of his sketching was done when he could steal a few minutes from the trail. Even then he had to hurry before the last wagon passed him by.

At the campsite, Blue Owl and Daisy had cooked a breakfast of coffee, bacon, and biscuits over the open fire. Jake had already eaten and was fixing the saddle blanket on his horse, Smokey.

"Finish yoking the oxen?" he asked Amos.

"Yes, sir."

Jake lifted the saddle and swung it over Smokey's back. "Maybe you can scout next trip. How does that set with you?"

Amos was wide awake now. "Yes, sir!"

"Of course, you'll just be learning, but I can teach you a heap." With that said, Jake mounted Smokey and rode off to meet Thomas and begin his day.

BLUE OWL started putting away the food while Daisy left to wash the dishes in the creek. She disliked the early mornings most. Even when she traveled with Jake, they hadn't risen in the dark. She was like the night animals, connected to the moon instead of the sun. When she heard the Elroy cat's guttural sounds each twilight, she longed to join in.

She watched as Amos met Homer to check the wagon. The boy was more like his father than he probably realized. Tender hearts mixed with strength. A troublesome combination. It was easier to be one or the other, instead of both. His choices would always be in conflict. This boy would have trouble crossing over to manhood.

Daisy interrupted Blue Owl's thoughts. She rushed over, flapping her apron at a flock of crows feasting on the biscuits they'd saved for noon.

"Shoo, shoo!" Daisy called out, stomping her feet at them.

From the looks of it, the crows had been at it awhile, pecking away at the biscuits that now resembled worn-out pincushions.

Blue Owl joined her, but it was useless. The birds had won this battle.

AT SEVEN O'CLOCK, the bugle sounded and the wagons broke their circle, lining up for the day's journey. It was the McBrides' turn to be first. Their wagon took off slowly and, one by one, the others followed suit.

The first day most of the walkers had stayed near their

own wagons, but that morning women and children drifted, visiting with their new neighbors. The mood was chipper, and they spoke in upbeat tones peppered with occasional laughter.

To Amos's joy, Jubilee and Elijah joined him. The three scouted for prairie dogs dodging in and out of their holes in the ground. When they spotted some, they pointed them out to Finn and Eliza, who dashed after the animals. They never caught any, but Amos and Jubilee laughed at their attempts. Penelope followed Eliza like a puppy, sticking her nose in the holes when the prairie dogs made a successful escape into their underground homes.

Isaac rode up next to Amos and smirked. "A typical second day, a day filled with optimists."

Amos felt optimistic himself, happy that Jubilee walked by his side while Jameson remained a quarter mile behind the wagon party.

When Isaac had made his speech the night before, Amos didn't ponder much on what it meant for the wagons to make better time. But later that day, he saw what it cost the pioneers. For miles, chifforobes, trunks, and rocking chairs littered the prairie, and before daylight burned out, Amos had helped Elijah and Mr. McBride push out the prized piano from the back of the wagon.

CHAPTER

19

THE VIEW REMAINED the same the first three days—flat vastness, no trees, just a sea of rolling grass. With each step, Amos's legs became heavier. He sure hoped something exciting would happen on this journey soon.

That night thunder roared across the prairie. Sheets of rain poured down. The folks who owned tents hurried to them. There was barely enough room for Blue Owl, Daisy, and Finn inside their tent, and provisions stored inside the wagon left no room to spare. So Amos, Jake, and Homer crawled beneath. They curled their bodies into tight balls and listened as the rain hit the wagon.

Lightning pulsed like a flickering candle. Deep blue patches flashed with each strike. The rain poured down so hard puddles formed quickly and the water spread underneath the wagon, soaking the men.

Jake quickly fell asleep. His body uncoiled and his left

side ended up exposed to the downpour. He began to snore, loudly and unevenly. The rain hit his face, and some of the drops landed in Jake's open mouth.

Homer whispered, "Are you sleeping, Amos?"

"Nope," Amos said.

"I couldn't tell. You had your eyes closed."

"Well, I thought if I pretended to be asleep, it might happen."

"Good idea. I'll try that." Homer squeezed his eyes shut.

But a moment later, he said, "Once when I was a boy, my pa threw me out of the house and bolted the door. It rained cats and dogs that night."

"What did you do?" Amos asked.

"Ran around the house, trying to stay warm until it stopped."

Amos tried to picture Homer as a boy, his skinny arms tightly wrapped around his body as he ran through sheets of rain. "Why'd your pa throw you out?"

Homer locked his hands behind his neck. "I guess I made him mad. He was always getting mad after Ma died. Always getting mad and drinking. Be glad your pa don't drink."

Amos had never given it much thought until now. But if Jake drank as much as he talked, Amos figured he might have thrown him out of the house, too. Or maybe he'd just talk Amos to death.

"Reckon why your pa don't drink?" Homer asked. He seemed determined to keep Amos awake.

Amos shrugged.

Just then Jake sat up and spat out the rainwater that had filled his mouth, bumping his head in the process. "Gawd a-mighty," he said, rubbing his crown. "I dreamt I was drowning."

CHAPTER
20

THE KANSAS RIVER

GWENDOLYN CRINGED while she watched her father make his way to the Indian. They had just reached the Kansas. The river was swollen from the hard rains. Isaac announced that they had two choices—build their own rafts or use the ferry run by some Shawnee. Just as she predicted, her father handed one of the Shawnee an envelope. The Shawnee peered inside it and abandoned the Elroy wagon that was to cross first. Then he motioned his helpers to the Winthrops' wagon.

Isaac Bolton noticed and headed toward Gwendolyn's father. "Winthrop, I don't know what you just paid that man, but you'll have to wait your turn."

Hale folded his arms across his puffed-out chest. "It's none of your concern if a man does business with another."

"Oh, you're dead wrong about that, Mr. Winthrop. Any business that goes on during this journey *is* a concern of mine. You'll have to wait."

Hale's back straightened, but try as he might, he could not reach anywhere near Isaac's six-feet-two frame. When Isaac stepped closer to him, Hale's eyes met Isaac's armpits. He stepped back to a safe distance from Isaac's reach. Gwendolyn wished Isaac would hit him. It would serve his arrogance right, trying to worm his way in front of that sweet family. They were all destined for the same place. Why did her father think he had to be the first to everything?

AMOS WATCHED Isaac's encounter with Hale Winthrop. He'd never known anyone like Winthrop. His cockiness seemed connected to the money belt bulging around his middle. During the confrontation, Mrs. Winthrop's cheeks turned crimson, but Gwendolyn stared at her father as if she were trying to pierce a hole big enough to drain every drop of blood from his body.

Mr. Winthrop tried to renegotiate the terms with the Shawnee since he'd lost his place at the front of the line, but when the Shawnee realized what was happening, he pushed past him and returned to the Elroys' wagon. The envelope of money Mr. Winthrop gave him earlier was tucked inside his jacket pocket.

Amos helped the men unload the wagons and remove their wheels. Then they carried the bodies of the wagons onto the ferry. Some of the Shawnee helped propel the ferry across with long poles. Others tied ropes to the oxens' horns and around the necks of the mules and horses so they wouldn't be carried away by the current when they swam across.

Finally, the last two wagons reached the other side of the river. After they reassembled them and reloaded the supplies, the Bolton party was on its way again.

JOURNEY TO THE PLATTE

The trail between Little Blue River and the Platte ran slightly downhill. Sandy mounds marked the way. Amos's mouth was parched. The lack of water and the way the sun struck the sand caused him to think the women and children walking ahead of him looked like giants twice the size of tall men. He swore he saw a lake just ahead, but he could never reach it. Even the oxen and mules seemed to be lulled into a dream state, their eyelids halfway closed.

Finn walked beside him, keeping pace in silence. Suddenly Eliza's head popped through the opening of the back of the Elroys' wagon.

She stood and waved. "Hi, Finn!"

Before Finn could answer, Eliza rushed to the front of the wagon and stepped onto the small seat as she'd seen Finn do dozens of times.

Mr. Elroy didn't see her. He was guiding the oxen. And Mrs. Elroy was walking one wagon ahead, as she held her baby and talked with Mrs. McBride.

Eliza turned to the side, stretched out her arms, and hollered, "Amos, catch me!"

Amos was watching her, but his head felt sluggish, and he didn't respond.

"Amos!" she yelled again.

Finn yanked at Amos's shirt. "Amos, catch Eliza!"

Amos saw Eliza clearly now, but before he could start in her direction, Eliza's legs wavered and her hands grabbed frantically at the air. Without uttering a sound, she fell over, headfirst. Her calico skirt flounced, turning upside down. Before Eliza hit the ground, her hem caught the axle. The wheel turned over her torso and the wagon dragged her across the grass. Eliza's tiny body looked like a rag doll's, flopping as the wagon moved.

Finn froze. Mrs. Elroy screamed. One by one, the wagons stopped.

Mr. Elroy left the oxen and hurried over to his daughter.

Finn stared at Eliza. Without thinking, Amos scooped him up and rushed away. They passed wagon after wagon—the McBrides', the Johnsons', the Winthrops'. Amos raced on. Faces became a blur. Questions fading into murmurs. Amos didn't stop running until they reached an open field away from the others.

When he finally collapsed, Finn rolled from his arms and into a ball. Amos stretched out on his back and stared at the clouds. A heaviness crushed his chest.

He had caused this. Amos showed Finn how to jump into his arms while the wagon was moving. Eliza would never have tried to jump if she hadn't seen Finn do it a dozen times. Back in Independence, Isaac had warned about the dangers of walking between the wagons, but Amos couldn't recall him ever saying it was dangerous to jump from one. He could still hear Eliza calling his name. "Catch me, Amos!" Amos covered his ears with his hands, but the words rang inside his head.

A group of sparrows landed nearby. Amos felt a need to strike something, and he sat up and swung at them. "Get out of here!"

The birds flew away.

Finn, who was still curled like a skein of yarn, began whimpering.

Amos rubbed his face and sat up, his back stiffened. "Finn, I know it's bad." He swallowed. "It's real bad."

"Is she broken?" Finn managed to ask.

"We better get back to our wagon," Amos whispered, though he didn't want to return.

Daisy met them halfway. The tall grass reached her waist and hid her skirt, but she was making a path through it, walking swiftly toward them. When Finn saw her, he took off running and didn't stop until he met her open arms.

THE COMPANY STOPPED their journey for the rest of the day. There was not a doctor among them, and Eliza died within an hour.

Amos felt helpless. He knew of nothing to do but draw. He fetched his sketchpad and found a spot away from the wagons. The child's laughter and songs echoed in his head while he drew her plump cheeks, wide eyes, wispy hair, and the sunbonnet that often hung loosely at the nape of her neck. His pencil flew across the paper, and he began to breathe easier, as if this single act held some power.

After he was finished, he started back toward their wagon to give the picture to Finn. He tried to avoid the Elroy wagon but couldn't. Their wagon was the next one over. He watched Mr. Elroy and Reverend McBride slip the little girl into the coffin his wife had made from a blanket. Back in Independence, she'd said, "in case the worst happens."

With needle and thread in hand, Mrs. Elroy settled on the ground. Mr. Elroy laid the blanket with his child's body on her lap.

Mrs. McBride stood close by, her hands fidgeting at her side as if they were fighting to stay put. Finally she bent over Mrs. Elroy, trying to grab the needle. "Let me do that."

Mrs. Elroy pulled the needle away from Mrs. McBride's reach, then hid it behind her back the way a naughty child would conceal a stolen biscuit.

"I'll do it," Mrs. Elroy snapped. Then she softly added, "Thank you." She hovered over the blanket and sewed the opening together. The top of Eliza's head was visible and Amos could not help but fix his eyes on it. Mr. Elroy knelt behind his wife and steadied his hand on her shoulder. Her mouth formed a tight, thin line as she pushed the needle into the fabric and pulled it through to the other side. Then, stitch by stitch, Eliza's golden hair disappeared from their sight.

Mrs. Elroy's shoulders lowered and her lips trembled. She dropped the needle and leaned her cheek against her husband's hand. Nearby, the two older Elroy girls stood silently watching. The eldest girl held Lou Ann on her hip. Amos wished the hours would turn back to the time they were the four silly Elroy girls.

Finn was resting his head on Daisy's lap when Amos returned to their wagon. He handed Daisy the picture. She studied it and nodded to Amos. Then she gave the picture to Finn.

When Finn saw who Amos had drawn, he sat up straight and held the picture to his chest.

AMOS HAD NOT realized Gil was a gifted speaker until he heard Reverend McBride stammer at the late afternoon burial. The reverend stopped occasionally to flip through the Bible, searching for a verse. When he settled on one, it didn't seem to fit the situation at all.

After he finished, Mrs. Elroy gave Mrs. McBride their remaining blanket coffins. "We won't be needing these. We're heading back."

Mrs. McBride seemed a bit startled by the gift, but accepted it anyway.

Mr. Elroy traded his team of oxen for Mr. Sanford's mules. Mr. Sanford had regretted not buying oxen. "They'll endure the long trip better. I know that now," Mr. Sanford said. "And the mules will get you home faster."

The Elroys said their good-byes to the wagon company.

Lou Ann sucked her thumb as she slept on Mrs. Elroy's lap. A moment later, she opened her eyes and gazed at Amos. Her eyes were Eliza's, that same hazel with gold specks. The two older girls climbed inside the back of the wagon. Just as they were about to take off, Finn hollered, "Wait!"

He went to Mrs. Elroy's side and held up the drawing of Eliza.

When he realized what Finn was doing, Amos tried to stop him. It was too late. Mrs. Elroy stared at the picture. She covered her mouth with her hand, but a dry sob escaped anyway.

Amos felt his heart twist and whispered, "I'm sorry."

Mrs. Elroy clung to the picture. "Amos, it's the spitting image of our Eliza. I'll treasure this forever."

The Elroys' wagon pulled away from the pack, turned around, and headed in the direction of Independence.

Soon Amos heard the snap of their reins, as if haste could carry them away from any more harm.

A few moments later, the journey began again for the remaining travelers. Until then, Amos would have never believed thirty-nine wagons would seem like a lot less than forty. After a few miles, he discovered the Elroys' blanket coffins on the prairie. Mrs. McBride had shed the unwanted reminder of what happened on the trail. Or maybe a warning of what might come.

CHAPTER
21

NO ONE TALKED about what happened to Eliza Elroy, but Amos noticed how mothers stayed closer to their children, as if death might snatch them up while the mothers weren't looking.

Amos felt weighted down by the burden of Eliza's death. His mind constantly played a game of *what if*. What if he hadn't shown Finn how to jump from the wagon? What if he'd hurried to Eliza's side and caught her? What if he had not been busy looking at giants and lakes that didn't exist? *What if? What if?*

All he could do now was fiercely guard Finn. He'd dreaded the task before, but now he did it like a debt he needed to pay. He promised himself that he'd never let anything bad happen to his cousin.

"Hello, Amos," Gwendolyn said.

Amos was so preoccupied with his thoughts that her greeting startled him.

"Hello," he said, staring down at the shadow under him.

"Do you know when we'll get to the Platte?" Gwendolyn asked.

"Nope," he snapped, "I haven't been this way before." He felt a bit guilty for his tone because he knew, if Jubilee had asked him, he would have answered more kindly.

"I guess I assumed you'd been this way since your father is a scout."

"I didn't go out West with him."

"Did you stay with your mother?" she asked.

Rebecca's face flashed in his mind. "Something like that."

"Blue Owl is beautiful. What tribe is she from?"

Amos frowned. Surely Gwendolyn didn't think Blue Owl was his mother? Then he softly answered, "She's a Shoshone."

"The way the sun shines down on her hair reminds me of the sunlight hitting a raven's wing—almost blue."

He was still staring down at the ground. Gwendolyn's shadow moved closer to his. He didn't say so, but he'd also often thought Blue Owl's hair reminded him of a raven's wing.

Suddenly he heard Jubilee's voice. "Hi, Gwendolyn. Hello, Amos. The clouds are rolling in. Do you think it will rain?"

Amos looked up at her, smiling. "Hopefully not before we make camp." He glanced at Gwendolyn. Now she was studying the ground. He should have been more friendly, but he was afraid to be kind to her. She might make more of it.

A hard slap met his back. He stumbled, but caught himself.

"Elijah!" Jubilee's fingers moved quickly.

Her brother ignored her, grinning.

"Amos, that was fine of you to give that picture of Eliza to Mrs. Elroy." Jubilee practically skipped as she spoke.

"Finn gave it to her."

"But *you* drew it, Amos," Jubilee said. Then she asked Gwendolyn, "Did you know that Amos has an artistic gift?"

Gwendolyn shook her head, then stole a glimpse at Amos's hands.

"Jameson must get tired of all that dust," Jubilee said, staring back at the line of wagons that seemed to stretch forever.

"Expect so," Amos said, only to be interrupted by a flying buffalo chip thrown by Elijah.

"Elijah!" Jubilee grabbed hold of his shoulders and turned him toward her. "Maybe Amos doesn't want to play all the time."

Amos picked up the chip and threw it back. "Not much else to do."

Although that evening there was plenty to do. He had to unyoke the oxen and gather buffalo chips for the fire.

BEFORE JUBILEE had joined them, Gwendolyn had tried to convince herself that Amos's replies were not harsh. He was just shy, she decided. And he had been somber. Those few quick moments they walked alone, she studied his face. It was the closest she'd ever been to him. His eyes were like the cornflowers that grew in window boxes outside their London home. His lashes were long and not at all usual. They were light brown with golden tips. Even as he stared down, she could see them just as plain as day. And the back of his neck was tanned from the sun. How she wished to kiss it. She'd finally smelled him, but for once, she was baffled. His was a pure clean scent, but not at all like soap.

Gwendolyn listened as Amos spoke to Jubilee in such a cheerful way that she was forced to admit the harshness in his tone when he'd answered her. Jubilee smelled sweet with a hint of spice like cake made with ginger. A sadness grew deep inside Gwendolyn, but when she dared to glance their way, she noticed Jubilee did not look at Amos in the same longing way he looked at her. She smiled as she spoke, but Jubilee had a joyful spirit when she spoke with every-one. It was her nature. Although when Jubilee mentioned the cowman, Jameson, Gwendolyn heard something lift in Jubilee's voice.

While Gwendolyn pondered Jubilee's feelings for Jameson, it came to her. *Water.* Amos Kincaid smelled like water.

A woman with wild scarlet hair appeared in front of them. Had Gwendolyn not recognized her, she would have thought she was one of the women in their wagon party. The woman turned and smiled at Gwendolyn. The smile had a black tooth and an empty space next to it, but it was a nice smile just the same. Gwendolyn smiled back. A tiny sliver of hope hung before her now. Then the woman disappeared and a flock of sparrows swept down and took her place.

THE NEXT DAY Amos thought he saw a lake. But this time it was the Platte glistening below them. The river was wide and muddy. Homer said it looked like moving sand. They'd heard the river was hard to cross, contained few fish, and was too dirty to bathe in. But the Platte served as an arrow pointing their way West. Land bordering the river offered more wildlife than they'd seen in the hundreds of miles they'd traveled so far.

"I wish we could stop and hunt," Homer told Amos when they passed a group of antelope.

They camped that night on the riverbank. The bank was as flat as a floor, providing an easier journey. Isaac hoped to make good time now, eighteen miles a day if they pushed, but some of the women complained that they needed a day to catch up with the laundry.

Soon they reached a creek that flowed into the Platte. The water was clean there, and Isaac announced that they would spend a full day off the trail. Later he told Jake and

Amos, "I'd rather lose a day than hear a bunch of women squawk about dirty clothes."

So while the men hunted, the women washed. Amos, Elijah, and a few other boys were ordered to stay and help the women. That annoyed Amos until he realized maybe he could help Jubilee. Jameson and Reverend McBride were asked to stand guard.

"I've never hunted a day in my life," Reverend McBride told Amos. "I wouldn't know where to begin."

Amos wondered how the reverend planned to protect them if he'd never shot at a wild animal. And he'd never known a man who would have admitted not knowing how to hunt.

"Sometimes I don't know why we bother to wash clothes," Daisy said, swatting at a fly. "They just get dirty again from the dust while they dry." Then she added, "At least stopping a day gives them a chance to dry in the sun and fresh air."

Mrs. McBride was feeling ill, and Amos helped Jubilee carry the oak bucket to the river to fill with water for washing. Blue Owl made a tea from some roots and dried leaves she carried in a pouch. By noon, Mrs. McBride was up and moving as easily as a younger woman. Amos couldn't tell she'd been sick at all.

When it was time for the men to bathe, Amos took Finn. They stayed in the shallow part, since Finn had never learned to swim. Nearby Jake headed toward the deep end with other men and boys. If they had time, Amos would teach Finn to swim as Jake had taught him years ago. Though he didn't enjoy swimming, he'd improved over the years. Jake had seen to it. Still, the water made him uneasy, and dreams of drowning came far too often for his comfort.

Homer shed his clothes, then told Amos, "I can stay with Finn."

Finn grabbed hold of Amos's arm. "I want to stay with Amos!"

"He'll be fine with me," Amos said.

Homer nodded his thanks, jumped in the water, and let out a, "Weesh! Shoot dang, it's cold!" Then he swam toward the other end of the creek.

After bathing, Amos felt like a new man. He almost hated to put on his dirty clothes. Before he did, he smacked them against the grass a few times, shaking off some of the dust.

Finn picked up his pants and did the same. Suddenly he screamed, "Snake! Snake!"

A rattler slithered near Finn's feet, and before Amos could think of what to do, a shot rang out. The snake's body jumped a few inches and landed on the ground, dead. Finn froze and Amos looked up.

There stood Jake, bare naked with a pistol in his hand. "Stay out of tall grass," he said. Then he placed his pistol on top of his pants and went back into the water.

AFTER DINNER, the music began, but Amos had to help Jake check their wagon wheels. When they discovered one had shrunk away from the rim, they removed the wheel and soaked it in the creek to expand it. Then they drove pieces of wood between the rim and the fellow. That would have to do until they reached the next fort.

From underneath the wagon, Amos watched couples twirling by in the center of the corral. He caught a glimpse of Jubilee's calico skirt. His eyes followed her until he noticed Jameson spinning her. The glow of the campfire cast a golden pink on their faces, and Amos couldn't miss the way their eyes locked as they danced. They acted as if they were alone. Amos felt like someone had kicked him in the gut.

Without moving his focus from the wheel, Jake said, "When I was a young man about your age, there was a pretty little gal who lived two farms west of us. I got in my head that I had to have that gal. But that gal didn't want me."

Amos wondered why Jake had to turn everything into a story. Why couldn't he just say something outright?

Jake sighed and continued. "She wanted the boy that lived two farms over to the west from her. They eventually got married, had a mess of kids, then she ran off with a man traveling through. I reckon she made his life miserable, too."

ACROSS THE CORRAL, Blue Owl showed Mrs. McBride how she could use buffalo dung for a fire. Some of the other women at nearby wagons looked on at her demonstration and moved in closer. They amused Blue Owl. She suspected they didn't want her to teach them anything because they thought she was nothing but a dumb Indian, but wood was scarce on the prairie and the flint kits they brought would probably run out before the trip ended. In times of desperation, a dumb Indian could show them a thing or two.

Jubilee rushed up to the campfire. Jameson followed her. "Hello, Mother. Hello, Blue Owl."

The girl's cheeks were pink from dancing, but Blue Owl noticed the sparkle in her eyes, too. That was not from dancing. Blue Owl thought of Amos. Jubilee was not the girl for him. She wished she could take away his pain once he knew this. She only hoped he didn't make a fool of himself before he accepted it. From what she'd witnessed, most white men did.

ALTHOUGH AMOS had a rough night, tossing and turning thinking of Jameson and Jubilee dancing, most people looked refreshed the next morning. The break at Spring Creek had been worth the time off the trail. But just as the circle broke and the wagons lined up, word traveled that Ebby Goforth had passed on. Isaac said they would have a quick burial and leave after eating at noon.

Ebby Goforth was an old lady, traveling with her son and his family. Her heart had simply played out. Amos could recall seeing her only once. When Jubilee told him that the Goforths had asked if he would draw a picture of her, Amos snapped, "I don't even remember what she looked like." He felt like shaking her. Didn't Jubilee know she was tearing him apart?

"I remember what Mrs. Goforth looked like," said Finn.

"You do?" Amos was suspicious. "How?"

"She was scary like an old witch. Me and Eliza used to spy on her."

"Why?" Jubilee asked. "Mrs. Goforth was a nice woman, Finn. She gave my family a jar of apple butter she canned from her Missouri farm."

"She had a long skinny nose with a hairy brown mole on her chin," said Finn. "Like a witch!"

Amos looked to Jubilee, who nodded. "I'm afraid so."

"She had beady eyes," Finn said.

"Small brown eyes," corrected Jubilee.

"Like a witch!" said Finn.

And so it went, Jubilee and Finn describing Ebby Goforth's every inch and Amos drawing until they both nodded in agreement.

There was nothing joyful about death, but there was not the dark cloud hovering over the old woman's funeral as there had been at Eliza's. Her son spoke about how his mother wanted to take that long journey West because it would be something exciting. "'It will be my last great adventure,' she'd said."

After the funeral, the wagons rode over the burial site,

pounding down the earth to make it difficult for coyotes, wolves, or Indians to notice it. Before they left, Amos gave the drawing of Mrs. Goforth to her son. His voice broke when he said, "Thank you, Amos. It looks just like her." Amos was glad he'd left the hairy brown mole off her chin.

CHAPTER
22

IF ANYONE had wanted to know what could be seen on the trail, all they'd have had to do was thumb through Amos's drawing pads. There they'd find prickly pear cactus, thistle, yarrow, and primrose. He'd also drawn buffalo, antelope, wolves, and coyotes. The birds intrigued him the most—owls, turkey buzzards, woodpeckers, ravens, and crows.

Sometimes he only had fleeting moments to observe them. So he learned to quickly take in as much as possible. He became skilled at memorizing detail in one swift glimpse, holding the vision in his mind's eye until he was able to meet up with his pad again. He certainly enjoyed drawing those subjects more than the dead.

The sun seemed to set on the same day for the next week—the same river, running along the same flat land, the same clouds casting shadows on the covered wagons.

Amos's shadow became his walking companion when Finn rested and Elijah was nowhere to be found. Although when he was alone, he always sensed someone watching him, studying his every move. Sometimes he felt a prickle on the back of his neck.

EVER SINCE Jubilee had mentioned Amos's talent, Gwendolyn had become obsessed with his hands. They were long and graceful, not feminine, but in a way that made them appear as if they were dancing when he sketched. The middle finger had a tiny callus on the side, probably from holding a pencil. The sparse blond hairs contrasting against his tanned hands fascinated her.

She noticed how he'd made a habit of finding a spot away from the wagons to draw until the last wagon passed. Then with sketchpad in hand, he'd race to the front of the wagon train again. He was ahead of their wagon now. She quickened her pace to get a closer view.

Back in Spring Creek, she'd seen Jubilee dancing with Jameson. The sight of them together had given her cause to hope, but now thinking on it, she felt sad. Amos would never look at her the way the young couple stared into each other's eyes that night. Not in a million years. Some things could never change. She touched the side of her face. She wondered, If her scars were gone, would she be pretty?

Finn walked beside his mother. He turned and stared. Then he stuck his tongue out at her.

She couldn't stand that little brat. If anyone would remind Amos of what she looked like, it would be him. She slowed her pace and hung back near her parents' wagon.

TOWARD THE END of the next week, they entered Ash Hollow and their surroundings changed. Within a few days, Chimney Rock appeared. At first, the formation seemed a mere stitch on the horizon, barely recognizable. Although as the wagons rolled forth, the rock grew until it resembled the giant haystack Amos had heard about. Chimney Rock represented the five-hundred-mile marker of their journey from Independence.

But first they came to Courthouse Rock. Amos squatted and Finn straddled his shoulders. Elijah and Jubilee joined them as they ran away from the wagons and toward the rock. The more they ran, the farther away it looked. They slowed their pace to a brisk walk, eventually making their way to the foot of Courthouse Rock.

Amos realized right away that the climb would be too dangerous for Finn. "Go on ahead," Amos told Jubilee and Elijah.

Elijah didn't understand and looked to Jubilee, two vertical lines forming between his brows.

Jubilee didn't explain. Instead she said, "Amos, please, go with Elijah. I'm not up for the climb."

Amos didn't know if she was saying that to be kind or because she really didn't want to climb to the top of

Courthouse Rock. He looked up. The yearning to climb pulled strongly at him and he turned to join Elijah.

"Wait for me," Finn cried out.

Jubilee fixed her hands firmly on her hips. "Now, Finnegan Johnson, don't tell me you would leave a lady unescorted."

Finn nodded. "Yep, I would."

"We'll write our names down at the foot," she told him. "Look, hardly anyone has carved their name here."

Finn lowered his shoulders. "Oh, all right. I guess I gotta protect you."

And with that, Amos was off.

Up there on Courthouse Rock, he could see everything—Chimney Rock and all the way to Scotts Bluff! He wondered if this was what God felt like looking down on the world. The view was the most magnificent sight Amos had ever seen. He could see the Bolton party below, and a wagon train that was about a mile behind them.

From below, two small figures waved their arms at them. Jubilee and Finn had backed up enough to be seen by the boys.

Elijah got excited and waved back, sweeping his arm high. Then he opened his mouth and let out a sound that was somewhere between a scream and a screech.

The sound came out of nowhere and was so unexpected that Amos had to steady his legs to keep from falling. When Amos stared at Elijah in disbelief, Elijah laughed. This high up, Amos felt free, almost as if he could fly like a hawk. Maybe Elijah did, too.

Amos dug in his pockets and pulled out three pieces of sharpened buffalo bone he'd saved for this very moment. He also had a small satchel that held a mixture of gunpowder, tar, and buffalo grease. He wrote Elijah's name for him, then went over the letters of both names. He wanted to make sure people would see their names a century from now.

Soon the boys climbed down and the four of them dashed off to catch up with the wagons. They weren't alone. Quite a few members of their party had also ventured out to see the world from God's eyes.

Elijah raced Finn back, running slower so that Finn could stay even. Amos decided to take advantage of his time alone with Jubilee. "Something happened up there on Courthouse Rock. Did you hear Elijah scream?"

Jubilee frowned. "Yes. How could I not? Did he scare you?"

He *had* scared Amos, but Amos said, "Nah, but I wonder why he did that?"

"I think my brother has a lot of pent-up feelings. If only Mother would let him go to a school."

Amos stayed quiet and listened to Jubilee explain how Reverend McBride had researched schools for the deaf. "There are a couple in the East. They're expensive, but Father found one in Ohio. They could teach him so much that we can't."

"But you taught him how to talk with his hands."

"We made up that language. We're the only ones who can understand it. At the schools, they teach a sign language and learn to read lips. Some students even learn to talk."

"Why won't your mother let him?"

"She's babied him since she found out that he was different. He'd have to live apart from us if he was to attend those schools. It's not that she means him harm, but I'm afraid for his future. How can a boy become a man with a mother who holds on so tight?"

Amos realized that was something he would never know.

CHAPTER
23

A FEW NIGHTS after they passed Chimney Rock, they happened on a clean spring. The only problem was that three
other companies were camped beside it, leaving no room
for the Bolton party. They stopped to fill their canteens, but
had to cross Horse Creek two miles away to set up camp.

Fort Laramie occupied the talk that night. Folks had a
lot of business to take care of there. A couple of the wagons
had repairs to make. The horses, mules, and oxen needed
to be shod again. Provisions needed to be resupplied.

"I hope there's a doctor there for Mother," Jubilee said.
"Every day the sickness returns. And she is having such
terrible dreams. Wicked dreams." Jubilee shuddered.

"What kind of dreams?" Finn asked.

"Oh, evil dreams. I shan't tell you lest they make you
have bad dreams."

"I have bad dreams all the time," Finn said.

Amos raised his eyebrows. He knew Finn did not like to be outdone, even while he slept. "What are your dreams about?"

Finn stared down and dug his toe in the dirt. Then he softly said, "That I'm dead."

They were quiet then, and Amos felt a knot form in his belly.

THE NIGHT BEFORE they reached the fort, it rained with such a force that even those in the wagons could not escape getting wet. The next morning, the sun shone so bright it was as if the downpour had never happened. But there were signs of it everywhere—the damp grass, the emigrants sneezing and coughing, Gwendolyn Winthrop's curls turning into a fuzzy orange dandelion.

When they arrived at Fort Laramie, some of the men told them, "First rain we've had since last September. Three years ago, it didn't rain a drop."

The fort didn't have a doctor, but an agent with a bit of medical experience in the war tended to the sick. Some of the women came with their children to find relief from their colds. The agent went to a shelf and took down a satchel. He pulled out some dried herbs that resembled those Blue Owl carried.

"What's this for?" one of the women asked suspiciously.

"Dried leaves and roots, such as that," the agent told them. "Get it from the Indians. Works pretty darn good."

Every head swerved in Blue Owl's direction, then quickly snapped back. Blue Owl seemed unaffected, but a smugness grew inside Amos. He figured the women were getting their fill of scandal, what with all the former trappers working at the fort who lived with Indian wives.

When Amos saw a thin old man, he called out, "Pirate Paul!" but the man swung around and two good eyes stared back at him. Feeling a bit foolish, Amos realized that he hadn't seen Pirate Paul in six years. The old man could be dead by now.

They stayed at the fort the next day, too, camping on the opposite side from the Indians. When they got back on the trail, Amos discovered two wagons had decided to return to Independence.

"Always figured them for turn-backers," Jake said with a scowl.

"But they've come so far," Amos said. "Why would they come all this way just to turn back?"

Jake rested his foot on a nearby stool. "They know they ain't got the backbone to face what lies ahead. Getting to Independence Rock is a pretty rough journey."

The wagon party left Fort Laramie and headed toward Laramie Peak and the Black Hills. The grass quickly vanished. Sagebrush and rock became plentiful, making the walking hard and nourishment for the animals scarce. Amos wondered if the turn-backers had been the smartest people in their party.

TWO WEEKS AFTER they left the fort, they had to cross the North Platte at Deer Creek. They'd been warned about the river back at Laramie. The emigrants made it to the other side, although two mules were lost in the process.

They had discovered plenty of buffalo on the trail, but since Fort Laramie they'd gone without seeing any. So when Jake spotted a herd a half mile off the trail, Isaac recruited a few of their best shots to help Thomas hunt some for dinner. Thomas had spent a year as a buffalo hunter after his trapping days ended. He had a quick, steady aim, which was a good thing because buffalo proved difficult for the emigrants to shoot. Blue Owl said that Thomas's Indian half had won over his white blood. Amos hoped that Isaac would pick him, but he chose Jameson and two other men instead. It tore at his insides to see Jameson ride off with Thomas.

The men would only have a short time to hunt because the wagons kept going forth on the trail. Isaac called the journey off an hour early to let the men catch up. A couple of hours later they rode up dragging two dead buffalos behind them.

Jake told Amos, "Come help me skin them. You can help, too, Elijah." Jake hadn't learned to face Elijah so that he could read his lips. So Amos repeated the offer to Elijah, whose skin paled as he shook his head. Then he took off for his wagon, throwing a sly glance over his shoulder to Amos. Homer and a few other men came near to help. The blood didn't bother Amos, but he would have preferred the hunting to the skinning. Jameson and the other men received echoes of gratitude and slaps on their backs. The glory belonged to the hunter.

While the meat cooked, Jubilee and Daisy helped Blue Owl stretch the hides, tying each corner with a thin leather strap to a wood stick hammered in the ground.

Amos didn't care much for buffalo. The meat tasted drier than beef. But he decided it was certainly better than beans.

CHAPTER
24

JULY 1848

WITH THE SLOW start and the extra days at the Kansas and the creek, Isaac had expressed doubt that they would make it to the marker in time. "We need to reach Independence Rock by the fourth of July. That way our chances are better that we'll beat the harsh winter weather. If we reach our goal, we'll take a day off."

Independence Rock was more than eight hundred miles from where they'd begun. The wagon train arrived there before noon on July third. Isaac kept his promise, and they stopped to celebrate. He announced, "We'll camp here along the river until the fifth."

The Sweetwater ran along the base, while mountains and other rocks kept it company. Grass had been scarce ever since they'd left Fort Laramie. The rib cages on the oxen and the other livestock were visible. Now they had plenty of grassy mounds to graze.

The women started cooking the minute the wagons formed their corral. They had saved preserves, sugar, and spices for this celebration. Much to Blue Owl's delight, Daisy had hidden a jar of honey between two quilts. While the women prepared for the next day, the men looked after the wagons.

Amos, Elijah, and Jubilee planned to wake early the next day and climb Independence Rock to carve their names on the stone.

Finn had started coughing that week, but when he caught word of Amos's plans, he told Daisy, "I'm climbing Independence Rock with Amos tomorrow."

"Oh, no, you're not," said Daisy.

Finn's cheeks puffed out and he started to cry.

"Buddy, listen to your ma," Homer said. "You've got a bad cough."

"Amos, tell them, I'm not sick," Finn begged.

"I'm afraid your ma and pa are right," said Amos.

Homer knelt by Finn so that they were eye to eye. "Rest up tomorrow. If you feel better the next day you and me could go fishing in the Sweetwater." The river ran along the base at one end of the rock.

Finn folded his arms across his chest. "I wanted to carve my name."

"I can do that for you," said Amos.

Frowning, Finn asked, "You will?"

"I sure will."

"Will you put Finnegan Johnson, not just Finn?"

"Yep," Amos said, relieved that Finn gave in so easily.

"And the date? You gotta put the date under my name."

Amos grinned. "Now, don't tell me you want me to write a poem, too?"

"Well . . ."

"Finn." Daisy slapped his knee, playfully. "You are a varmint."

Homer told Finn, "You better quit nagging or Amos will change his mind."

The next morning Amos got up at five o'clock, grabbed a biscuit, and walked quietly to the McBride wagon. Most of the women were up, getting their campfires started. Soon the aromas of coffee and bacon stirred the air.

Amos found the reverend sitting by the fire, staring at his coffeepot. The coffee was bubbling up and escaping from the lid, running down the sides of the pot.

"Morning, Amos," he said in a hushed tone.

"Reverend, your coffee is boiling over," Amos told him.

Reverend McBride hopped to his feet and grabbed the handle with a pot holder. He moved it away from the flames and rested it on the ground. "Thank you, Amos. Seems you're always saving me from some dilemma or another."

Jubilee showed up, smiling weakly at Amos. She always looked so freshly scrubbed in the mornings, even though she bathed as infrequently as Amos. And she smelled good, like fresh-baked gingerbread. Rebecca had made it for Christmas one year, and he had never forgotten the scent.

"Mother is feeling poorly again, and I guess Elijah has caught her sickness. I knew that he was ill when he didn't want to get up for the climb this morning."

Amos was sorry to hear about Elijah, but now he'd have time alone with Jubilee. They weren't alone though. Many of the other emigrants had the same plan. Mr. Sanford and his son, Ker, walked with a group of men. As they made their way to Independence Rock, Amos tried to think of something fascinating to tell Jubilee.

"Did you know that it's about a hundred feet high?"

"That's what Jameson told me," Jubilee said. Then she turned her head as if to search for him.

"And it's about a half mile long," Amos added.

"Yes," she said.

Amos did not have to ask how she knew.

Ahead of them, Gwendolyn walked by herself at such a meandering pace that Amos was not sure if she was aiming for Independence Rock or just wandering about. When Jubilee noticed, she caught up with her. Amos reluctantly followed. He could predict where this was heading.

"Happy Fourth, Gwendolyn," Jubilee called out.

Gwendolyn smiled. "Hello."

"You have the most lovely curls," Jubilee told her. "Oh, how I wish my hair would do that without Mother twisting it with rags."

"Curls can be bothersome," Gwendolyn said with a bounce.

If they talked only of such things as curly hair, Amos thought he might desert them and join the group of men walking ahead. The heat already felt thick. He studied the sky. The sun was quickly floating up from the horizon.

Amos held out his hand to help Jubilee climb a couple of feet to a safe landing. He never knew touching someone's hand could give him such a thrill. Jubilee's soft skin made his entire body tingle. He hopped up, joining her on the landing.

When Amos reached her side, Jubilee's eyes widened. "Don't forget Gwendolyn."

Amos stepped back down and offered his hand to Gwendolyn, who smiled so broadly, he thought he was looking at Smokey's mouth.

"Thank you," she said, her gaze lingering long on Amos.

Suddenly Jubilee smiled and waved to someone. "Oh, look, it's Jameson. He said he thought he'd have to keep an eye on the livestock today."

This was not working out at all as Amos had planned. They waited for Jameson to meet up with them.

"G-Got the day off," he said, squeezing in next to Jubilee and pushing Amos closer to Gwendolyn. The four proceeded to climb.

Most of the names were within eight feet of the ground, and Amos felt disappointed when Jubilee announced, "How fortunate, here's a clear spot for us to sign on, and we don't have to climb any higher."

Anyone could sign their names at the foot of the rock. Maybe he'd finish the climb on his own. He suddenly missed Elijah. Then he thought about the sound that Elijah had made and how it had startled him.

They read some of the names. A few went all the way back to 1830. "Probably trappers," Amos explained. His eyes scanned the rock for the names that Jake mentioned in his stories. He'd almost given up when he saw *Paul Ferguson, 1842*. That was the year he'd last seen Pirate Paul.

While Gwendolyn and Jameson wrote their names, Jubilee and Amos wrote Finn's and Elijah's before writing their own. Amos carefully wrote *Finnegan Johnson, July 4, 1848*. After giving it pause, underneath he added, *A Poem*.

When Jubilee noticed, she burst into laughter.

Gwendolyn read the words and said, "I don't understand."

Amos explained how Finn had teased that he wanted a poem written under his name.

Gwendolyn's laugh startled Amos. It came from her belly and rang out with such joy that it didn't seem to belong to her. He turned to Jubilee and noticed the tip of her nose had turned pink even though she wore a sunbonnet. Amos wished he could kiss it. Jubilee didn't seem a bit aware of her beauty, while Gwendolyn seemed aware of her own lack of it.

When they finished, Jubilee stood and looked down on the wagon caravan. "I'm going to come back here one day with Elijah and show him his name. I may be an old lady, but I'll be back."

Amos looked into her eyes, and he believed she spoke the truth. He believed everything that came from the mouth of Jubilee McBride.

"I'll t-take you b-back here one day," said Jameson.

Jubilee smiled up at him.

Amos turned away.

Gwendolyn was staring at him. "Will you return here again, Amos?"

"As soon as we get to Oregon, I'll be coming back with Jake to scout." He had no idea if that would happen for certain, but he peered over at Jubilee to see if she was impressed. She was looking at the view with Jameson. She had not heard Amos.

But Gwendolyn had. "You're going to be a scout? How exciting and dangerous!"

"Not if you know what you're doing." Now Amos felt like an imposter.

Jameson was pointing out the McBride wagon to Jubilee so Amos looked at Gwendolyn. And when he did, her hand flew to the scarred side of her face.

"Let's f-finish the c-climb," Jameson said.

Jubilee smiled. "Of course."

Amos almost groaned.

After they reached the top, they returned to the McBride wagon to find Mrs. McBride up and moving nervously.

Jubilee touched her mother's hand. "Are you better, Mother?"

Mrs. McBride's forehead wrinkled. "Yes, but not your brother. I do wish we had a doctor in this group. Your brother is burning up with the fever."

"I could fetch Blue Owl," Amos said. "Maybe she could make some of her tea?"

"God bless you, Amos," Mrs. McBride said.

Amos took off. He passed quilts laid out on the ground, which the women were covering with food. Some of the men had gathered together and were tuning their instruments. All around him a party was about to start. Now, with Elijah sick, Amos didn't believe there was anything worth celebrating. That morning, he'd not known the seriousness of the illness. Amos had only been concerned with being alone with Jubilee. He was thankful when he saw Finn running about with some other boys.

Blue Owl made her tea, and the McBrides waited to see if it would be the miracle cure it had been for Mrs. McBride. They stayed at their tent instead of joining in the festivities.

Usually the families ate separately, but today their quilts touched, forming a patchwork map. The food was modest—dried beef, beans, potatoes, and bread. But there were plenty of honey cakes and Ebby Goforth's apple butter. Watching

Blue Owl devour three slices of honey cake made Amos smile and forget his worries for a bit.

At dusk, the music played and people danced. Amos stayed back, leaning against the right front wheel of their wagon, and stared across the circle to the McBrides'. Jubilee looked down at the ground, her shoulders lowered. He longed to reach out to her. But he felt helpless.

Then he noticed Jameson heading to the McBrides' wagon. A second later, Jameson slipped his arm around Jubilee's shoulders. She gazed up at Jameson with such tenderness that Amos clamped his teeth so tightly a pain shot through his jaw. He turned his focus to the twirling couples. Daisy and Homer were there. Tiny Daisy spun around by clumsy Homer. Daisy didn't seem to mind at all. Suddenly someone was calling his name, awakening him from his thoughts.

"Amos?"

It was Gwendolyn Winthrop standing before him. A blue ribbon held her curly locks.

"Do you dance, Amos?" she shyly asked.

He didn't answer. He just grabbed hold of Gwendolyn's hand and led her to the circle, joining the other couples.

GWENDOLYN DIDN'T KNOW what caused those fleeting moments of courage. She seemed to be two people in one. Most of the time she was so aware of her scars and other physical flaws that she felt like a little mouse trying to hide. Then every once in a while, like a gift, she forgot her shortcomings and something restless soared inside her. Usually those moments passed quickly and nothing could be done. But tonight, when she saw Amos alone, watching the couples, she snatched the courage. The words came easily from her mouth as if she'd rehearsed them. She hadn't. She didn't know how to dance. Since that first night on the trail, she'd studied the couples and practiced alone in the dark.

Her heart beat fast as her feet tried to keep up with the music. She could feel herself smiling. She was afraid if the music kept this fast pace, the evening would be over too soon. She looked at Amos. He was staring into her eyes with such surprise that she quickly focused on the view over his shoulder. He's realized what he's done, she thought. He's realized that he's dancing with the ugliest girl on the trail. Still they danced. And still Gwendolyn wished the evening would not end.

AMOS DID NOT know what had come over him when he accepted Gwendolyn's offer to dance. Or had she even asked him to dance? No. She'd merely asked if he danced. He had not thought about it. Dancing just seemed the thing to do. He needed something to do after seeing Jameson put his arm around Jubilee.

But what had been unexpected was that before the first dance had ended, Jubilee had slipped from his mind. He found himself wondering about Gwendolyn. How did she get scarred? How old was she when it happened? Would she work in her father's store?

Her hands felt damp and cold. Or were *his* hands damp and cold? He wanted to wipe them on his pants but was afraid it might offend her if he did. He was new to dancing, but he felt like an expert compared to her. She'd stepped on his feet twice and each time he'd twirled her, he could tell it had taken her by surprise. Still, he hoped the musicians didn't quit any time soon.

CHAPTER
25

THE NEXT DAY the Bolton party made their way around Devil's Gate, where the Sweetwater shot through a narrow crack in the tall rock. As they continued on to South Pass, word traveled around the company that Elijah wasn't doing well.

Around the campfire that night, Mrs. McBride said, "If Elijah could just hold on until we get to Fort Bridger. I've been giving him cups and cups of Blue Owl's tea. I'm even giving him doses of vinegar as if he has scurvy."

"He's got the typhoid," Jake said. "I've seen more than a few trappers come down with it."

Mrs. McBride's mouth fell open. She lifted her apron and hid her face.

"Are you sure, Jake?" Reverend McBride asked.

"Yes sir, that's what it is," Jake said. Then as if he'd realized the impact of his words, he quickly added, "But he's a strong boy. He'll pull through."

Elijah wasn't the only one who'd met up with typhoid. Isaac ordered the families who had someone with the fever to keep a quarter mile behind the rest of the party. At night, the typhoid wagons made their own circle. Isaac said it was the only way he knew to keep the typhoid from wiping them all out.

Amos could not understand what had happened. Elijah had been healthy the last time he'd seen him. They'd walked side by side, tossed buffalo dung, raced after Finn. How could sickness grab hold of him so quickly? Amos was relieved that Finn's cough had stopped.

Then Amos remembered how quickly the smallpox came upon Rebecca. She might have died from the disease if the Otoe hadn't killed her. . . . Something just never seemed right about that day. He couldn't put his finger on it, but the details festered inside him. Back then, Sparrow Hawk and the Otoe had been their friends. How could friends become enemies in such a short time? And why would they kill Rebecca? As a child, he'd accepted what he was told. But every time he'd allowed himself to think of it in the last few years, what they'd said didn't ring true.

That night when Jameson ate dinner with him, Amos asked if they could walk alone. A full moon hung in the sky, and he could clearly see Jameson's face.

Amos did not waste time getting to his point. "What happened to Rebecca?"

Jameson quit walking and faced Amos. "She g-got the smallp-pox. Remem-mem-ber?"

"I'm talking about *how* she died. Who shot her? Was it the Otoe?" Amos was not a boy anymore. He needed the truth.

An owl hooted nearby. Jameson turned his head to the right, then left, as if searching for the bird. He took a deep breath, then another. "G-Gil shot her. She b-begged him, Amos."

Amos's heart stopped. He knew. Somehow he'd always known. And now he knew for certain.

BLUE OWL moved to the outside of the corral so that she could see Amos and Jameson. Whatever had been said upset Amos. She knew this from the way he backed away from Jameson, taking long strides as if he'd been slapped by the words. It was probably about Jubilee. Amos had to face it sooner or later. The girl was good, but she would bring bad to him, like too much rain on a river causing a flood—one heartache after another. Better one big heart-ache now.

Amos would heal. She knew this in her bones. He'd danced with the other girl, the girl whose face told the story of many broken hearts. This could bring good.

THE JOURNEY from Independence Rock to South Pass took six days, and by the time they arrived, four people had died of typhoid. Elijah was not one of them. He had not gotten any better, but he had not gotten any worse. The burials and funeral services were swift, because Isaac said they must push forward if they were to stay on schedule and beat the snow in the Rockies. So the men dug holes while Amos drew the dead.

The children proved resilient, pulling through just when it looked like they might not. Violet Simmons's death bothered Amos the most. He didn't know her, but she was not much older than Daisy. She left behind a husband and two young children. Amos wondered how Finn could stand to live without his mother. He hoped Finn never had to find out.

They stopped for the burial. A few men were helping Mr. Simmons, who insisted on digging his wife's grave. While they worked, Amos tried to remember every detail he could about Violet. He thought of her brown hair that she wore in a bun and her slender frame. But he couldn't remember her facial features because he had not looked at her closely. He was thinking on that when Gwendolyn walked up.

"Are you drawing Mrs. Simmons?"

"Yes," Amos said, staring out toward the wagon train. "I can't remember her face." He looked down at the empty spot above the neck he'd drawn.

Gwendolyn settled on the ground, across from him. "She had lovely green cat eyes."

On another sheet, Amos sketched an eye and held it up for her to see. "Like this?"

"That's the shape, but a bit larger."

To the side of the one he just sketched, he drew another.

Gwendolyn smiled, nodding. "Yes, exactly."

"Do you remember her nose?"

Noses were hard to remember unless someone had an unusual one, but Gwendolyn said, "It was small and turned up a bit. Not so much that it looked snooty, but cute, child-like, I guess."

Amos grinned. He, too, had thought about how physical features made a person appear to have a certain personality trait.

Without Amos asking, Gwendolyn added, "And her lips were thin. The top one hardly existed at all."

Under Gwendolyn's guidance, Amos drew. She described Mrs. Simmons's small ears and high cheekbones. Then when she softly said, "Her skin was flawless," Amos looked up at her.

Gwendolyn's hand flew to her face.

Amos leaned toward her, gently took hold of her wrist, and pulled it away from her cheek. "It's not that bad."

She stared the other way. "You're just saying that."

"I don't just say anything," he told her.

She turned back toward him and smiled. Her smile started small but grew until her teeth showed.

It startled Amos because her teeth didn't appear long and bucked as they had before. Gwendolyn's smile was lovely.

THE SOUTH PASS opened to them like a wide gate, providing a way through the Rocky Mountains. Reaching it should have been a joyous event. They'd come a thousand miles, their halfway point. But the deaths and sickness were with them now. They wondered who would be next.

Amos could not keep his mind from Elijah. He hadn't seen him since the day before they arrived at Independence Rock. These last three months, they'd walked miles together. He'd learned to communicate with him, not only facing him so that he could read his lips, but using his hands and fingers, also. He knew only simple signals—eat, juggle, tired, sleep—but they had helped bridge their friendship.

Amos hadn't talked to Jubilee since they'd found out about Elijah. He'd seen her from a distance, though. She walked with her mother alongside the wagon in the day, and at night Jameson made his way to her side. Each time Amos noticed them together, a bitterness rose from his gut until he needed to spit upon the ground. Although that didn't ease his hard feelings. Jameson had betrayed him, allowing him to believe that Rebecca had been killed by the Otoe. And now Jameson was spoiling any chance Amos might have with Jubilee.

Then, somewhere between the Sweetwater and the Big Sandy River, it occurred to Amos that it was not too late. He had never been able to say quite the right thing to Jubilee, but this day, he would. He thought on it some and decided he'd chance it. Maybe he'd find the right words when he saw her. Besides, he wanted to know how Elijah was doing.

The crisp night air filled his lungs, and his steps felt

light as he made his way to the other corral. Ten yards from the McBrides' wagon, something stopped him cold. At first he could only see two forms moving in the dark. Then he focused his eyes and realized it was Jubilee and Jameson. He was lifting her. Her shoes dangled at his knees, and her arms were locked around his neck. They were kissing.

Amos turned to run. He accidentally kicked a pail, causing a loud thump.

Jubilee called out, "Wait!"

He slowly turned, facing them.

She'd moved away from Jameson. Now fear tinged her voice. "Wait, Amos."

He couldn't escape, but he didn't move toward them either.

Jubilee walked up to him. Her voice shook. "Amos, did you come about Elijah?"

Amos didn't say anything.

"How good of you," she said. "I'll tell him."

Jameson called out, "How are you d-doing, Amos?"

He hated Jameson. He wished he'd never kept that giant. It was a foolish, childish thing to do. He should have tossed it away years ago.

Jubilee stepped closer to Amos and touched his arm. "You have been such a good friend to Elijah." He didn't want to feel anything, but her touch made him tingle like the day he touched her hand at Independence Rock. His chest felt tight. He couldn't breathe. He wanted her. Without thinking, he grabbed hold of her wrists, pulled her to him, and pressed his lips against hers.

Jubilee squirmed and Amos held tighter. He could feel her trying to push him away, but he kept a firm grip. He needed her to want him. Suddenly he was grabbed by his shoulders and his hold on her was broken.

He swung around, and when he tried to strike, Jameson caught his arm. "D-D-on't, Amos!"

He felt like that little boy at the mission again. He bent toward Jameson's hand and bit down.

Jameson hollered, rubbing his hand. "D-Dang it, boy!"

Amos wanted him to strike back, but Jameson didn't. He kept rubbing his hand, staring at Amos with a baffled look. Jameson's resistance made Amos more angry. He stepped forward and pushed Jameson with all his might.

It didn't work. Jameson hardly moved. So Amos tried again.

This time Jameson drew back his fist and punched Amos in the chin.

Amos fell to the ground, flat on his back. Then he got up and walked swiftly away.

"Amos," Jubilee called after him.

By then he was running. He reached the other corral, but kept on. Amos made a path around the outside of the wagons. He passed Blue Owl and Jake, who sat by Daisy and Homer near their campfire. He didn't stop until he reached the Winthrop wagon. He didn't know why, but when he'd started running, it was as if he knew he would end up there.

He called out, "Gwendolyn."

Mr. Winthrop stood from where he'd been sitting in front of the fire with his wife. "What do you want with my daughter?"

From the other side of the wagon, Gwendolyn appeared. She stared at Amos. "It's okay, Father. I asked Amos to come by."

"Gwendolyn," Hale said with a sharp tone, "a proper young lady does not ask a young man to drop by."

Gwendolyn went to Amos. "Next time I'll ask an old man, then."

Mrs. Winthrop quickly reached up and touched her husband's hand. Then she looked toward her daughter. "Only for a little while, dear. Don't wander too far."

To Amos's surprise, Hale didn't object, although he locked his jaw and glared at him.

They walked until they escaped from the light of the Winthrops' campfire. Gwendolyn didn't ask why he was there. She didn't speak at all. She stopped walking and lightly touched his chin. It still ached, and her cool fingers felt soothing. He wished they were Jubilee's. And when Gwendolyn removed them, he was tempted to grab hold of her hand and place it back.

"My father loses his temper sometimes, too," she said.

Amos was puzzled at first, but then he realized she

thought Jake had struck him. He didn't explain that she was wrong, but now he had another reason to dislike Hale Winthrop.

They looked toward the corral. There was no music, but they could see Daisy and Homer dancing with Finn, forming a circle as they moved around the campfire.

"They're the happiest couple I've ever seen," Gwendolyn said.

Amos hadn't thought about it until then. He supposed that Blue Owl and Jake were happy, too, but there was something joyful about Homer and Daisy.

Suddenly, Gwendolyn asked, "Do you like petunias?"

"What?" Amos laughed.

"Petunias," she repeated. "They're flowers. I'm going to plant loads of pink petunias when we get out West. When I was seven, my mother took me to the ballet. The dancers wore pink tutus. Every time I saw a pink petunia after that, it made me remember and I got happy all over again." She sighed. "I should get back."

Amos watched her until she disappeared from his sight. His chin hurt. So much had happened that evening, but all he could think about was what tutus and petunias must look like.

The next day, the news about what had happened the night before spread from wagon to wagon. Not about the fight, but about Jubilee McBride and Jameson Block. They were engaged to be married.

CHAPTER
26

JAKE DIDN'T SAY anything about Amos's chin. He just shook his head when he noticed it the next morning. Homer whistled and started to comment, but Daisy poked him in the ribs with her elbow.

Homer scowled and rubbed his side. "Shoot dang, Daisy! I was just going to tell him how I got a shiner from pining over a girl years ago."

Daisy poked him again. This time, Homer winced and pressed his lips together.

Finn awoke and peered through the tent's opening. "What happened to your chin, Amos?"

"You are just like your pa," Daisy said. "Get your clothes on and come eat."

"But what happened to his chin?"

"Get your clothes on," Homer told him.

Blue Owl made a paste from her herbs and told him to

cover the spot with it. The herbs created a cool sensation, but soon began to feel hot. Maybe Blue Owl was part witch with all her potions. If she was, he didn't care. Her potions always seemed to work.

The engagement announcement brought on mixed feelings for Amos—oddest of all, relief. The restlessness he'd felt since Jubilee and Jameson met was replaced with a peace like the quiet after a storm. He only wished he could forget the foolishness from the night before. He hoped Elijah would get well, but he was thankful that their wagon rode in the typhoid train. That way he wouldn't have to face Jubilee.

But a few days later the McBride wagon rejoined their train. Elijah sat in the wagon next to Mr. McBride. When Elijah saw Amos, he raised his arm and swung it high and wide. Amos rushed over to him and tugged at Elijah's pants hem.

"Good to see you, Amos," Reverend McBride said, "but you might want to keep your distance from Elijah for a while. Just to be sure."

Amos nodded, smiling.

"Glad that chin's doing better," Reverend McBride said with a wink.

Amos's ears burned.

The reverend turned when he noticed Amos's ears. He focused straight ahead as he spoke. "I wouldn't want Mrs. McBride to know this, but before the Lord sent her into my life, I pined for another. The young lady had a beau who was visiting his cousins in New York. I seized my opportunity and tried to court her. I wrote her a poem. When she read it, she laughed. I even baked her a cake. She spat it out. But the worst was when her beau returned and beat me up so bad I had to stay in bed for a week."

"Sorry to hear that," Amos said. He walked away wondering if all men made fools of themselves. And why did they need to tell him about it?

He glanced over his shoulder and saw Elijah, again waving his arm against the sky. Amos waved back and glanced around, searching for the Winthrop wagon.

AS CRAMPED as it was, Gwendolyn stayed inside the wagon, reading books. The bumpy ride made it difficult, but she wanted to hide from Amos. She was full with all that had happened in the last few weeks with him—the dancing, helping him remember Violet Simmons, and the stroll in the dark. And now Jubilee and Jameson's engagement. She didn't trust this much happiness. She was afraid it would vanish like a field of dandelions, displaying golden petals one day and blowing away the next.

More than anything, she worried Amos's kindness was merely pity. By staying away, she'd avoid getting hurt with the truth and she'd keep her cherished moments with him.

CHAPTER
27

MID–SEPTEMBER 1848

THE WAGON TRAIN followed the Snake River. The ground was rocky where it dipped into the canyons, and a few young children cried because they'd cut their bare feet. Like the children, many of the animals were now shoeless, and blood streaked the trail for miles. At times, Amos had trouble seeing because of the dust. He and Finn tied kerchiefs around their heads, covering their noses to their chins.

One night the mosquitoes swarmed so thick, Daisy pinned a petticoat over a hole in the tent to keep out the bugs. The men had to sleep in the open air. Jake snored away, but Amos and Homer were restless. Homer rolled up tight in his quilt. Along with constant outbursts of *"shoot dang!"* he wiggled so much from the bites, he resembled a giant caterpillar.

Amos curled up under his quilt. The bugs still nipped at his neck and hands, causing him to slap and scratch for hours.

Worse, the horses cried out all night in agony. Amos couldn't stand it any longer. He got up and used his quilt to smack the bugs off Smokey. It was useless. The bugs returned to the horse after a detour to Amos's face. Finally he fixed the quilt over Smokey's back and gave up.

BLUE OWL was used to the rocks, dust, and mosquitoes. She was home. Her people had lived along the Snake River for generations. She knew by heart the way the sun shimmered on the river and the way the moon drifted between the night clouds. As a girl she had worked harder than any of the others, especially her sisters. They had been cursed with beauty. Their good looks had made them favorable to men, but also lazy. Still, as they moved along the river, she watched for her family.

A few days later, they came upon a group of Shoshone, but she didn't recognize any of them. They dressed in various pieces of white people's clothing—buttoned shirts, long pants, and boots. One man even wore a pipe hat and suspenders. They were willing to trade for more with their strings of salmon. Blue Owl didn't know about the rest of the travelers, but she was sick of dried beef and beans.

Some of the Shoshone touched the white women's dresses or skirts as if trying to swap the frocks right off their bodies. The Shoshone startled the women, but then Blue Owl told the Shoshone to approach them like they would a darting fish—slowly and with patience.

They immediately dropped their hands to their sides.

"They want trade," Blue Owl told the white women.

"Goodness," said Mrs. O'Neil. "This is all I have left. The other dress looks like an old rag after traveling this long." Then after a quick pause, she asked, "Do you think they'd want to trade for that?"

Blue Owl shrugged. "Try."

Mrs. O'Neil rushed into her wagon and returned with a faded calico dress. A deep tear was near the hem. She held it out to the women who spread the skirt of the dress like a cloth, admiring the piece. The Shoshone woman took six salmon from her catch and offered them to Mrs. O'Neil.

"I got five young'uns," Mrs. O'Neil said. "I'll need seven fish." She held up seven fingers.

The Shoshone woman added another fish, and Mrs. O'Neil gave her the dress. The other women went to their wagons to hunt for more trades.

Jake shook his head and snorted. "Just goes to show, women don't need no mercantile store to shop."

Finn raced over to Daisy. Breathless, he said, "I want to trade."

"What have you got to trade?" Daisy asked. "You're not trading any of your clothes."

"How about socks?" Finn asked. "I got lots of socks."

Daisy fixed her hands on her hips. "You ain't got that many socks, Finn. And what would those Indians do with your itty-bitty socks?"

"Please, Ma. Can't I try and trade?"

"Oh, go ahead. You're just gonna keep begging till you try."

Finn slipped out of his moccasins and yanked off his socks. He ran over to the man with the pipe hat and suspenders and held his socks out to him.

The man, who stood with his friends, stared down at Finn holding up his tiny socks. In Shoshone, Blue Owl told the man that Finn wanted to trade. The man took the socks from Finn and held them up. He laughed. Then everyone laughed except Finn.

"Whatcha gonna trade 'em for?" asked Finn.

The Shoshone took one of the salmon off his line of six, then he cut the fish in two pieces and held out one half to Finn.

Finn folded his arms in front of his chest. "That's all you're gonna trade me for them socks? That ain't fair. Them's good socks."

"You could have at least offered him some clean ones, Finn," Homer said.

Then the Shoshone man in the tall hat picked up his line of salmon and handed the entire catch to Finn.

"Well, that's more like it," Finn said.

BY THE TIME the trading ended, it was midday, so Isaac said they would noon there. Everyone ate their meal of salmon and bread. The food was a welcome change from bacon and beans. Amos decided he liked salmon as much as any meat.

After the meal, Amos sneaked five spoonfuls of sugar into a cup of coffee and stirred. He'd never much cared for the taste of it before the trail, but somewhere between Chimney Rock and Fort Bridger, he'd picked up the habit of drinking a cup each morning. Across the fire Daisy licked the corner of her apron and dabbed at Homer's face. After she finished, she quickly kissed his cheek. Gwendolyn was right. Daisy and Homer were two of the happiest people he'd ever known.

Except for a brief glimpse here and there, he hadn't seen Gwendolyn for weeks. When Amos noticed her carrying dishes to the river, he dumped the rest of his coffee and rushed over to meet her. The Winthrops were the only family with real china, and she was carefully balancing three cups atop a stack of plates.

"Can I help with those?" he asked.

"I've got them," she said, but the cups started to slide.

Amos caught them before they fell.

"Thank you," she said, smiling.

That was when Amos noticed her eyes. Hadn't the left one been larger? Maybe he'd imagined that. Because now it was clear to see. Gwendolyn's eyes were green as summer grass. And they were equal.

CHAPTER
28

WHEN THEY CAME to the crossing at the Snake River, Isaac recommended that the wagons cross two at a time, placed abreast of each other, to fight the raging water. There were thirty-nine wagons, though. One would have to go alone.

Folks exchanged glances and no one said anything. Amos figured it would be their wagon since Jake was a scout.

Then Hale Winthrop rested his hands on his waist where the money belt was hidden under his shirt. "I'll go alone as long as my wagon can go first the rest of the journey."

Isaac said, "You can start going first now."

Mr. Winthrop and his family headed toward their wagon. He climbed in and drove it to the river's edge.

Isaac met him. "I'd suggest you lead the animals across. Let your wife or daughter drive."

Mr. Winthrop's face went pale and he paused. Then he said, "Very well," and jumped from the wagon.

Gwendolyn was sitting in the back, but she quickly came to the front and squeezed in next to her mother. "I'll drive the team."

Mrs. Winthrop didn't even blink. She sat stiff as Gwendolyn took the reins.

Mr. Winthrop walked to the left side and took hold of a lead mule's harness.

The others waited for him to cross. Amos watched Isaac fold his arms across his chest and his mouth twisted into a smirk. "Slow and easy," he shouted to the Winthrops.

Amos's heart pounded. He was afraid for Gwendolyn, but she stayed focused and held the reins as if she'd driven the wagon from Independence.

The mules would not budge at first until Mr. Winthrop said, "Snap the reins!"

Then they took off. The water was shallow at first, but the river rushed on, rising the more they moved away from the bank. Mr. Winthrop held tighter to the harness. The mule kept shaking his head as if he was trying to escape. Then Mr. Winthrop lost his hold and slipped.

Gwendolyn's mother screamed and a few folks on the riverbank gasped.

But her husband straightened and caught hold of the mule's harness. He waved with his other hand. "I'm steady now. Not to worry."

Gwendolyn had not seen the mishap. Her concentration seemed to be on the other side of the riverbank. Amos felt a huge admiration for her.

The mule calmed. But when the water reached almost a foot above the wagon bed, and touched Mr. Winthrop's shoulders, the animals stopped. Mr. Winthrop teetered and stumbled, letting go of the harness.

With a mighty force, the current carried him downriver. His arms flapped, but he disappeared below. Hale Winthrop's hat sailed along at a swift pace. All eyes focused on the hat as it rode the river, it hit a fallen log, until becoming trapped in the crook of a forked branch.

No one moved. No one said a word. There was only the rushing of the river and the snap of the reins as the Winthrop wagon continued to the other side.

Amos watched the back of the wagon, silently willing it to the riverbank. Then he heard the sound of someone breaking the water. It was Homer. He was heading in the direction of Hale's hat. The water's depth rose to Homer's neck, and he began to swim.

"Get back here, Homer!" Jake hollered.

If Homer heard, he ignored the warning. For a moment it seemed like it could be possible, Homer saving Hale Winthrop. Homer swam and swam. And when he reached the hat, he stood and lifted it as if Hale Winthrop would be directly below. Then he stepped in the direction of the river's flow and sank beneath.

"Homer!" Daisy screamed and ran toward the river. As she reached the water, she lifted her skirt, exposing her skinny calves.

Blue Owl raced after Daisy and grabbed hold of her just as she entered the river.

"No!" Daisy yelled, trying to escape Blue Owl's grasp, but Blue Owl was strong and she pulled Daisy to the bank. The hem of Daisy's skirt was soaked, and she leaned forward, moving as if her body was heavy.

"Ma!" Finn wailed, running to meet her.

Amos felt helpless watching. He tried to think of what to do, but he was paralyzed. Then Jake ran into the river and swam toward the spot where Homer had gone under. He ducked beneath the surface. The world above went still. It seemed as if Jake were under an hour before he came up for air. On and on it went—Jake fighting the current, swimming back and forth, above and below. Isaac called out for him to stop, but Jake continued.

Finally Jake gave up and swam back to the riverbank. When he emerged, Amos noticed blood flowing from a deep gash in Jake's left leg. At the water's edge, his knees buckled and he collapsed, face forward. Amos raced to him and quickly removed his own shirt. He rolled it up tightly and tied it around Jake's wound. Reverend McBride met them, and with Jake between them, Amos and the reverend managed to get him to the wagon.

"It's as if he's disappeared," Jake said, shaking off the water from his hair.

Finn clung to Daisy, who stared at the river as if she were waiting for Homer to emerge any second. Amos could hardly stand the pain of it all. He turned away, and, when he did, his gaze landed on Gwendolyn and Mrs. Winthrop. They'd lost everything—Hale Winthrop, and every bit of their money that had gone down the river secured around his belly. Head held high, Gwendolyn stood tall, her arm surrounding her mother's shoulders. Amos decided he'd never seen a braver person in his life. Then as if sorrow had cracked open the sky, rain began to pour down on them all.

CHAPTER
29

THE MCBRIDES SET UP their tent, and Amos helped Jake inside. Isaac dug in his saddlebag and pulled out a pint of whiskey. "He'll sure need this." Then Isaac left to watch over the wagons' crossing.

Blue Owl held the bottle to Jake's mouth, and for the first time ever, Amos witnessed Jake take a drink. He quit after three swigs, but Blue Owl kept the whiskey to his lips and ordered, "More!"

Jake raised his head, took another swallow, then rested back on the ground. Between his quick shallow breaths, he said, "You better sit on my arms, boy."

Amos settled across one of Jake's thick arms. Elijah sat on the other, while Reverend McBride held down Jake's legs at his ankles. Blue Owl placed a cloth on the wound to soak up the blood. Then she splashed whiskey over the spot and poured some on the needle before threading it.

Jake squeezed his eyelids shut.

And Blue Owl began to sew. *In and out. In and out.*

"Gawd a-mighty," Jake muttered.

Elijah passed out and fell across Jake's chest. The reverend leaned toward his son, but he kept holding Jake's ankles. Amos tried to keep both arms down while he watched Elijah's body rise and fall with each breath Jake took.

Blue Owl didn't break her focus. She continued sewing with the black thread until the eight-inch gash was closed.

Then Jake asked, "Is it done?"

Blue Owl nodded. "Yes."

Jake's eyes rolled back in his head and he passed out with Elijah's body still across him.

THE BIRDS were making a racket, squawking from the branches, the ground, the sky. Some of the young children covered their ears. The boy's mother spirit was there, too, standing in a tree, shaking its branches. Blue Owl turned toward the water. She wondered if her return to Snake River had cursed the day's events. She'd so loved Bittersweet Creek that she'd forsaken her own homeland. But as she watched Jake wince from the pain of his leg, she knew where her heart belonged. It belonged with Jake's people. They had become her own.

Blue Owl had been with Jake for nine years now, and even though there had been no baby, she did not feel childless. She longed to gather all the pain from this day and tightly wrap each despair together until they formed a stone. Then she would toss that stone of misery into Snake River, with hopes that it would swallow every bit of sadness.

When their time came to cross, they decided to partner their wagon with the McBrides'. Reverend McBride would guide his team of oxen, but Amos would have to ride Smokey since Jake was injured. So Jameson volunteered to lead their team while a farm boy rode his horse. Jameson's offer caused Amos even more shame about what had happened back at Independence Rock.

Jake rode in the back with Blue Owl while Daisy sat up front, holding Finn. As they crossed, Daisy stared down at the water as if she were still searching for Homer. If things had been different, Amos knew Finn would have been chattering away about the excitement of the crossing. But he hadn't uttered a word since the drowning.

Their wagons had been the last to cross. Once they'd reached the other side, Isaac said they'd take a few hours off before moving on.

After the announcement, Finn took off running. Amos tied Smokey to the back of the wagon and chased after him. He was surprised that he had trouble catching up. When had Finn gotten so fast?

"Stop following me!" Finn hollered. They were on a knoll above the wagons. "Why can't I find a tree?"

"Why do you need a tree?"

"I need to kick something," he snapped.

"Then kick me," Amos told him.

Finn swung his leg back and kicked Amos in the groin.

Amos fell back on the ground and curled up in a tight ball. "Not there!" he managed to squeak.

Finn bent over him. "Did I hurt you?"

"Yes."

"Good." Then Finn flopped on the ground beside Amos. They were both quiet for a long while, staring at the clouds rushing through the sky.

Then Finn broke the silence. "Do you think my pa hurt before he died?"

"I don't know," Amos said.

Finn's chin quivered.

Amos regretted his answer, but the words had been spoken. Then he added, "I think the water was probably a peaceful way to go, kind of like floating to Heaven."

Finn rubbed his eyes with his fingers. "Do you believe in Heaven?"

"Sure," Amos said, but that day he had his doubts.

"If my pa hadn't tried to save that ugly girl's pa, he'd still be here."

He knew Finn's words came from anger, but he couldn't leave it be. Amos told him, "Her name is Gwendolyn, Finn. And remember she lost her pa to the river, too." Amos's words didn't seem to make Finn feel any better.

The afternoon was scorching, but when they returned to the wagon, Jake sat on the bench huddled under a quilt. Isaac was talking to him about making camp there. That way, he said, they could have services for both of the men.

Daisy was absentmindedly unraveling the hem of her skirt, but when she heard, she spoke up. "Ain't no need for that."

Isaac lowered his eyebrows and frowned. "Don't you want Homer to have a service right here by the . . . river?"

"I don't need to be where my husband took his last breath. He don't need no funeral."

Shivering, Jake shook his head. "Now, Daisy, you just ain't thinking straight."

"Homer is dead," she snapped. "No words gonna change that."

Daisy made perfect sense to Amos. No words would bring Homer back. Amos's groin still throbbed, but when he looked at Finn, viciously plucking grass blades, he decided he could deal with the pain.

Mrs. Winthrop felt differently about a ceremony, and Hale Winthrop had a send-off at four o'clock. "Teatime funeral," muttered Isaac. "That's fitting for your highness."

Gwendolyn stood next to her mother while Reverend McBride read scripture. Amos wondered how she and her mother would get by. Then he remembered the money hidden in his art pouch. He had not thought about it much on the trail. But now he had Daisy and Finn to help. The money would need to stay with him.

After the ceremony, the wagons lined up. They'd be lucky to cover a few more miles before they'd have to make camp, but at least it would get them two miles away from the crossing at the Snake River.

The drownings had cast a shadow over them. If they had not been this far into the journey, Amos suspected many would have turned back. For they still had other crossings and worse, they would have to tackle the Columbia.

KER SANFORD had offered to drive the Winthrop wagon, and Gwendolyn's mother had accepted. Ker was sixteen, thin, and gawky. His grammar was atrocious. Gwendolyn doubted he could read, but she forgave him because of his kindness. A few times, she noticed him staring at her, but his focus always seemed fixed below her neck. That made her skin crawl, and she had to restrain herself from saying something. She hated being at anyone else's mercy.

When night came, Gwendolyn brushed her mother's hair. The small act brought her comfort. In the last two days, her mother had looked to her as if she had all the answers. If only her mother had asked her advice before her father's drowning. But then they would never have left England and she would never have met Amos. Her heart ached for him and his family. Homer was the sort of man who would leave a hole.

She tried to think past her father's abuse, searching for some moment in her memory to cause her reason to grieve for him. Finally she recalled the plays, the ballets, and the musical performances he'd taken her to see. Of course her mother had suggested the events. But he had not objected. There, she thought, now she had something worthy to miss about him. Her father had exposed her to culture.

Gwendolyn knew it was wicked not to mourn her father's death, but she felt like someone who had been choking all of her life and could suddenly breathe without effort. Still there were facts to face—they were penniless and they were heading West, where every man would receive free land, but not one woman.

CHAPTER
30

A WEEK PASSED and there had been much talk about trying out the Barlow Road instead of riding the Columbia. But Isaac wouldn't hear of it. "I've heard stories of deaths on that road, and I won't risk it. We could run into an early snow in the mountains."

Amos worried about Jake, whose leg grew worse each day. His fever climbed so high, he talked out of his head. He obediently drank Blue Owl's teas, but nothing helped. Amos hoped they would find a doctor at Fort Boise.

When they crossed the Boise River, Amos saw the fear in Daisy's and Finn's eyes. He worried about how they would handle the Columbia.

Fort Boise was disappointing. Located on the north bank of the Boise River, the fort was nothing more than a tiny rectangular building surrounded by adobe walls. Even more devastating was the lack of provisions—two wagon parties had reached the fort a few days before them, and they'd practically wiped them out of all flour, beans, and coffee.

Tempers raged among the emigrants. Amos even overheard Reverend McBride snap, "It seems like you'd be more prepared than this, since you're the last trading post left until we reach the Dalles."

The trader scowled at the reverend. "I guess the same could be said for you, mister."

Reverend McBride's temples pulsed, but he nodded and said, "That's true, sir."

From a corner in the store, Amos watched Gwendolyn and her mother approach one of the men who worked there. Ker followed them as if he were their assigned protector. Amos couldn't hear all that was said, but he gathered enough to realize Mrs. Winthrop was trying to sell their nonfood supplies and wagon.

"There ain't no reason to do that, Missus," Ker told her. "I aim to drive it fer you."

"I can't pay you," Mrs. Winthrop whispered. A harsh tone tinged her words, and Amos figured it was from embarrassment. His hunch had been right. All the money they had in the world was somewhere at the bottom of the Snake River.

How would they survive? The men could claim land when they reached the valley, but what would two women alone do once they arrived there? Maybe they could go back East and return on a ship to England. Maybe some relatives would support them in London. But that option required money. There was so much to think about—the Winthrops, Daisy, Finn, and Jake. Amos's head could not hold it all.

Isaac found the only person who had any medical experience at the fort. Hap Giller was an old trapper who claimed he'd sawed off the limbs of several of his trapping companions. "A few of 'em are still living and breathing to this day."

He glanced at Jake's leg where pus had begun to form over the area near Blue Owl's black stitches. "Yep, that leg needs to come off."

Jake spat on the ground. "Gawd a-mighty! You must think I'm a damn fool."

But after Isaac examined Jake's calf, he concurred. "Jake, gangrene is setting in. You'll be a dead man if that leg doesn't come off soon."

So more whiskey was brought in to pour on the wound and down Jake's throat. They laid Jake across the table while Hap went after his saw and knife. Amos noticed a twinkle in Hap's eyes like he couldn't wait to cut off Jake's leg, one more lost limb to brag about. When he returned, he said, "You already had two toes missing on that leg. At least I'm leaving you with the good one."

Amos left the room. Even though Blue Owl, Isaac, and Reverend McBride were there, he felt like he was abandoning Jake. But he couldn't bring himself to stay. He hurried through the opening in the adobe walls and passed the campsite where some of the tents were already set up. He rushed by their wagon and ended up at the river. Still, his journey did not take him far enough to escape Jake's screams.

THEY STAYED at the fort for three days to allow Jake a chance to rest without the bumps and shaking of the wagon moving along the trail. He remained in the room where they removed his leg. Blue Owl and Daisy took turns tending to him.

Amos had not seen Jake yet. Whenever he considered visiting him, he quickly changed his mind. Instead he spent his days looking after Finn, taking care of Smokey, and hunting rabbits. He was afraid of what he'd find missing from Jake besides his leg. For what would Jake do now that he couldn't scout? He couldn't dowse either, even if he'd wanted to.

The last morning at the fort, Amos watched Daisy as she warmed up beans for breakfast. The jagged edges of her skirt hem brushed against the dirt. When she leaned over the fire, he realized her belly had a thickness he'd not noticed before. She was with child. He was certain of it. And by the looks of it, she had been for a while. Suddenly he felt the weight of the world on his shoulders.

What would happen to *them* without Jake earning money? At least the three hundred dollars he'd hidden in his art pouch would help them until he figured out what to do next.

The whole while he pondered this, his focus stayed fixed on Daisy's belly. He glanced up at her face, and she told him, "I've known for a while. I wish Homer had known. I was waiting until we got off the trail. He made such a fuss when I was carrying Finn."

Amos could think of nothing to say. He just dug his heel in the dirt.

"Me and Homer were never married," she blurted out. "Not officially, anyway. Oh, we tried to get married. We walked all the way to Independence, but the minister told me to run back home and grow up."

Amos stayed quiet, listening.

She lifted the lid and stirred the beans. "Not a soul in this world know'd except us. Now that Homer's gone, I didn't like being the only one. So now you know, too. I hope you don't feel burdened by it."

THERE WAS NOTHING much left except for beans, bacon, and coffee. Amos had been bored of biscuits by the time they'd reached South Pass, but now he daydreamed of them by the panful—crusty around the edges and soaked with butter.

Having fewer provisions meant there was more room for Jake in the bed of the wagon. His leg had been cut above the left knee. Thomas made him some crutches, though he couldn't use them yet. Thomas, Reverend McBride, and

Elijah helped Amos carry Jake to the wagon. Blue Owl created a pallet of quilts for him to rest upon. When Amos first saw him after the operation, a heavy guilt overwhelmed him.

"How are you doing?" Amos asked him, avoiding Jake's stump.

Jake raised his hand from the wrist and nodded.

Hap came over and took a long last look at his handiwork. "I figure he's got a fifty-fifty chance. Them's my odds, anyway."

At camp that night, Amos listened to Reverend McBride talk with Isaac. "I'm sure glad you insisted he pour whiskey on that saw and knife. That man acted like he'd never heard of such a thing."

Isaac shook his head. "I was afraid he was going to spit on it before starting in. Maybe with your prayers, Jake will make it through this."

"He could use your prayers, too," Reverend McBride said.

Isaac cleared his throat. "Er . . . yes, sure."

Two days later, Jake's fever broke. Now he had to heal. He endured the bumpy trail each day, and every night Blue Owl changed the dressings on his leg, covering the area with a thick layer of the same herb paste she'd used on Amos's chin.

As the days passed, Jake seemed better, but he still didn't talk much. Amos decided he'd have to figure a way to support everyone. Every adult male in the Oregon Country could get free land. But Amos hated farming. He remembered plenty from the hard work at the Block farm. Even if he decided to farm, how could he do it by himself? That night he dreamed as he often did so many nights. He dreamed of water. By the time the wagon train reached the Dalles, he knew what to do. He would dowse.

That settled, he now fretted over how Daisy and Finn would handle traveling down the Columbia. As it was, Finn had nightmares every evening about drowning. He wanted to ask Jake what to do, but he had enough just fighting to stay alive. That gave Amos something else to fret about. And how would Jake do, riding the rough current flat on his back?

They needed to stay at the Dalles several weeks to build enough rafts for the wagons to ride down the Columbia. Some of the folks still argued about Isaac's choice to take on the river, since there was another option.

"I heard a man at the fort say that most folks were traveling the Barlow Road these days," argued Mr. Sanford.

"Heard the same thing myself," said Mr. Porter, who'd hardly spoken the entire trip.

Isaac reminded them that they'd promised to stay with him the entire way when they signed on with his party. But after the fourth man brought up the Barlow Road, he called the emigrants together and announced, "I release anyone who wants to go at this time."

Most of the people shut up then, but the Sanfords got

ready to head toward Barlow Road. Now without a wagon, Gwendolyn and her mother had been taken under their wing, so they would go, too. The families said good-bye to the ones who remained. Gwendolyn nodded toward Amos, then turned to join her mother.

Amos wanted to say something, but couldn't find the words. He glanced down at Finn, but Finn had left his side and was running toward Gwendolyn. When he reached her, he stretched up and tapped her back. She turned. Finn opened his arms and hugged her legs, pressing his cheek against her skirt. "I'm sorry about your pa," he cried.

Gwendolyn lifted his chin and gazed down at him. "And I'm so sorry about yours, Finn. Your father died a brave man. Always remember that."

She knelt down and wiped his eyes with her sleeve. Then she stood to leave. Amos watched her walk away until she disappeared from his sight. He wondered if he'd ever see her again and was surprised by the sudden emptiness he felt.

As they left, Isaac shook his head and sneered. "They'll be wishing and praying they'd stayed with our company. If they're alive long enough to wish and pray."

The next few hours, Amos helped the men build rafts, but he felt a struggle within. He stopped his work and studied the river. The soft roar of the Columbia echoed inside his head. The sun caused the water to sparkle as the river went forth with its steady, swift flow. The water could be so deceiving. For the Snake had taught them that a river could rage like a hungry mountain lion. It could reach out and take. He looked over at Daisy. She was biting her lower lip, staring at the Columbia. Finn held her hand, his head turned away from the water. Amos had found his answer.

He walked up to Isaac and heard himself say, "I think it's best we join the Sanfords."

Isaac squinted down at Amos. "What are you talking about?"

Amos tried to breathe before saying, "We can't risk another river . . . and . . . with Barlow Road, we don't have to."

"That road has its own set of dangers," Isaac said.

Amos studied the ground.

"Your pa isn't dead yet," Isaac added. "Think of him."

Amos was thinking of Jake. If anything happened on that river, Jake would have no way of saving himself. At least staying on land would keep him from drowning. Everyone stared at him except for Reverend McBride, who was looking toward the Columbia.

Amos's mind flashed back to the day he begged Gil to let him stay at the Block farm. He had stood alone then, too. Trying to swallow the fear lodged in his throat, he turned right and left, searching for her. There she stood, apart from all the emigrants. Blue Owl had not changed much from the day he'd met her—beads and feathers tied to her long dark hair, moccasin boots on her feet. But something about her was different. Then he realized it was not her at all, but him. He had not known it until that moment. What she thought of him mattered. When her eyes met his, he caught the strength she was sending his way. Even though she stood far from him, he could almost feel her firm hold on his shoulders.

"Did you hear me, Amos?" Isaac asked. "Your pa isn't dead yet."

He lifted his chin and managed to say, "I'm trying to see that he stays that way."

Reverend McBride stepped forward. "Amos is making sense, Isaac. My family will be joining him." He looked at Amos, adding, "I've done well listening to this young man."

Isaac pushed up his sleeves, staring straight at Jameson. "Well, don't think you can leave with them. I'll give Jake his pay once we meet up in the Willamette Valley. But I won't pay a deserter. You signed on for this trip as my cowman."

Jubilee fled to Jameson's side. "I won't leave without him, Father."

That was how Jubilee and Jameson came to marry at the Dalles. Right as the quick ceremony was about to begin, Jameson turned around and faced Amos. "W-Wait," he said.

Amos didn't move. Jameson had been like a brother to him. He'd protected him at the mission and cheered him up when he was sad. He had a kind heart and deserved a kindhearted woman. Amos wanted Jameson to know all of this. But he didn't know how to begin to tell him. For now, he would listen to what Jameson had to say.

Except for the sound of the river rushing by and Mrs. McBride's sniffling, it was quiet as everyone waited for Jameson to speak. Finally he said, "Amos, w-would you be our w-witness?"

Jubilee smiled his way. "Yes, Amos, would you please?"

Something eased inside of Amos. Then he stepped forward and said, "It would be my honor."

Moments later, Jubilee hugged her family farewell. Then with Amos riding on Smokey, the two wagons parted, leaving the others behind. Now Amos knew what it was to feel courage and fear at the same time.

CHAPTER

31

TRAIL TO BARLOW ROAD

MOMENTS BEFORE Amos stood up to Isaac, Blue Owl had noticed Delilah standing behind her son, her hands firmly fixed on his shoulders. But when Amos's eyes met Blue Owl's, the boy's mother had slowly backed away and disappeared. She was like the wind in a storm that had suddenly become so calm no one could remember it having been any other way. Now Blue Owl had no recollection of her, but she sensed something had changed.

The boy had become a man. Blue Owl thought about his transformation as they left the others at the Dalles. She knew the hardships had shaped him. She also knew hardships could turn a boy into a man only if he was ready. Amos had been ready.

There was an old story her grandmother had told her

about a group of girls who had been left behind when a tribe had to move quickly. The girls came upon an injured wolf. They nursed him back to health, and in return, a pack of wolves adopted them. They protected the girls and saved them from many dangerous situations.

Amos was a wolf.

Before Homer's drowning and Jake's injury, Blue Owl would have chosen riding the river instead of traveling the Barlow Road. Before then, she didn't believe mountains were meant to have roads carved through them. But the hardships had changed her, too.

As much as she craved silence through the years with Jake, it was unsettling to her now. He seemed to prefer the dream world, sleeping away his days and nights. She looked to the place where his leg had been. His left pant was tied in a knot below his stump. Better a leg than his heart. He meant as much to her now with one leg as he had with two. But Jake was the sort of man whose worth came from his work. He was like a bear that took pride in his hunts. And how could a bear survive without one of his paws?

NIGHTFALL CAME UPON them and they still had not met up with the Sanford party. They made camp, but started out before daybreak. Amos rode atop Smokey, fretting about whether he'd made the right decision. If only he could ask Jake.

Amos considered asking Reverend McBride's opinion, but the reverend was a man of the city. He didn't even know how to shoot a gun. He was counting on Amos.

A piece of blue fluttered from a branch ahead of Amos. He rode up to it and pulled it loose. It was a ribbon, the blue ribbon Gwendolyn had worn in her hair the night they danced together. He tucked it in his pocket and hurried back to his spot in front of the wagons.

"What was that?" Finn asked. He was walking with Elijah.

"Someone lost a ribbon," Amos said.

"Can I have it?" Finn asked.

"Nope."

"Why not?"

"Okay," said Amos, "but only if you let me tie it in your hair."

Finn didn't ask about the ribbon again.

At noon, Amos suggested they forge ahead instead of stopping to eat in hopes that they might catch up with the others. He wanted to join them before the Tygh Valley.

"Sounds like a good plan to me," the reverend said. "We don't have to answer to any bugle calls now."

The plan paid off. An hour later, they came to a clearing and discovered the Sanford wagon stopped along a creek. From the looks of it, they'd just finished their noon meal. Mrs. Winthrop and Mrs. Sanford were folding the blankets, and Ker was leading the oxen away from the water. From his saddle, Amos scoped the site until he found Gwendolyn near the creek.

GWENDOLYN WAS WIPING the tin plates when they rode up. She heard the oxen hooves clopping against the rocky road. She blinked three times before she allowed herself to believe it was Amos riding toward them. He was waving something blue above his head. As he neared, she recognized it. She had not even known her ribbon was missing.

Amos dismounted his horse, and while the others went to the wagons, he walked up to her, holding out the ribbon. "Did you lose this?"

"It seems I did." She took the ribbon from him, but let her eyes linger on his fingers.

"You should wear it more often," Amos told her. "Then maybe you wouldn't lose it."

She gathered her hair back and secured it with the ribbon, tying it into a bow.

They settled on the rocky ground. He sat a few inches from her, so close she was able to breathe in his scent. There was the water, but also something else she'd not detected before. He smelled faintly of pine and earth, like someone else she'd known, but now could not recall.

Amos told Gwendolyn all that had happened after she'd left with the Sanfords—the decision to take Barlow Road, Isaac's reaction, and the wedding.

"Was it a beautiful wedding?" she asked.

Amos laughed. "Well, it wasn't a church wedding. There wasn't any music, just the river."

"I'm sure Jubilee must have been beautiful." Gwendolyn's face felt hot. Why had she said that? Of course Jubilee was beautiful. Jubilee was always beautiful. Gwendolyn's hand aimed toward her face, but Amos grabbed hold of it before she could touch her cheek. He held her hand for a few seconds and stared at her with a softness. Gwendolyn figured it was because he didn't want to hurt her feelings. She didn't press him for more details about the wedding. Instead she said, "You must be hungry. Come, I'll get you some beans."

GWENDOLYN SEEMED so fragile to Amos when she asked about the wedding. As she questioned him, he found himself studying her features. The way the sun hit her hair caused it to look like a harvest moon, shiny and orange. How had he not noticed that until now? Her green eyes gazed at him with such honesty that he felt safe, like he could say or do anything and she would remain a loyal friend.

And when she'd mentioned Jubilee's beauty, he couldn't help himself. On impulse, he looked at the left side of her face. To his surprise, the scars had faded. They were mere shadows of what had been there before.

CHAPTER
32

THE BARLOW ROAD was not the godsend the folks at the fort had said it was. Every day Amos questioned his decision. He wondered how the rest of the Bolton party was doing, rafting the Columbia. Since meeting up with the Sanford wagon, his burdens had only increased because now he worried about Gwendolyn, too. Yet despite her city privileged upbringing, she proved not to be a helpless girl. She cooked along with the women and insisted on cleaning the dishes alone after every meal. Her boots had holes worn through the soles, but she never complained as the road zigzagged through the rocky terrain.

But Amos cared. A day after they left the Tygh Valley, making their way through the Cascades, he looked back at her so often it caused him to slide off his saddle once. She was walking beside the Sanford wagon next to Ker. The road was on a steady incline and even though her skirt covered her legs, he could tell she was tired by her wobbly strides.

He turned Smokey around, and when he reached Gwendolyn, he dismounted and said, "Here. Get up."

Her eyes bulged. "I don't know how to ride."

"I'll lead him. All you'll have to do is hang on to the saddle horn." He guided her foot into the stirrup and told her to swing the other leg over Smokey's saddle.

Ker stood by, frowning, with his arms at his side. Then Amos took hold of the reins. As he led Smokey behind the wagon, he noticed Ker narrowing his eyes at him.

It didn't occur to Amos what was wrong until right before sleep that evening. Ker must have been sweet on Gwendolyn. Ever since Mr. Winthrop's death, he'd probably fancied himself as her protector. He empathized with Ker, remembering how it was with Jameson. But Amos had no plans to give up his new role. Gwendolyn was under his watch now.

AT THE END of the week, they reached a steep slope.

"Mercy," Reverend McBride said.

"Damn," said Mr. Sanford.

"We should have rode the Columbia," Ker said. "This ain't good." He glared at Amos as if it was his fault.

For a long moment, they all stared at the chute in disbelief. The decline must have been almost three hundred feet. Finally Finn asked what was on everyone's mind. "How are we going to get down there?"

After Amos pointed out the rope burns around some

trees growing near the chute, Mr. Sanford decided they would use the trees to help lower the wagons. First the men pushed logs between the spokes to keep the wheels from turning. They thought of attaching the oxen to the back of the wagons to help slow the descent, but changed their minds.

"If we lost the wagon, we'd lose the animals, too," Mr. Sanford said.

Instead they cut down some pine trees and used them. They tied ropes to the backs of the wagons. Then they wrapped the other ends around the standing trees to use as pulleys.

Before the wagons were lowered, Jake would have to be slid down the hill. Amos, Elijah, and Ker built a stretcher from pine logs. The men placed Jake upon it and Amos tied him securely to it. Jake squeezed his eyes shut as Amos made each knot.

Then Amos went with the women and Finn who made their way down by walking. They watched for holes as they wove between large rocks, holding on to narrow trees when they could.

Finally on the ground, they waited as the men lined up behind each other, holding the rope and lowering the stretcher. Even at the slow pace, it was not a smooth ride. The stretcher spit pebbles and dirt on its journey downward. Then when Jake was fifty feet from the landing, the knot loosened from the abuse of constant rubbing.

Amos saw, but it was too late. The rope slipped off.

Amos's heart pounded as he witnessed the stretcher pick up speed and jolt its way down. A cloud of dust kicked up around the stretcher but didn't hide Jake's good leg now hanging off the side. The leg bounced with each jerk. Everyone watched helplessly as Jake narrowly missed a tree. Daisy gasped loudly and covered her eyes with her hands. Amos held his breath.

Then the stretcher stopped at the landing a few yards from the group. They ran to Jake and stood over him. Blue Owl sighed and Daisy burst into tears. Amos started to breathe again.

Jake looked up. He had been quiet for weeks, but now said, "Whoo-ee! First time I ever prayed for mercy. When them clouds went to parting, I thought I was seeing Heaven opening the gates."

Through her sobs, Daisy managed to say, "Jake, if you die, I'll kill you."

Everyone laughed, even Blue Owl. Amos's faith was renewed. Despite the rough narrow roads through the Cascades and the constant hunger pains kicking his gut, they would make it to the Willamette Valley. Amos was certain of it, just as sure as he knew now that Jake would survive.

It took hours to lower the wagons and walk down the animals. When they finished, they were tired and hungry.

Their food supply had grown dangerously low, but Mrs. Winthrop had saved a slab of bacon, and they boiled it in a kettle over the fire that night. After what they'd been through that day, the meager broth tasted like a feast for kings.

A FEW DAYS later, the temperature dropped quickly. With a quilt surrounding her, Gwendolyn noticed Elijah shivering as he walked a few steps ahead. She caught up with him and tapped his shoulder. He turned and she opened the quilt, beckoning him to join her. They wrapped the quilt tighter as they walked, their shoulders touching. Gwendolyn didn't mind, and neither, it seemed, did Elijah. They were grateful for the added warmth.

It was not snowing, but Gwendolyn could smell snow. Her thoughts wandered back to a London Christmas when she was four. Her father must not have been drinking yet, because the beatings had not started. Snow began to fall on Christmas Eve that year. The next morning, her father awoke her at dawn. They sneaked out of the house and built a snowman for her mother. They used two pieces of coal for his eyes and drew a smile with a stick that became his nose.

Gwendolyn could still see her mother peering through the window, smiling and waving when she discovered the surprise. Then her father took off his hat and placed it on the snowman's head. Later they drank hot chocolate to celebrate. She didn't recall any of the gifts she'd received that morning. But she did remember her father laughing and giving her and her mother a quick peck on the cheek.

Keeping in step with Elijah, Gwendolyn began to cry for what had been lost a long time ago.

THE FOLLOWING DAY they left the Cascades. The rocky road with its switchbacks lay behind them as they emerged into the Willamette Valley. It was as if they'd been trapped in a box the last few weeks on Barlow Road and someone had finally removed the lid. A massive group of ravens had gathered on the ground ahead. When the group approached, the birds parted, leaving enough room for the wagons to proceed between them.

Mrs. McBride cried, "Dear Lord, we made it."

No one else said a word. They just stood still and admired the town before them. It was dusk, and the sun was nowhere to be found. Strings of smoke curled through chimneys of the houses and buildings along the river threading through the rocky canyon. Even with the roar of the river falls, they could hear the faint sounds of dance-hall music playing on a piano.

"Never thought I'd be so thankful to hear a drinking song," Reverend McBride said.

Under different circumstances, they might have laughed, but they were all silent. They had traveled two thousand miles. They had walked the flat prairies, tromped through mud, crossed rivers, and made their way through mountains. They had lost loved ones and pieces of themselves along the way to gain this moment.

"Did you feel that?" Gwendolyn asked Amos.

"What?" Then something cold and wet hit his nose.

It was snowing. Big fat flakes fell from the sky, like sugar sifting into a cake bowl. Amos looked back at Jake. He was sitting next to Blue Owl in the front of the wagon. Snowflakes stuck to his wild hair and beard, causing him to sparkle. Nearby, Finn and Elijah darted back and forth with their heads up and their tongues out, while Daisy leaned against the wagon, smiling and softly crying.

Then Amos turned to Gwendolyn. She stood a few feet away, arms outstretched and hands cupped. She brought her hands to her nose and smelled the snow. When she dropped them to her sides, she laughed, that joyful, free sound that at one time Amos didn't believe could possibly belong to her. But standing out there with his back to the mountains and the valley before him, he knew that laugh was every bit hers. He watched Gwendolyn for a moment, wishing he could grab hold and kiss her lips. Then as he tried to memorize every inch of her, he suddenly felt as if his breath had been squeezed from him. Her scars had completely disappeared. Gwendolyn Winthrop was a beauty. She was beautiful all the way to her soul.

CHAPTER
33

OREGON CITY, NOVEMBER 1848

WHILE THE FAMILIES set up camp outside town, Amos grabbed his art pouch and went to find a place for Jake to recuperate. The waterfalls could be heard everywhere. He walked along the streets and asked the first person who looked him in the eye, "Could you tell me where I could find an inn?"

The man adjusted his hat, squinting. "There's one around the corner." Then he rushed away.

Amos realized he probably hadn't bathed in weeks. There was no telling what he smelled like. He considered finding a place to bathe before entering the inn, but surely the owner would be accustomed to people ending their journey on the trail. And besides, Amos had the money.

A sign hung over the door: THE INN AT THE END OF THE

TRAIL. He went inside and discovered an old man leaning over a desk. The man must not have heard him because he didn't look up when Amos walked in.

Amos cleared his throat. "Excuse me, sir?"

The man glanced up with one eye. A patch covered the other.

"Pirate Paul?"

The man grinned. "Well, if it ain't Amos Kincaid, as I stand here breathing. What brings you to the Oregon Territory?"

"Territory? Oregon's a territory?"

Pirate Paul nodded. "As of this summer."

The words rushed from Amos's mouth. Somehow he managed to tell the story of the journey in a few minutes. But he slowed down when he came to the drowning and Jake's injury.

When Amos was through, Paul said, "That's a shame about your uncle, but if I know your pa, he'll survive. I've come a long ways with just one eyeball. Where is that old fool, anyway?"

Amos remembered why he was there. "We need a room for him. For us. He needs a comfortable place to heal."

Paul nodded. "I've got a spare room upstairs. It's not fancy, but it's clean and comfortable. You can have it for no charge."

"I can pay," Amos said.

Paul leaned over the counter and narrowed his eye. "Now,

Amos, there are a lot of times you shouldn't take something for nothing. Most things ain't free. Like that six hundred forty acres all these men have risked their lives to get. That land ain't free. They'll be paying for it every damn day of their life with sweat. But I'm offering Jake a room for free in honor of the old times. I think that's a bargain. Don't refuse it."

"Won't your boss be mad?"

"My boss?" Paul chuckled, then he called out, "Fiddleless!"

A dark man appeared. It didn't take Amos but a second to realize that the first black man he'd ever laid eyes on was standing in front of him. He looked older, with silver dusted through his hair, but he was definitely the slave he and Samuel had met at the Missouri. The man who had saved his life.

"Fiddleless," Paul said, "Amos here wants to know if the boss will be mad if I give him a free room."

"No, sir. I don't believe he will." Fiddleless left the lobby and entered the back room.

"Is *he* your boss?" Amos asked. Maybe the West was the land of miracles.

"Fiddleless? No. Last I heard, that old boss of mine was trying to get by with one eyeball."

Amos felt his ears warm.

"No need to feel ashamed. Every room in this inn is mine. Mine to charge for, or mine to give away for free."

"Thank you," Amos mumbled, realizing he shouldn't be

so foolish with the money. Three hundred dollars would eventually run out.

"Fiddleless and I met up at the Kansas when I was scouting for Isaac. He was helping the Shawnee swim livestock across the river for a while. Isaac let him ride along and cook for him and the scouts. Sorriest cook I ever did know."

"What does he do at the inn?" Amos asked.

"Cook." Then Paul quickly added, "Hasn't improved a bit. He finally admitted to me that he was a runaway slave. All he does is moan and groan about how he gave some boy a fiddle his pappy made to keep his mouth shut. That's why I call him Fiddleless. I figure a fiddle is a small price to pay for keeping your head attached to your neck. But I reckon he don't see it that way."

Paul leaned way over the counter. He lowered his voice and widened his eye so that Amos could almost see the socket. "Fiddleless is a crazy old thing. He made a voodoo doll with some straw for the hair that he dyed with red berries. He said the boy that took his fiddle had red hair. Every once in a while, the cranky old thing goes to poking that doll in the side. He thinks that boy's side will go to aching every time he does it." Paul chuckled. "Ain't that the silliest nonsense you ever heard?"

Amos was thankful that Fiddleless hadn't made two dolls. He glanced at the clock hanging on the wall. "I should be heading back to get Jake. Do you have more rooms available?"

"Three more."

He asked him to hold rooms for the McBrides and the Sanfords. Then he paid for Mrs. Winthrop and Gwendolyn to have one for a few weeks, too. He started to leave, but before he reached the door, Paul told him, "Actually I was expecting to see you. Isaac made it in a few days ago and asked if I'd seen you or your brood."

"Isaac?"

"Yep. And he made a big to-do about there being no drownings on the Columbia." Paul snorted. "He neglected to mention the ones at the Snake. I got the feeling he wasn't happy with your choice to use Barlow Road."

"I guess I'll have to live with that," Amos said.

AN OAK VANITY sat directly across the room from the bed. Amos wondered if that bothered Jake, seeing his reflection without the leg. But Jake said, "Helps me get used to what is and what ain't."

But every day that passed, Jake seemed to withdraw more. After the town doctor examined Jake, he told him, "That old trapper saved your life."

Jake scowled. "Just what kind of life? I'm getting sores on my rear end from lying in this bed."

The doctor pushed at the bridge of his spectacles. "We can do something about that."

"What?" Jake asked. "A peg leg? How am I supposed to make a living with a peg leg?"

Amos had not told Jake that he'd planned to dowse. And

now didn't seem the right time to mention it. Jake needed to know there was something more for him. He needed a reason to get out of bed. That night Amos dreamed of water and wheels.

The next morning, he picked up his pad and flipped past all the pictures he'd drawn on the trail—the Elroy sisters picking wildflowers, the birds and plants, and the rock formations. When he reached an empty page, he began to sketch.

The wagon would be small and built close to the ground. The size would allow for a mule to pull it. He drew a dropback with hinges.

"What's this puny wagon for?" Jake asked after Amos handed the picture to him.

"You."

"Me? What am I going to do in a one-mule wagon?"

"Dowse."

Jake dropped the pad. "Them days are over. Everything comes to an end—the trapping, the scouting, and now the dowsing."

Amos picked up the pad and pointed to his drawing. "I'll be sitting here, driving the wagon. You'll sit backwards at the end so you can dowse. That's why I drew it with a drop-back."

Blue Owl walked across the room and studied the drawing from over Amos's shoulder. She folded her arms and stared straight at Jake. "Looks good."

Jake took the pad from Amos. He examined it a long time. Then he said, "Let me think on it some."

THOUGH FIDDLELESS stayed on at the inn, cleaning and doing odd jobs, he was replaced by Daisy and Blue Owl in the kitchen. As badly as he'd cooked, Amos and the others had figured Fiddleless's heart wasn't in peeling potatoes and stewing meat. But instead of being grateful that he could take off the apron, he seemed resentful.

"There's no pleasing him," Paul said, shrugging it off.

Paul hired Amos to help Fiddleless with some repairs around the inn. And Amos was reminded every day about the fiddle Samuel stole from him. Amos could recite the story by heart. Like Amos, Fiddleless had lost his mother when she died giving birth to him. His pappy had swore he heard fiddle music playing when his mother took her last breath so he figured it was his son's destiny to play the instrument. The master was not a bad sort of fellow, as far as masters go, and he gave Fiddleless's pappy some wood and even bought some violin strings from a local musician. "It took my pappy three years to make dat fiddle. He had to work seven days a week for da master, so he worked after dinner till dat sun went down."

Before Fiddleless grew into a young man, his pappy died, and a year later so did the master. His son was a cruel man, which was why Fiddleless ran away. The oddest thing was that Fiddleless told Amos the story all the way up to

Samuel taking his fiddle, but he never mentioned saving Amos's life.

Amos thought of telling Fiddleless that he was the other boy, but even as he and Fiddleless became friendly over the months of working together, Amos was afraid of Fiddleless's voodoo.

THE OTHERS who had traveled Barlow Road had also started their new lives. After a month in the Oregon Territory, the Sanfords decided to head to California. Daisy told Amos she thought they were fools. "I can't imagine traveling all this way, only to pack up and do it all again."

The Sanfords were not alone. Many of the emigrants from the Bolton party had gold fever. Empty cabins could be found throughout the territory. The McBrides took over a place left behind from a man "afflicted with gold greed," as the reverend put it.

"Then I guess we're benefiting from his ailment," said Mrs. McBride.

After they reached the territory, Mrs. Winthrop had surprised Gwendolyn with a new take-charge attitude. Her mother awoke one morning and said, "It is time to build a new life."

A mercantile store hired Mrs. Winthrop. She and Gwendolyn moved out of the inn and into a small place above the store. It was modest, a long way from their fine home in London, but they could afford the rent. Gwendolyn took a job as a seamstress at the millinery shop. Now she was making the kinds of fine hats she used to wear. It didn't bother her, though. Everything in her life seemed new.

Gwendolyn loved learning to sew and decorate hats. The owner, Miss Parsnip, always smelled like she'd just bathed in rosewater. She was a plump, pleasant woman, although she was very particular. She took inventory of her supplies every night before she closed the store, causing Gwendolyn to wonder if Miss Parsnip trusted her. But Gwendolyn soon realized the lonely old woman thought of her items as children. She was merely putting her hat pins and needles away like a mother tucking in her babies at night. Once before closing up the shop, Gwendolyn overheard her saying, "Good night, my sweets. See you in the morning."

Gwendolyn loved her job so much she went to sleep each night designing a new hat. But Amos always slipped into her dreams. Every morning she awoke with a smile on her face. And at work, she tried to resist glancing out the window to see if Amos might be walking by to wave at her. Every day he did.

At Christmas, Amos gave Fiddleless a brand-new fiddle. When Amos presented it, Fiddleless flipped it over, eyeballing every inch. "It ain't quite as good as da one my pappy made, but I sure am gonna try to make it sing. Dat's the best I can do with a gift from a boy dat I done saved his life." And with that, he tuned up the instrument and played it like he'd never missed a day doing so.

For a brief second, Amos thought he felt a pain in his side.

Fiddleless wasn't the only one who received a gift that Christmas. Daisy gave birth to the tiniest baby Amos had ever seen. When Jake first laid eyes on her, his face lit up and he said, "Well, she ain't nothing but a little bit. In fact, that's what I'm gonna call her, Little Bit."

Daisy held the baby close and told Jake firmly, "I'm going to call her Sarah. That's the name Homer wanted if Finn had been a girl."

Finn stroked the soft spot on his sister's head. "I'm gonna call her Sarah Little Bit." And that is who she became to them all.

Within moments of seeing her, Jake announced to Amos, "Spring better arrive soon this year. We've got work to do."

Jake had returned.

CHAPTER
34

MARCH 1849

THE DOCTOR HAD ARRIVED to help Jake with his peg leg, again. From the top of the staircase, Blue Owl saw Amos below. She motioned him up and watched as Amos climbed the stairs with dread. He was like her. He hated witnessing Jake's pain.

Blue Owl sat in the chair while Amos stood on one side of Jake and the doctor stood on the other. Jake's arms straddled their shoulders as they helped him move across the floor. Before they'd arrived in Oregon City, Jake had lost weight, but his appetite returned the day Sarah Little Bit was born. That was three months ago, and in that short time he'd regained every pound he'd lost. Amos and the doctor struggled to hold him up as Jake tried the peg leg out again.

Jake moved a few inches, then fell back, collapsing on the bed.

"Gawd a-mighty!" He pushed himself up to a sitting position, took a deep breath, and held out his arms. "Help me up."

Again and again, he'd take a step, fall back on the bed and insist on trying once more. Blue Owl felt sorry for the doctor. He was old. She called for Fiddleless, who took the doctor's place while Jake attempted again, cursing the entire time.

He cursed so much and so loudly that Blue Owl went over to the windows and shut them. As she pulled them down, she noticed people on the street had stopped whatever they were doing and were staring up at the window. When she stuck out her tongue, their heads snapped back in place and they moved along. She was glad Finn had taught her that gesture.

"We've done enough for today," the doctor said, still trying to recover from his session. "I'll stop back by tomorrow morning."

As the doctor left the room, Jake lifted his new limb and gave it a good looking-over. "Just call me Peg-leg Kincaid."

JUBILEE AND JAMESON had claimed land a few miles out of Oregon City, but had waited until spring before they decided to settle there. They stopped into the millinery store to tell Gwendolyn good-bye. Jubilee promised she'd come by and see Gwendolyn every time they came to town for supplies.

Jameson told Gwendolyn, "Tell us if you and your ma need anything." Gwendolyn noticed that Jameson hardly stuttered at all anymore. She figured that was what a woman like Jubilee could do for a man like Jameson.

Right before turning to leave, Jubilee said, "I love that blue ribbon in your hair, Gwendolyn."

Gwendolyn smiled. She'd worn it every day. She'd convinced herself that it had brought her luck. How else could she explain Amos's change of heart toward her?

Amos entered the store just as Jubilee and Jameson were leaving. They bumped into each other. The three of them laughed, but Gwendolyn didn't join in. She was too busy examining Amos's reaction to encountering Jubilee.

Jameson shook Amos's hand, and Jubilee touched his sleeve.

Amos tilted his hat and said, "Jake and I'll be out your way so he can dowse that well for you soon as he finishes with your father's."

They left after another round of good-byes. Then Amos turned and smiled at Gwendolyn. She felt her heart leap. Finally she asked, "How is your father?"

"Trying to walk with his peg leg." Amos shook his head and laughed. "That's not going too well."

"I've heard," Gwendolyn said, looking a bit regretful for saying it.

Then Amos laughed and she did, too.

"I just came from the wainwright," he told her. "Our wagon will be ready next week."

"Is that when Jake will start dowsing again?"

"That's the plan. There are a lot of people counting on him. I've gathered business all over this land. Some of the folks were on the trail with us."

"Will you be gone a long time?" She already missed him.

"Oh, we'll have to make camp most nights, but I've arranged it so that we'll be back that Saturday." Amos picked up a hat pin on the counter and started bending it.

"Oh?" Gwendolyn hoped she could straighten the pin before Miss Parsnip returned from lunch.

"Yep," Amos said. He stared at the pin that was folded completely in half now. He dropped it with a look of horror on his face. "Sorry about that."

"Don't worry, I'll fix it," Gwendolyn said, although she didn't know how she possibly could. "So you're coming back Saturday?"

"Yep," Amos repeated, glancing around the room like he was looking for something else to fidget with. He swallowed. "Um, there's a dance."

"Yes?" Gwendolyn forgot about the pin.

"There's a dance in town. Most folks are going, and since we've danced . . ."

Gwendolyn decided to save him. "Yes, I'd be happy to go."

Amos sighed, "Good." He backed away and softly repeated, "Good. Well, good day."

Gwendolyn watched him as he made his way out of the shop, but not before he knocked over a row of hats displayed on the counter.

CHAPTER

35

THE NEXT WEEK the trees began to bud, and Jake announced that it was time to go to work. He'd given up on the peg leg, preferring the simple crutches that Thomas made back on the trail.

Jake settled at the rear of the wagon, facing backwards while Amos drove the mule to the McBrides' place. A one-legged man riding in the small wagon built low to the ground must have been a sight. Over the recent months in the valley, Amos had grown accustomed to Jake's appearance, but now, as they rode through town, he was reminded of the injury. People stared as they passed, and some of the children pointed in their direction. Amos felt relieved when they left Oregon City.

A few miles outside of town, they came upon the McBrides' place. Even though patches of grass were still brown and many of the trees still bare, Amos could see the beauty in their land. Elijah and the reverend greeted them as they rode up.

"Come inside and warm up," the reverend told them.

Amos tied the mule to a nearby tree while Jake struggled to walk on his crutches.

The reverend had wasted no time starting a church. It was an outside church like Gil had back at the mission— no walls, just a cover made from lumber. "Only a few families have managed to make it the past two Sundays, but I'm sure we'll have more soon."

He pointed to the spot where he and Jameson would build the church. "I plan to grow some apple trees. I got word of a man who carried some trees all the way from Iowa."

Jake looked at Elijah, pretending to bite into an apple. "Now, won't that taste good, Elijah? A fresh crispy one."

Elijah smiled and nodded.

Mrs. McBride served them coffee inside the small cabin.

"I chose this place because of the cabin," Reverend McBride said. "We need to get through the winter."

They gulped down their coffee and went outside to begin. Amos had fretted so much over getting Jake back into dowsing that he'd forgotten there would be other barriers to cross. Jake would need to learn to dowse backwards, sitting down. He would have to grow accustomed to giving Amos orders. Amos hoped he had not been too foolish in thinking that this new way would work.

Jake settled in the back of the wagon, his one leg dangling over the edge.

Amos took off with a jolt.

"Slower!" Jake snapped. "I gotta get the feel of this."

Amos drove the wagon across the land while Jake held the dowsing branch in front of him. When an hour passed, more doubts flooded Amos's head. What if Jake's gift had left him along with the leg? Maybe *he* should have been dowsing instead of Jake. But maybe he didn't have the gift. Maybe that was just a boyhood dream. After all, it had been years ago when he picked up that branch.

The air was cool, but they both sweated buckets as they struggled to find a rhythm. *Forward, back around, slow, slower.* Amos was thankful that the reverend stayed inside his home, since Jake had a few cursing fits out of frustration. Amos had to bite his tongue to keep from joining in.

Then Jake yelled, "Stop! Stop right here!"

Amos swung around, wondering if Jake had decided to give up. He couldn't see his face, just the back of his wild hair and broad body, sitting perfectly still. His arms were straight in front of him, but Amos couldn't make out the branch. Maybe Jake had dropped it in defeat. Amos jumped from the wagon and went around to see for himself.

Jake's eyes had gone wet. His hands were shaking.

Amos looked to the branch. It was pointing down. Every fear and doubt left him. He was still the dowser's son.

CHAPTER
36

TEN YEARS LATER MARCH 1859

THE DOWSER PACED and paced. He held the branch as his father had done, as his father had done before him. Palms up, thumbs out. The sun crawled up the sky. Then just when he was about to give up, fearing the gift had left him, the energy flowed through his fingers and traveled up his arms. He stared down at the branch now pulling toward the ground. It was like this every time he dowsed, a slow start and then eventually the sensation of water. The gift had never failed Amos.

Unlike Jake, Amos welcomed the dowsing gift. He liked the way folks counted on him. Water was their lifeline, and he gave them a way to it. Amos marked the spot with a stake, then set out to find the cross stream.

He smiled to himself, remembering how at one time he

believed the three hundred dollars he'd carried with him from Bittersweet Creek would make him rich. In a way, it had. He'd helped Gwendolyn and her mother when they first arrived in Oregon City. He'd paid his debt to Fiddleless. And then there were the cabins. It was as if the tree at Bittersweet Creek had sprouted fruit.

Amos walked some more. As usual, the cross stream didn't take long to find. After marking it, he mounted his horse and hurried home. He needed to get ready for the celebration.

BLUE OWL walked across the entire length of the wood floor. Then she turned around and traced her steps back. She began each morning this way, a tribute to the wood floor she'd wanted for so long. Four years ago, Amos had built a home for her and Jake. It was the year following Jake's stroke. Jake had been dowsing when it happened. The doctor said he'd live, but never talk or walk. Blue Owl thought that they might as well have dug a hole and buried him, but Jake had surprised her. He had found a quiet contentment in these late years of his life, watching his family grow around him.

The day after Jake's stroke, Amos had ridden back to the field and done what Blue Owl had suspected all along. He could find water, too. Word of the young man with the dowsing gift spread throughout the Oregon Territory. His reputation grew larger than Jake's. She believed that was probably because Amos accepted his gift. He saw the good in it.

Blue Owl opened the door and threw bread crumbs on the porch. She and the birds had made peace long ago, although she occasionally dreamed of cooking a pot of mockingbird stew or dumplings soaked in a gravy made from the drippings of roasted doves.

She settled on the porch and waited for Daisy to walk the well-worn path between their cabins. Amos had built their homes close by. They had become a tribe, and he had taken care of each of them. This was no surprise to Blue Owl. Amos was a wolf, after all.

FROM THE FRONT window, Gwendolyn watched Finn race his horse across their land. The boy could ride a horse faster than anyone she'd ever witnessed. He'd taken after Daisy with his good looks. He was seventeen years old, and he'd broken every young girl's heart in a twenty-mile radius. No wonder he rode fast. No girl was going to tie him down— he'd made sure of it.

Sarah Little Bit was the only girl who could tell Finn what to do. Sometimes when Gwendolyn looked in her eyes, she could swear she saw Homer staring back. It made her want to cry for all that Sarah Little Bit would never know. Every time some single man had checked into the inn, Daisy received a new marriage proposal. But she turned each of them down, claiming, "There was only one man for me, and the river swept him away."

One day Gwendolyn would tell Sarah Little Bit that her parents had a big love and were the happiest couple she'd ever known. Until now.

Sometimes Gwendolyn didn't think she deserved such joy. How could someone who looked like her have all this?

She stared at the picture hung next to the window. It was a drawing of Amos's mother. The first time she saw the image, the woman had looked familiar, and even now Delilah's image stirred things inside her that she could not quite understand. She decided the feelings were attached to her love for Amos. He was a part of Delilah. Even death could not erase the bond between a mother and her son.

Finn had disappeared from Gwendolyn's sight, but she continued watching. Soon she noticed Amos making his way across the valley. He'd left two days ago to dowse the Reynoldses' farm. Now his horse had begun to gallop toward their cabin.

She scooped up Ezra and held him to the window so that he could see. And when her sweet boy clapped his hands and called out, "Papa!" the thoughts Gwendolyn had mere seconds ago disappeared. Her life *was* true and purposeful. She deserved this moment and all the moments that would follow. Ezra was proof of that.

Gwendolyn opened the door and went to meet Amos coming home.

THE CELEBRATION was winding down. The McBrides and Blocks had just ridden away in their wagons. Gwendolyn's mother and stepfather had headed back to town. It was still the same Oregon to Amos, but the new statehood had given them an excuse to get together with the families. The women were gathering the dishes and Finn took Sarah Little Bit for a ride on his horse after a warning from Daisy to ride *slow*.

Ezra had fallen asleep, his head resting on Amos's shoulder. Amos took his son into the house and gave him to Gwendolyn. Before Amos turned away he touched her cheek and she pressed against his hand. He watched her as she placed their son in the cradle and even when she left to join the other women, he watched her still. Then he walked to the porch where Jake sat. Instead of settling next to him, he paused in the doorway. The sun was going down, and he could see the pink clouds peeking behind the mountains. Looking at Jake sit there staring at them tugged at his heart. He suspected the mountains would always be calling out to Jake.

His own wanderlust had been replaced by something more. Something that eased the yearning he'd had as a boy. When Rebecca died, Amos thought he'd never again have a family. But he'd had one all along. From where he stood now, he could see them—Gwendolyn and Blue Owl, shaking out the blankets; Daisy, her hand blocking the sun as she watched Finn and Sarah Little Bit; Jake sitting on the porch, his eyes fixed straight ahead.

Amos pulled up a chair next to his father and sat. The

quiet between them felt good and comfortable, but he needed to speak. "Jake, remember when you were with Isaac in the Rockies in thirty-three?"

Jake nodded and the right corner of his mouth curled up a bit.

"Remember," Amos continued, "when you came upon that bear and you told Isaac, 'It's either gonna be me or that bear standing'?

"And then you said, 'If I have anything to do with it, it sure as heck ain't gonna be that bear'?"

It was an old story. They'd both heard the tale many times. But a good story traveled like water, constantly flowing, making rivers from one person to the next, returning and filling them up all over again.

ACKNOWLEDGMENTS

This story started around the dinner table when my husband mentioned that his father showed him how to dowse. I'd never heard of dowsing and was both fascinated and astonished that he'd never shared the tale with me. "You don't know everything about me," he said. So it seemed I didn't. But that is why Jerry deserves my first thank-you. Without him, this story would never have existed.

After me, Shannon Renee Holt, has read this story more than anyone. This book is better because of her skilled eye, smart suggestions, pep talks, and talent. She internalized my story so much she wrote a beautiful "front porch" to the book. I'm blessed to have her as a daughter for so many reasons. Traveling with me on this journey is only one of them.

The Retreat Girls—Kathi Appelt, Jeanette Ingold, Rebecca Kai Dotlich, and Lola Schaefer gave encouragement and time to reading part or all of the manuscript. On her second reading, Kathi made a remark that made me rethink a pivotal thread, and Rebecca's simple comment, "I think Delilah will always be a part of the story," proved powerful and prophetic.

Charlotte Goebel read an early draft and despite the bumps and holes, still said she liked it. A year later when I told her I might have taken on a story that I just wasn't capable of writing, she smiled and assured me I was wrong. Thank you, dear friend, for being a cheerleader.

Another optimist was my mother, Brenda Willis, who welcomed me to send an early draft, a few chapters at a time. I'm certain the reading was sometimes painful. Thank you for never letting me know.

This story takes place over twenty-six years and I collected quite a library of research about the West. I returned to some of those books again and again. One of those was William E. Hill's *The Oregon Trail, Yesterday and Today.* Imagine how thrilled I was when Bill agreed to serve as historical fact-checker of the manuscript. I owe him a huge debt of gratitude for pointing out my oversights and making recommendations. At times I chose a different option for the sake of the story. If there are any historical errors, they are mine.

It's comforting to know I have Amy Berkower looking after my interests. Amy proves that you can be successful in business and still be nice. I'm grateful that this very busy agent made a bit more room on her client list for me.

In 1998 Henry Holt and Company published my first book. They have demonstrated, book after book, that there are a lot of people behind a story. Thank you for the care you invest with this and all of my books.

The most important person on that team, to me, is my editor, Christy Ottaviano. She has embraced my work with a passion that many writers can only dream of having in an editor. I have grown as a writer because of Christy's advice and guidance. When I rewrite, it is her voice I hear. She is an editor who truly loves editing. Thank you, Christy, for allowing me to be a recipient of your gift for all these years.

And my last thank-you is to you, cherished readers. You make it possible for me to do what I love every day. Thank you, all, from the bottom of my heart.

SQUARE FISH

DISCUSSION GUIDE

THE WATER SEEKER
by Kimberly Willis Holt

Discussion Questions

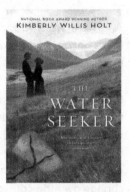

1. Jake Kincaid was known as a dowser. However, he preferred being a trapper. Why did Jake try to ignore his gift of dowsing in favor of spending long months trapping animals?

2. Delilah's image appears to many characters, including Henrietta and Rebecca. Who else witnessed Delilah's vision and how did they respond?

3. When Gil and Rebecca started the mission at Pretty Water, they had hopes that the Otoe would attend the church and the schoolhouse they had built. What were some of the challenges and barriers Gil and Rebecca encountered in life at the mission?

4. Jameson Block became a central figure in Amos Kincaid's life. How did Amos meet Jameson? What was the artifact that bound them together? And how did their relationship change over the years?

5. In *The Water Seeker*, birds offered comfort, created an annoyance, or resulted in food for the trappers and pioneers. What was the significance of the birds to characters such as Delilah and Blue Owl, as well as to others?

6. What was a day like in the life of a member of the wagon train on the Oregon Trail? What role did men, women, and children play as the settlers moved west?

7. There were many hazards on the Oregon Trail. What were these hazards and how did they affect the members of the wagon train?

8. When Amos first encountered Gwendolyn, "he wondered if she was born that way. In his entire life, he'd never seen anyone so horrifying" (p. 145). As the story progresses, Amos begins to view Gwendolyn differently. Did Gwendolyn's appearance change or was it the way Amos viewed her? How did their relationship change over the course of the book?

9. Many characters experienced the loss of a loved one—Amos never knew his mother; Daisy lost her husband, Homer, in a tragic accident; and darling Eliza became the victim of a terrible misfortune resulting in profound grief for her family. How did these characters respond and cope to the losses they endured?

10. Readers are introduced to protagonist Amos Kincaid as a baby. How does Amos evolve as a character? What events impacted him as a boy and as a man?

GOFISH

QUESTIONS FOR THE AUTHOR

KIMBERLY WILLIS HOLT

© Shannon Holt

What did you want to be when you grew up?
A writer.

When did you realize you wanted to be a writer?
In seventh grade, three teachers encouraged my writing. That was when I first thought the dream could come true. Before that, I didn't think I could be a writer because I wasn't a great student and I read slowly.

What's your first childhood memory?
Buying an orange Dreamsicle from the ice-cream man. I was two years old.

What's your most embarrassing childhood memory?
In fourth grade, I tried to impress the popular girls that I wanted to be friends with by doing somersaults in front of them. (I never learned to do cartwheels.) They called me a showoff, so I guess it didn't work. If only I'd known how to do a cartwheel.

What was your worst subject in school?
Algebra.

SQUARE FISH

What was your first job?
I was in the movies. I popped popcorn at the Westside Cinemas.

How did you celebrate publishing your first book?
I'm sure my family went out to dinner. We always celebrate by eating.

Where do you write your books?
I write several places—a soft, big chair in my bedroom, at a table on my screen porch, or at coffee shops.

Where do you find inspiration for your writing?
Most of the inspiration for my writing comes from moments in my childhood.

Which of your characters is most like you?
I'm a bit like most of them. However, I fashioned Tori in the Piper Reed books after me. But Tori is bossier than I was and she certainly makes better grades than I did.

When you finish a book, who reads it first?
My daughter listens to me read my first draft.

Are you a morning person or a night owl?
I'm a morning person.

What's your idea of the best meal ever?
That's a toss-up. My grandmother's chicken and dumplings, and sushi.

Which do you like better: cats or dogs?
I'm a dog person. I have a poodle named Bronte who is the model for Bruna in the Piper Reed series.

What do you value most in your friends?
Loyalty and honesty.

Where do you go for peace and quiet?
Home.

Who is your favorite fictional character?
Leroy in *Mister and Me* because he is forgiving. And that's a trait many of us don't have.

What are you most afraid of?
Anything harming my daughter.

What time of the year do you like best?
Fall.

What is your favorite TV show?
CBS Sunday Morning.

If you were stranded on a desert island, who would you want for company?
My husband and daughter.

What's the best advice you have ever received about writing?
A writer once told me, "Readers either see what they read or hear what they read. Writers have to learn to write for both." When I started following that advice, my writing improved.

What do you want readers to remember about your books?
The characters. I want them to seem like real people. I want them to miss them and wonder what happened to them.

What would you do if you ever stopped writing?
I plan on dying with a pen in my hand.

What do you like best about yourself?
I'm honest.

What is your worst habit?
I eat too much.

What do you consider to be your greatest accomplishment?
I gave birth to a wonderful human being.

What do you wish you could do better?
I wish I could do a cartwheel.

What would your readers be most surprised to learn about you?
I send gift cards with positive messages to myself when I order something for me.

SQUARE FISH

Young Tiger Ann Parker will do just about anything to get out of her rural town of Saitter, Louisiana. And when Aunt Dorie Kay asks her to come live in Baton Rouge, Tiger finally has a way out. But will Tiger be able to leave the only life she's ever known?

Find out in

MY LOUISIANA SKY

by Kimberly Willis Holt.

one

Folks around Saitter don't understand why parents would name their daughter Tiger. But Daddy says it's because of love. Momma had a kitten named Tiger when she was a little girl. She loved that kitten so much, she hugged it too hard and it died. Momma wasn't going to let that happen again, so when I was born she was real gentle with me.

Some people in Saitter say Momma and Daddy should have never been allowed to get married because they're different. Folks around here call it retarded, but I like "slow" better.

Even though Daddy got through twelve years of school, most folks say teachers felt sorry for skinny Lonnie Parker. Just passed him from grade to grade like they do some of the basketball players. Momma never went to school, but Granny taught her to read.

With those kind of odds, I should be dumber than

an old cow. But I'm not. In fact, my classmates' parents are still scratching their heads trying to figure out how I got straight A's and won the spelling bee five years in a row. It's even harder for them to believe Momma taught me to read. But she did. Momma likes reading comic books. I read about Superman and Donald Duck when I was four. Now Momma likes me to read to her because I can read the words she can't.

It rained every day the week after I finished sixth grade. The clouds hung low in the gray sky and the raindrops poured down, hammering our roof with a constant patter. But by Saturday, the day Aunt Dorie Kay came to visit from Baton Rouge, the sun came out in all its glory and the sky returned to a brilliant blue. When we heard her car drive up near the gate, Momma ran out of the house like a little kid. She grabbed hold of Aunt Dorie Kay so hard, my aunt wobbled on her high-heeled shoes.

"Whoa, Corrina." Aunt Dorie Kay caught her balance and smoothed her dark hair back in place.

"Oh, Dorie Kay, I missed you so much," Momma squeaked. She stepped back with her dirty bare feet, admiring Aunt Dorie Kay from head to toe. "You're as pretty as a picture in a fancy ladies' magazine."

Aunt Dorie Kay was Momma's younger sister. To me, she was the most sophisticated person I had ever known. Today she wore a tailored navy blue suit that matched her shoes and she smelled better than the perfume counter at Penney's. She wasn't beautiful like Momma. Momma's long dark hair fell to her shoulders, and her body curved in all the right places. But somehow Aunt Dorie Kay's flat chest and narrow hips appeared stylish in her pretty clothes. She wore more makeup than any Saitter woman dared to, except for the women who went to the Wigwam honky-tonk on Saturday nights. But while their faces looked caked on, hers looked glamorous.

Aunt Dorie Kay gently cupped my chin with her hands. "Twelve years old. Tiger, you are growing up into such a young lady."

Her voice was smooth like a deep, calm lake. I wanted to dive right in and let it work magic on me. Turn me into someone I wasn't. But as I looked at my reflection in her eyes I was reminded of what I saw in the mirror. I saw Daddy. He was tall and skinny with thin red hair and a long neck. His narrow eyes squinted when he smiled and his nose took up a lot of room on his face. But folks say kids change a bunch before they finish growing. Especially in the summertime.

In the afternoon my best buddy, Jesse Wade Thompson, stopped by to say hello to Aunt Dorie Kay. He and I were sitting on the living room floor, drinking Grapettes and listening to Elvis on the radio, when we heard someone drive up.

Aunt Dorie Kay leaned forward, causing our tweed couch to squeak. She drew back the calico curtains. "Why, Tiger, look. Are you expecting something from an Alexandria store?"

I rushed to the window. A Mitchell's Appliance delivery truck screeched to a stop in front of our gate. Jesse Wade and I dashed to open the screen porch door for two men carrying a bulky box. Two weeks ago we received a box of twenty-four baby chicks Granny had ordered. But this box was almost as big as our woodstove.

I held the screen door open for the men. "Excuse me, sirs, but do you have the right house?" Brando, our one-eyed cat, leaped from the swing and pranced off the porch.

The taller man with a harelip exchanged smiles with his stocky helper. "I don't know. Whose house is this?"

My breathing was hard and fast. "This is the home of Jewel Ramsey and her kin." Jewel Ramsey was my grandma. I hoped the box was for us, but I knew it had to be a mistake.

They carefully lowered the heavy box onto the porch. The harelip man wiped sweat from his brow with his handkerchief and dug out some folded papers from his back pants pocket. He unfolded a yellow slip, then slid his finger to the bottom of the page. "Well, let's see here. You say Jewel Ramsey and her kin?"

I hunched my shoulders. "Yes, sir. That's what I said."

He frowned and shook his head. "Nope. I don't see anything that says that."

My heart sank. "It's probably for your family, Jesse Wade." Mr. Thompson owned the plant nursery where Daddy worked. They could afford things that came in big boxes.

Jesse Wade leaned his curly black head against the doorway. "We're not expecting any deliveries from Mitchell's."

Aunt Dorie Kay walked onto the porch while the man continued to study the papers. He frowned, shaking his head. "Nope. This here paper says for the family of Jewel Ramsey *and* Lonnie Parker." The corners of his mouth turned up into a slow grin.

The other man laughed loudly and slapped his knee with his hat. "Fooled ya, didn't we?"

My heart felt like it flew plumb out of my chest. I raised my chin and stood straight. "Yes, sir, that's my grandma and daddy. Right this way, sir. Can I get you some iced tea?" The men followed me inside, carrying the box. It took up so much space in our plain little room.

Momma darted out of the kitchen with a half-peeled potato in her hand. The spiral peeling bounced as she ran toward the box. "What is it?" she asked. "What's in that box?"

"Hold on, Corrina," Granny said, walking slowly behind and wiping her hands on her apron. Her black hair was pinned in its usual tight bun, but some fine locks stuck to her full face. Aunt Dorie Kay stood near the window, smiling as she watched us.

Daddy, returning from the garden, clopped up the porch steps. He started to walk in, then looked down at his muddy boots, backed out, and pulled them off. He walked in the house with white socks on his feet, rubbing a dirty hand across his red chin. I couldn't tell if his face was red from the sun or because two strangers stood in our house. He studied the box, then shyly peered at the men. As always, he spoke slow and cautious. "What's this box doing in our house?"

"It's for us, Daddy. The men said it was for us."

The deliverymen headed toward the front door. The stocky fella tipped his hat and said, "You folks have a good day."

The screen door squeaked open and shut as I examined the puzzled faces in the silent room. I dashed out the door before the men reached their truck. "Wait a minute, sir. Who is this box from?"

The tall man opened the truck door. "It's on those papers we left with you."

I ran back to the house and grabbed a paper stamped INVOICE off the box. It said Doreen Kay Ramsey. Aunt Dorie Kay bought it! I whipped around. "Oh, thank you, Aunt Dorie Kay!" It was just like Christmas.

She yanked gently on my long pigtail. "Don't you think you better see what it *is* you're thanking me for?"

Momma's focus didn't stray from the box. "Open it," she demanded. "Open it, Lonnie."

We all stood around Daddy while he drew his knife from his front pocket and carefully cut into the box. Cardboard sides flapped to the floor and revealed an object I had seen only in stores and Jesse Wade's living room. Dark oak surrounded a wide green screen. A brand-new RCA television set!

Momma jumped up and down, squealing like a baby pig. Daddy stepped back, stunned, brushing the hair from his eyes as Jesse Wade whistled approvingly.

Then, as if we all planned it, everyone, except Granny and Jesse Wade, grabbed Aunt Dorie Kay and hugged her until she lost her balance and fell to the couch, laughing.

"Thank you! Thank you, Aunt Dorie Kay!"

Momma raced to the TV and stroked it like a puppy. "Thank you. You're the best sister in the whole world."

Daddy clasped his hands together, cleared his throat as if to begin a speech, and said, "This is mighty nice of you, Dorie Kay Ramsey. It must have cost you a whole lot of money."

Aunt Dorie Kay must have made a big salary working as a secretary in Baton Rouge.

Granny frowned, turned on her heels, and marched to the kitchen, her apron bow riding high over her huge hips. A hurt look spread across Aunt Dorie Kay's face as Granny walked away.

I wondered why Granny wasn't happy like the rest of us. There weren't many families in Saitter with a television set.

"It's a beauty," Jesse Wade said. "Make sure you put a lamp on top. Momma says that helps you see better. Speaking of Momma, I better get on home. She'll be hollering for me if I don't."

My eyes were so fixed on that TV, I hardly noticed him leave. Daddy plugged it in, then Aunt Dorie Kay helped connect the rabbit-ear antennas. When they finished, she asked, "Tiger, would you like to turn on the television?"

"Yes, ma'am." I turned the knob to the right. We waited and waited. Maybe Marlon Brando would be on TV. My knees grew weak from the thought of seeing his dreamy movie star face right in the middle of my living room.

Finally the screen lit up like magic. Soon we saw a man in black and white like some of the movies I'd seen at the picture show. His lips moved, but we couldn't hear anything. We stood there with our mouths open, watching the man talk. Aunt Dorie Kay bent down and turned another knob. The man's voice boomed from the set. "And that's the news for June 1, 1957."

Everyone but Aunt Dorie Kay jumped back. Granny started out of the kitchen, frowning with her hands on her hips.

"Volume," Aunt Dorie Kay explained as she adjusted the knob that lowered the sound.

Daddy and Momma exchanged puzzled glances. Then their faces smoothed out. Momma smiled and Daddy nodded with a grin.

Later the   came on. Daddy settled on the couch, clapping offbeat to the music, while Momma and I held hands and danced around the living room. Floorboards creaked as our steps thumped against the wood.

Aunt Dorie Kay perched on the arm of Granny's lumpy lounge chair, her eyes glazed as if she were miles away from our living room. Every once in a while she batted her eyelashes.

While Momma and I danced, Granny entered and sank into her chair. She stared at the TV, but a film covered her eyes like the times right before she fell asleep in church. She and Aunt Dorie Kay seemed to be in worlds of their own.

Then Granny spoke. "Don't you have better things to spend your money on besides a noise box?" Last year when Granny learned Aunt Dorie Kay hired a colored maid to clean her apartment, she'd said, "That gal thinks money grows on trees."

Now Aunt Dorie Kay said, "Oh, Ma, lots of families are buying televisions."

Granny shook her head and walked back into the kitchen. Her large, lumpy hips reminded me of two fighting cats trapped in a sack.

I sat down and offered a silly grin to Aunt Dorie Kay. She smiled back, but her eyes looked sad. Granny's comments spoiled the gift for me, but Momma kept dancing by herself around the room.